P9-DHH-112

DECEPTION'S DAUGHTER

ALSO BY CORDELIA FRANCES BIDDLE

The Conjurer

Murder at San Simeon

Beneath the Wind

WRITTEN BY CORDELIA FRANCES BIDDLE

WITH STEVE ZETTLER AS NERO BLANC

A Crossworder's Delight

Another Word for Murder

Wrapped Up in Crosswords

Anatomy of a Crossword

A Crossworder's Gift

Corpus de Crossword

A Crossword to Die For

A Crossworder's Holiday

The Crossword Connection

Two Down

The Crossword Murder

Cordelia Frances Biddle

DECEPTION'S DAUGHTER

Thomas Dunne Books

ST. MARTIN'S MINOTAUR

NEW YORK

THOMAS DUNNE BOOKS.
An imprint of St. Martin's Press.

www.thomasdunnebooks.com
www.minotaurbooks.com

Design by Maggie Goodman

Library of Congress Cataloging-in-Publication Data

Biddle, Cordelia Frances
Deception's daughter / Cordelia Frances Biddle.—1st ed.
p. cm.
ISBN-13: 978-0-312-35247-9
ISBN-10: 0-312-35247-6
1. Young women—fiction. 2. Upper class—Pennsylvania—Philadelphia—Fiction. 3. Philadelphia (Pa.)—Fiction. 4. Kidnapping—Fiction. I. Title.
PS3552.I333D43 2008
813'.54—dc22

2008013627

First Edition: August 2008

10 9 8 7 6 5 4 3 2 1

For Cordelia Dietrich Zanger

daughter, friend, reader, writer

"Love all things, so your heart is shown."

ACKNOWLEDGMENTS

MY ABIDING THANKS TO MY enthusiastic editor, Marcia Markland, to her equally supportive assistant, Diana Szu, to India Cooper, copy editor *extraordinaire,* and to David Baldeosingh Rotstein for his magical cover art. I am fortunate indeed to have such a caring, savvy, and attentive team. You allow Martha Beale to walk into the modern world.

Gratitude also to Jax Lowell and Pozi Jensen, fellow artists, hand-holders, and advisers without par. And, of course and always, to Steve.

Oh Yet We Trust

From *In Memoriam A.H.H.*

ALFRED, LORD TENNYSON

Oh yet we trust that somehow good
Will be the final goal of ill,
To pangs of nature, sins of will,
Defects of doubt, and taints of blood;

That nothing walks with aimless feet;
That not one life shall be destroy'd,
Or cast as rubbish to the void
When God hath made the pile complete;

That not a worm is cloven in vain;
That not a moth with vain desire
Is shrivell'd in a fruitless fire,
Or but subserves another's gain.

Behold, we know not anything;
I can but trust that good shall fall
At last—far off—at last, to all,
And every winter change to spring.

So runs my dream: but what am I?
An infant crying in the night:
An infant crying for the light:
And with no language but a cry.

DECEPTION'S DAUGHTER

IN THE WIND, GHOSTS

THE GUSTS GROW IN STRENGTH and purpose, swirling over the ground in rust-colored eddies that pluck up and then discharge particles of desiccated leaves, ocher-brown twigs, gritty pebbles, and the sere, yellowish grasses that were once the verdant summer-scented lawns and meadows of Beale House. When the breeze spins away in order to buffet another area of the property, the wake smells acrid, brittle, and dead, as if no flowery plants had ever graced its path, no fresh green shoot had ever ripened, no inch of soil had ever yielded up a nurturing loam and the dense aroma of burgeoning life.

Standing on the veranda of her father's country estate—her house and property now—Martha raises a hand to her bonnet as she gazes past the gardens with their artfully arrayed statuary, past the *jardinières* imported from Europe, past the formal promenades and rose walks until her view takes in the fields and woods that stretch down to the Schuylkill River's distant banks. *And yet the heavens are blue,* she thinks, *and the river, half full and sluggish though it may be, is as azurine as hope.* Despite the scorching September afternoon, despite the sun and cloudless sky, she shivers.

Then a voice calling her from within disturbs her reverie; and she turns, as she always does, in habitual and brisk compliance. It will take her many months or many years to unlearn the patterns of her youth.

"Mother," she hears again, and Ella flies outside, her high-buttoned boots tapping across the stone flags, the skirts of her traveling costume creating miniature storms from the powdery soil that has blown up against the house. "Must we leave? Must we? And why today? Why?"

Martha's green-gray eyes don't lose their clouded apprehension, and her long, aristocratic face retains its pensive stamp, but she smiles for the child's sake. "We must return to town for your schooling, dearheart. As you well know. For your schooling and for Cai's."

Ella's expression remains defiant. Since she became Martha Beale's ward seven months before, the eleven-year-old's sallow complexion has grown pink with health, her thin shoulders have rounded, and her hair has taken on a lustrous flaxen hue; but her eyes can still spark with mistrust as though she cannot help but anticipate the loss of everything she has come to know and love.

"All pleasant occasions must come to an end eventually," Martha continues, her words accompanied by a frown that for a moment replicates Ella's.

"But why? We're happy here. You and I and Cai."

"Mistress Why and Wherefore." Martha tilts her head and smiles in earnest. "Because the summer has reached its conclusion as it does every year, and always will. And we three must leave the countryside and journey to our home in the city. But we'll return here. This house and these barns and fields won't vanish. They'll patiently await our coming again, just as they awaited me during the times I traveled back and forth to Philadelphia with my father. There will be many more holidays, and many more hours of idle pleasure. Now, you go and find Cai, and then we can have a final tramp in the gardens while the footmen load the trunks into the carriages in preparation for our departure."

"He's with Jacob and the dogs" is the short reply. "Cai was crying. Jacob took him to see the hens in order to cheer him."

"Just so." Martha nods in agreement with this decision. Jacob Oberholtzer is the estate's head gardener and was one of her father's most faithful servants. The old man, for he surely is that by now, will know precisely what to do with an unhappy five-and-a-half-year-old boy. "Well, you go and ask Jacob if he can spare our Caspar for a few moments."

But before Ella can do as she's bidden, the wind kicks up again, racing across the veranda where the two stand and beating hard against Martha's dark purple *peau de soie* skirts. They fly out stiff and loud while her bonnet, too loosely tied, flies upward before crashing earthward and rolling end over end across the bristled lawn.

"Oh, this wretched wind," she mutters through clenched teeth as she smooths and rewraps her tangled mantilla. Her hands, unfashionably bronzed by a season spent out of doors, are tense. "And no rain in sight. What will become of the crops? What will become of the wild creatures who dwell in the woods?"

"But the wind cannot be wretched, Mother" is Ella's staunch reply. "It bears the ghosts of all the souls who have gone before us."

"Who says such things?" Martha's voice is unexpectedly sharp.

"Miss Pettiman. She told me that is why I hear howling in the chimney flue in my bedroom or in the day nursery. She says it's a soul crying out, but it cannot make human noise until it enters a human dwelling."

"That's nonsense, Ella. When people die, their souls escape to either Heaven or to Hell—"

"Not all of them, Mother," her adopted child argues in return. "Miss Pettiman said there are folk who cannot quit the earth, that either anger over some outrage accomplished during their lifetime, or grief at forever forsaking loved ones, holds them here. Miss also said that's why Cai is so often quiet and why he sometimes falls into that awful trembling state, because he's listening to the murmurs of the parents he cannot recall. It's doubly hard for him, she told me, being a mulatto child and being born so frail and sickly and everyone believing he was no better than a deaf mute."

"Oh, goodness me! What foolishness is that nursery maid teaching you?" Martha's cheeks are flushed with irritation. She relinquishes her place on the stone veranda floor and marches away to retrieve her wandering bonnet while Ella, now chagrined and a little frightened by her adoptive parent's quick wrath, trudges warily behind.

"And are Miss Pettiman's heedless words the reason Cai is weeping with Jacob?" Martha demands as she swoops up the dark headdress and thrusts it haphazardly onto her ringlets, retying the long mulberry-colored ribbons in a tight and clumsy knot.

"No. He doesn't want to leave the countryside. And neither do I." The tone, however, has lost its boldness. Ella has reverted to the supplication and hesitation that were the mark of her younger days. Then she regains a little of her bravado. "Is it because of Mr. Kelman that we're returning to the city?"

"Is that Miss Pettiman's opinion you're quoting?" Martha demands with more warmth than she intends, and Ella's reaction is swift contrition.

"No. It's mine . . . because he was a guest here on occasion. And he hasn't visited us in a long while."

"Mr. Kelman was helpful to me during a difficult period in my life. Of course, I would be grateful for his friendship—and happy to see him, as well," Martha states, although by now her cheeks are very red, and she realizes she's doing precisely what she's warned the children against: She's lying. The problem of her relationship with Thomas Kelman is very much on her mind.

"Cai likes Mr. Kelman," Ella continues.

"I hope Cai will like many people. And that you will, too" is the ambiguous answer; then Martha adds a more forthright "Now please fetch Caspar, or we will be late for our departure."

BUT LEAVE AT THE HOUR allotted, they do. The servants, both the house and grounds servants, line up in front of the entry portico to bid farewell to their young mistress, her two wards, and their nursery maid, who, in a breach of custom, has been consigned to the second carriage with Martha's lady's maid and the various trunks and valises that have accompanied the group for their summer sojourn. Miss Pettiman has already taken her place among the piled boxes, staring straight ahead as if she were studying a distant mountain, although no such heights can be found on the banks of the Schuylkill River.

The housemaids and the cook drop curtsies as Martha passes; the stablemen and farmers bow bared heads, their caps twiddling in their calloused fingers, their eyes fixed to the dirt of the drive. Every face evinces sadness at Martha's leave-taking. Her father garnered respect but a dearth of kindly thoughts from those who served him; the daughter has gained loyalty because all employed at Beale House, from the youngest scullery maid of thirteen to the senior laundress or the most laconic groom, carry in their hearts a desire to please her. She shakes each hand: wide, narrow, rough-skinned and red, or hard and smooth as stone; and extends her thanks on behalf of herself and the children.

Then a footman helps her into the coach, decorously offering her long skirts into her lace-gloved hands before he closes the glossy door. Ella clambers in at the carriage's other side, followed by a silent, stricken Cai. The coachman cracks his whip; the four black geldings strain forward in their traces; the wheels, crafted of wych elm, heart of oak, and ash, begin to turn; and the procession commences.

Martha looks backward as Beale House dodges out of sight: its Gothic Revival turrets and stone tracery, its slate roof and clipped boxwood hedges, its kitchen garden and outlying buildings hidden for a moment and then springing back into view as the carriages proceed along the dappled and winding trail. The unexpected angles are disconcertingly unfamiliar, as if the house were in the midst of being reformed and refashioned.

She turns her head this way and that, pondering the strange mutations to a place she knows so well. Then a gust catches a tree bough, pushing it downward with a sighing snap. The horses start in fear at the creaking wood and the sudden roar of wind rioting in the neighboring branches. The coach buckets from side to side; and Cai, now Caspar Beale, begins to whimper about invisible demons winging through the air. For an anxious moment, his hands quiver spasmodically as though one of his epileptic fits were imminent. Martha coos to him, stroking his fingers, repeating his name, and gazing into his eyes until the threat passes. Then she tries to convince him that the unseen spirits are not ghouls or wraiths come to haunt and harm him, but angels with enormous and shining wings flying close to earth in order to protect him. Cai remains steadfast in his belief that ghosts are riding in the wind.

THE JOURNEY BACK INTO PHILADELPHIA consumes over two hours; a man on horseback would require an hour or a little more, but the roads in the area known as Falls of Schuylkill are often no better than cart tracks, and the large, laden carriages must go slowly. Inaccessibility is precisely what drew Martha's father to the spot where he built his grand and aloof mansion. In the Philadelphia in which he rose to fortune and fame—as in the current city of 1842—the country estates of the prominent were customarily chosen for their convenience to visiting friends and acquaintances; such was not the desire of Lemuel Beale. When he removed himself and his only child from their house in town, he expected no one to follow.

Within the drowsy heat of the carriage, Martha alternatively watches the passing scenery and the children, who are now asleep. As he slumps in a doze, Cai's expression remains fearful, his brown face wizened and preternaturally aged as if no amount of healthy sustenance and kindly encouragement will ever be enough to satisfy or fully cure him of his brain disease. Ella looks merely vexed; her legs kick in time to the coach's jouncing motion.

Martha sighs and shakes her head, wondering again—as she does at least once every day—how she can gain the necessary wisdom to raise these two needy children. For a moment, she considers whether her decision to bring them into her home was a wise one, then immediately counters the question with a brisk *But what could I do? Leave them on the streets? Let them starve? Kittens and horses are rescued; shouldn't children be, too?*

So debating with herself, she removes her bonnet, gloves, and mantilla, tosses them aside, then briefly touches the elaborately curled braid that lies at the base of her neck. Finding the plait has come unpinned and the chestnut-colored locks in which she takes secret pride are tumbling down her back, she mutters in frustration as she stabs the long hairpins back in place. *Ringlets, braided bands, hats, capottes, petticoats, and stays despite this grueling heat . . . an underskirt and overskirt, and a flannelette chemise. It's a wonder ladies do not expire in such voluminous and ill-considered costumes!* She fans herself energetically, switching her skirts from side to side, but instead of cooling the coach's cabin, the cloth turns as dusty as the air, which increases her irritation. At the august age of twenty-six, she knows she should behave with greater decorum. No man wishes a wife who's as careless and precipitous as a child. Not even the daughter of the illustrious Lemuel Beale.

But that reminder leads directly to her quandary over Thomas Kelman. For Ella is correct in guessing that her adoptive mother is far happier in his company than without it. *Oh, Thomas!* Martha's brain demands. *Where do we stand, you and I? I believed we'd reached an understanding, but was I wrong? Has your time in my company been no more than empathy for my father's death? Or a noble sense of duty? Or can it be that the great Beale wealth prevents you from seeking my hand? Or . . . or perhaps, the opposite is true, and my sole attraction is—?* Here her thoughts crash to a halt, leaving her to stare disconsolately at the passing scenery until she becomes aware that the carriage has reached the northwestern outskirts of the city.

Where the road winds close to the river's tree-dotted banks, the Schuylkill is clearly visible. In the small, rock-strewn pools that lap the stream's earthen borders lie puddles of yellow sycamore leaves. Against the slowly swirling water and the dense green of the reeds and riverine grasses, the leaves gleam like purest gold, and Martha cannot help but feel her spirits start to revive. She's ordered the coachman to follow the river rather than turn eastward into the heart of the town, reasoning that Ella and Cai would enjoy the longer journey, but it's Martha who takes pleasure in the sight.

As she watches, a figure catches her notice—a woman on the opposite shore, standing upstream from where the ferry crosses from Philadelphia's prosperous environs toward the almshouse built in the pastureland along the Darby Road. She's yellow-haired and hatless in the sun, and although her clothes are drab she carries herself with purposefulness and pride. In her hands is a new wicker-ware basket; she lowers it to the water's edge, then bends to reach inside. As she does, the light from the liquid at her feet spills upward into her face, turning it an incandescent white.

Wading ankle-deep in the water, the woman propels the basket along, then spins backward, startled; and Martha follows the unknown female's gaze. On the promontory above her ranges a group of boys. All are raggedy; all are barefooted; all are thin. They call down to the rocky strand, and the object of their attention appears to respond before turning away and continuing her progress through the shallows.

Then the sight is lost as the carriage and river road part company, and the city's streets begin in earnest. Martha straightens her spine against the horsehair cushion, then reaches for her cast-aside bonnet and mantilla, pulls on her gloves, and begins to awaken the sleeping children.

WHEN THE PAIR OF RESPLENDENT coaches with their equally grand steeds and obviously wealthy passengers vanish among the trees, the boys' shouts intensify. In frustration, they throw clods of earth, stones, sticks, and handfuls of brittle grass down upon the wading figure, howling for her return.

Her response to their shrieks is to sing in a soft, unfocused lilt.

"Hush! my dear, lie still and slumber;
Holy angels guard thy bed . . .
Soft and easy is thy cradle;
Coarse and hard thy Savior lay . . ."

The boys know the hymn well. They're forced to sing it every night by the warders in the children's asylum of the almshouse as they pace among the rows of beds, exhorting their charges to greater heights of ardor with a rod each man carries in his right hand. The fact that their quarry can so heedlessly warble the detested words makes the boys all the more fierce in their determination to call her back. None can venture down to the river, however, because none can swim, and they've learned by heart the tales they've been taught: how devils lurk in the Schuylkill's depths waiting to snag a foot from a slippery rock, or suck the mud beneath your legs; and how once you are pulled into the waves, the devils work in consort to drag you down to their black and lethal lairs.

The boys wail out their distress, their bodies crouching forward while their prey's indifferent voice continues to assail their ears.

"May'st thou live to know and fear Him,
Trust and love Him all thy days;
Then go dwell for ever near Him,
See His face and sing His praise."

With that, she sets the basket adrift, pushing it well beyond her reach with a mighty shove that seems to take all her diminishing strength. The basket bobs and spins, dips to one side as the burden within rolls in response to the sudden motion. The high-pitched mewl of a newborn infant rends the air; and the children on the embankment scream at the cry, raining down a fresh avalanche of missiles. "You will burn in Hell forever for what you've done!" the eldest of the pack bellows.

But the threat goes unnoticed. Her tormentors cannot know that her mind is envisioning not a river in Philadelphia on a hot September day but the far-off land of Egypt and the baby Moses set adrift on the stream. Set adrift to be discovered by the daughter of a mighty king.

"See His face and sing His praise," she repeats in a singsong fashion that has now become tuneless and weary. Then she adds a whispered "*A morte perpetua . . . ab omni peccato . . .* That thou would'st spare us . . ."

She watches the basket take to the currents; she hears another milky cry, imagines the red and wrinkled face, the miniature hands, the legs still sticky with blood. Then she walks deeper into the water, slipping on the slimy stones, falling and righting herself until she sets herself adrift.

AS ONE BODY THE BOYS run, then stop as one body. What can they do? They, who have defied all rules to follow the woman and her baby. Surely the punishment meted out for such an infraction will be terrible. Fear of those who rule the almshouse paralyzes them. Then the threat of eternal damnation sends them on their way again. If they say nothing, the infant and its mother will surely drown. Why, the two may be dying already! The devils might already have lured them to their nasty graves!

By now the bare and filthy feet are flying along. In panted breaths, it's agreed that the eldest among them, a runty and cunning boy who goes by the name of Findal Stokes, will sound the alarm alone—while the others creep away and return to such pastimes as they've stealthily forsaken.

As Martha's twin carriages arrive in noisy splendor at the equally grand house on Chestnut Street, young Findal reaches the less consoling destination known as Blockley House.

A TRICK OF THE LIGHT

THE BOY WAS ALONE WHEN he came upon the mother and her child?" It's Thomas Kelman who poses this question while he, the constable in command of the day watch in Blockley Township, and the president of the Humane Society, whose mission it is to rescue drowning persons, wait on the almshouse portico. It's a space designed by William Strickland and so graced with Doric columns and commanding such a pleasing view of river and meadow that it appears to be fronting a country estate rather than an institution for the destitute.

The physical elegance of Blockley House combined with its distance from the city never ceases to perturb Kelman; one hundred eighty seven acres encompassing kitchens, washhouses, workhouses, a surgical amphitheater, and a chapel: all built of stone and at vast expense, although, the poor within its protection subsist on gruel and exhortations to improve their slothful habits.

"The boy was alone" is the constable's guarded answer. Unlike Kelman, who is tall and uncompromising in his stillness, the constable jerks with movement, like a hedgehog trying unsuccessfully to roll itself into a ball. True, he would rather the infant and mother had taken themselves to another part of the river—to be dealt with by another member of the day watch—but he especially wishes he weren't under the scrutiny of Thomas Kelman.

The man's black eyes and steady stare, his somber clothes, his habit of quiet vigilance would make anyone nervous, but it's Kelman's association with the mayor that causes the most anxiety. With no unified police force, the constable knows, the mayor privately relies upon Kelman to sort out criminal matters that lie beyond the scope of the day and night watches that have patrolled the city's districts and boroughs since colonial days. But who tells Kelman if he's correct or not when he claims a person is guilty? If he were to declare a member of the watch derelict, who could argue against the charge? Not a mere fellow who lives on sleepy Darby Road. No wonder the constable wishes he could transform himself into a prickly circle of fur and hide under the nearest bit of shrubbery.

Instead, he begins rattling off information. "Findal Stokes, twelve or thirteen years old according to what history the authorities were able to procure when the lad first came here. Of slight stature. He arrived malnourished, so his age is hard to gauge. One parent, a father, residing in the men's ward. Findal and his father have been at Blockley two years. The parent works now and then, sometimes displaying a strong desire to quit the place and resume his former trade, but more often succumbing to lethargy and drunken oblivion—which in turn depletes his meager coffers. The boy insists he was alone. He shouldn't have been wandering from the institution grounds, and has been disciplined for such infractions and other misdemeanors many times in the past."

Kelman makes no comment, but the president of the Humane Society does. Easby is his name, and he's an avuncular figure, exceedingly portly, with a weakness for colored silks, elaborate waistcoats, and satin cravats. It's as if his nature were warring with itself, and he would rather organize a dancing school for cultured young gentlemen and ladies than urge his fellow missioners to retrieve the bodies of the despairing from the river. "We owe that boy a debt of thanks. It was most fortuitous that he spotted the woman and her baby when he did. Else we could not have rescued the child. It's tragic about the mother, of course. She must have filled her pockets with stones to have so successfully vanished from view, although I imagine her body will resurface. They generally do."

Kelman doesn't respond to this final comment. Instead, he turns away from his examination of the deceptively benign vista—the far-off city no more than colored air, and the river like a soft silk sash. "And this young Findal Stokes can't describe the missing mother?"

"He said the glare was playing tricks on his eyes," the constable answers with regimental swiftness.

"Is he poorly sighted, then?"

But any reply is interrupted as the main doors to Blockley House open, admitting the three visitors, who are then escorted to a second-floor office where the boy himself is waiting.

Amid the comfortable appointments provided for the institution's director, the handsome Turkey carpet and burnished mahogany of the furniture, Findal is an anomaly. It's clear he's been in this room before, for his eyes don't dash about in wonder at the richness of his surroundings. But neither do they rest. Fear is what Kelman reads in the child's expression. Fear whose refuge is deceit.

The boy looks at the constable with eyes that are as pale as standing water, then at Easby, sizing up the lazy girth of the latter and the fretfulness of the former, but the colorless eyes avoid Kelman's unflinching gaze. Kelman notes that the boy makes much use of his hearing, that his head tilts and twists with minute but intentional motions, and that his ears have an oddly pointed quality like those of a bat.

"Did you take anything from the missing woman?" Kelman asks before the director has time to make the appropriate introductions.

Findal's head snaps upward, although he doesn't regard his interlocutor. "How could I, with her already down in the water and me atop the embankment?"

"Sir," the director barks. He raps the boy's ankle with a cane, and Findal automatically stiffens and straightens.

"Sir . . . Didn't I say I spotted her in the river, trying to drown her poor newly born babe? That's a crime, that is. Murdering an innocent who's naught but a few moments old."

Easby sighs in gargantuan empathy, and the boy's quick ears hearken to the sound. "I was right to come running, wasn't I, sir? If I hadn't, that wee infant would be dead, too. And now I must suffer for my good deed." He looks at Easby with practiced appeal; the president of the Humane Society seems on the verge of making a conciliatory remark when Kelman interrupts.

"But you would have pilfered something if you could. You've been disciplined before for stealing from your fellow inmates, have you not, Master Stokes?" Kelman doesn't wait for an answer; instead, he produces another query. "What were you doing outside the institution grounds?"

"Running away." The response is daring. Findal's bat ears flush pink; his eyes stare Kelman full in the face as if defying further interrogation. Noting the thin white scar that cuts across the man's left cheek, however, the boy reflexively reaches up to his own cheek, and an expression like admiration flits across his brow.

"Leaving your boots and your worldly possessions behind?"

In answer, Findal's gaze slides toward Easby, who has now

squeezed his bulky frame into a chair and is rapidly fanning himself with a handkerchief whose color is the crimson of fire. "If it weren't for me, that baby would be no more alive than his mother," the boy whines. "I should be praised for my act, not punished. He'd be feed for the fish, were it not for me. Or the bog demons would have got him."

"For someone who claims to have been at a distance when the act occurred—and to be unable to identify the mother—you seem quite certain the child is not only a newborn but a boy. When the basket was found, the baby was tightly swaddled in a cloth. Perhaps you could explain these riddles for us? Or how you came to know the child had been newly birthed? And don't tell us you were blinded by the glare."

The boy opens his mouth, then pinches it shut again. It's obvious that no amount of browbeating will elicit further information.

AS HE RETURNS TO THE sternwheel paddle steamer that will carry him and Easby back to the Schuylkill's eastern shore, Kelman parts company with the constable, whose relief is all too apparent. "A female vagrant," he speculates while his body gratefully uncoils itself and his gaze seeks out the welcome path toward home. "We get them out here now and then—even along the Darby Road. Escaping rough treatment at the hands of her family or masters. Likely, this one was turned out for immoral behavior and she was journeying into the city's anonymous streets when her labor pains came upon her—"

"Ah, yes," Easby concurs as he steps into the welcome shade of an elm growing beside Blockley's chapel. "What you say makes perfect sense. And having given birth, the poor soul places her baby in the basket she was carrying when she fled her dwelling place. Then, in a fit of melancholy and terror at an unknown future, takes herself down into the river. It's not uncharacteristic for new mothers to behave irrationally. Indeed, for some months following parturition their humors can be quite inconsistent." Easby nods as though agreeing with another's observation, then hurriedly shakes hands with the constable. Both men are now so anxious to be finished with the dilemma—and with Kelman—that their leave-taking has a disconcerting air of jocularity.

The Humane Society president carries this convivial humor through the rest of the almshouse's spreading grounds, past the stables and kitchen gardens down to the river and the ferry.

Not Kelman, however. While the boat slips over the heat-flattened waves, he responds to Easby's remarks with fewer and fewer words. Instead, he gives himself to brooding over the boy Stokes and his father, and the vanished and most probably drowned mother of the infant.

Then, eschewing an offer to ride in Easby's waiting phaeton, Kelman begins retracing his steps into the city. As he walks he reflects on the changes time has wrought upon it. In ten or twenty years, he knows, little will remain of William Penn's "greene countrie towne" or the peaceable waterways that border it. Instead, there will be additional wire suspension bridges like the one constructed the previous winter, more coal barges churning through the canal, more pleasure steamers spewing smoke above the falls at Fair Mount. From the banks of the Delaware to the rocky cliffs of the Schuylkill, the city will be nothing but hard, paved streets, brick and stone buildings lined cheek by jowl, abattoirs, woolen mills, match factories, tanneries—and the children of the poor.

For a moment he pauses, recalling the scenes of his youth. *Was I any different than young Findal,* he wonders, *running barefoot through these vanishing fields? Wild and untamed, and filled with the same hard-won valor. True, my father was never relegated to an almshouse, but was that because he was a wiser man than Stokes senior—or merely more fortunate? For he was no saint. Nor any remote approximation of one, either.*

Kelman marches on, his shoes chafing at the dust and weeds of the dirt road, his black jacket prickling with heat. By now the elegant homes of the wealthy are beginning to dot the streetscape: new mansions and walled gardens filling what was once open grazing land. It's all he can do to prevent his path from turning in the direction of Martha Beale's residence on Chestnut and Eleventh streets. He knows she was expected home the day before, but he has been purposely keeping his distance. *Better for her that I remove myself from her acquaintance,* he recites in bitter silence. *Better that she has a clear choice in a husband and companion, someone of her own means and background. I only cloud the issue. She must forget me. She'll be happier for it. Happier and more content, by far.*

AS KELMAN TRUDGES EAST, MERRIER feet than his flutter through less gloomy air, passing down a set of freshly washed marble stairs that front a home on lower Pine Street. This is Theodora Crowther; and she, in the company of her parents, Mr. and Mrs. Harrison Crowther, is on her way to visit the newly established daguerreotypist on High Street. The city is abuzz with this marvel—freshly arrived from France, of course, while the man who owns the gallery boasts a name full of hyphenations and ducal-sounding associations: Monsieur Jean-François Baptiste-Gourand, who learned his craft from M. Daguerre himself.

Theodora, or Dora, for this is how her mother and father call her, is nineteen and affianced to Percy VanLennep, who like her is fair-haired and given to quick flushes of embarrassment and impetuous bursts of enthusiasm. Together, they are like fledgling chicks, bobbing up and down with hopeful hops; apart, they are more restrained. Dora, in her parents' company, can seem no more assured than a girl of fourteen.

"Oh, do come, Mama," she now trills, lifting her little heart-shaped face, which today is framed in a bonnet of pale pink satin. Like her walking dress, the hat is piped in violet satin and trimmed with silk flowers; and she fairly spins in pride at this new ensemble. Excitement shivers across Dora's lilac-hued shawl, down her arms in their tight sleeves, and makes her lace gloves dance in the air. "Mama! Do come! Else we'll be late!"

Georgine Crowther appears in the doorway at that moment. She precedes her husband, whose tall hat rises less than an inch above the top of her own bonnet. Mrs. Harrison Crowther is a commanding presence. Where her daughter dances along the brick walkway, she promenades in a measured gait, with a frame so much broader and higher that she looks as though she might be descended from another race of peoples altogether. Dressed head to toe in moss green, Georgine Crowther resembles a leafy tree moving toward the street.

"Mama, do come!"

But the party is called back again as Harrison Crowther's elderly maiden aunt Lydia steps outside to stand on the topmost step. The aunt so perfectly resembles her great-niece as to appear a portrait of youth turned old—and at the age of eighty-two, she is indeed ancient. Where Dora's hearing is sharp though, Lydia's is failing. Despite repeated applications of Scarpa's Acoustical Oil, she exists in a realm that encompasses both past and present, and where the remembered conversations of her youth often have more relevance than present ones.

Now Miss Lydia, as the Crowther servants refer to her, totters down the stairs in order to embrace her great-niece and to remind her—loudly—to "mind her manners when in the presence of the general." Dora's mother starts to protest the interruption, but Miss Lydia continues speaking as if the tall lady dressed in green were invisible.

"He admires a pretty face," she states in a rapturous singsong tone, "but not a pert retort. Silence is advisable when in doubt, especially because he's so often burdened by affairs of state." The "general" is George Washington, dead for over forty years but alive in Lydia's mind—as is her father, who served as the great man's aide-de-camp. "I feel a plume in your hat might be better than those flowers," she adds, but Dora's mother interjects a domineering:

"Miss Crowther, we're tardy in keeping our appointment. Perhaps you could discuss Theodora's headdress upon our return."

The old lady can scarcely wave good-bye before her great-niece is hustled away, trailing behind her mother like a small boat sucked into the billowing wake of a larger one. Harrison Crowther tips his hat, and his aunt graces him with an inconclusive smile. She can't recall the short man with the square face and rectangular torso, but her aged fingers automatically stretch out on either side. If she weren't suddenly aware of standing beside a busy city street, she would attempt a curtsy. A full *révérence* straight down to the ground—as the general always desired.

THE RECEPTION ROOM OF THE daguerreian's gallery is so extravagantly furnished with damask-covered *tête-à-têtes,* with pier glasses and curio cabinetry, that Dora gasps in pleasure, hurrying into the already bustling space as though entering a *thé dansant.* Her mother, no less astonished but more circumspect, follows, bestowing haughty nods on several acquaintances while covertly examining the quality of fabrics and choice of color scheme. The crimson hues, vibrant greens, and splashes of gold meet her approval since they reflect an appropriately masculine taste. Given the fact that she considers the daguerreotypist's art no more than a passing fancy, she finds the surroundings surprisingly to her liking.

"Ah . . . good . . . good . . . Mrs. Crowther," her husband says, "what say you to the gallery? I trust that observing so many elegant folk has allayed your fears for our Dora." He doffs his beaver hat but then is forced to hold it in his hands—there being no servant present to receive it.

"Oh, Papa, do come see! There's a portrait of Becky Grey!"

Georgine Crowther stiffens, as any good mother would on hearing this disconcerting news. Becky Grey is an actress—or was until a foolhardy gentleman decided to make her his wife. As the gentleman is of the Crowthers' social sphere, his rash undertaking is all the more galling.

"Mistress Grey, indeed" is Harrison's jovial reply, but Georgine interjects a stentorian:

"How would you have possibly have recognized the woman, Theodora?"

"Oh, Papa took me—"

"Not to the theater, I trust!" Despite the turning of heads and tilting of curious bonnets, Georgine's voice is nearly a bellow. "And the lady is known as Mrs. Taitt now, Theodora, and that is how you should refer to her. If you must refer to her at all—"

"Dora and I happened to stroll by the American Theater on Walnut Street," Crowther tells his wife. "As you know, it's my belief that young ladies should learn the works of the great dramatists, and since Mr. Booth was commencing the role of Hamlet, and Mistress Grey was to play Ophelia, I felt—"

"Surely you did not permit her to view the production, Mr. Crowther?"

The father glances at the daughter. He's far from chastised; instead, he seems to be enjoying the public altercation. "Alas, the hours allotted for the tragedy weren't convenient. Another play was running in repertory—the comedy *A New Way to Pay Old Debts,* which didn't much interest either of us. And now, of course, it's too late to see Becky Grey in any role other than dutiful wife and future mother—"

"Oh!" Georgine's ruddy cheeks flush a deeper hue; her bosom, despite the creaking stays, heaves. She fans herself and stifles another noisy sigh. "Theodora, I will not have you attending theatrical productions."

"But Papa felt—"

"Your father does not appreciate the impropriety of young unmarried ladies witnessing—"

"Mistress Grey was also an unwed lady at the time," Harrison interposes; his boxy face beams complacency and bonhomie.

"If you please, sir, I know whereof I speak." Georgine turns her back on her husband. "Theodora, if your father proposed taking you to the Masonic Hall to witness the trickery and prestidigitations of the Fakir of Ava, surely it would not occur to you—?"

"Oh, Papa, might you?" Dora has completely misunderstood her mother's meaning; she pirouettes on her dainty heels as she gives her father a loving smile. "Hindoo Miracles, and costumes imported from Hindoostan. I read about the exhibition in your copy of the *Philadelphia Gazette.* The mysterious young lady who assists the Fakir, and a boy sorcerer with another foreign-sounding name. The card printed in the *Gazette* was most explicit in describing their acts of wizardry. I noticed it when I was reading a serialized tale entitled *The Fortune-Teller's Ring*—"

"Theodora!"

Too late, Dora understands her mother's meaning. She sends a frightened glance toward her father, who returns a conspiratorial wink, then strolls away on the pretext of admiring the likenesses framed upon the gallery walls. *Womenfolk and their foibles,* his stance attests, *mothers and daughters, aunts and nieces: What a good deal of fuss the distaff side fabricates.* When he spots a portrait of Becky Grey he pauses, fully aware of his wife's reproachful gaze. He settles his shoulders as though relishing her disregard.

WHEN THE CROWTHERS ARE CONDUCTED at length into the daguerreian's operating room, it's husband rather than wife who experiences misgivings. A slanting skylight smudged with dirt and ash blocks the sun, making the place appear somber and forbidding; the artist's backdrops drape the walls, their colors tomblike and eerie: bluish gray, dark Roman ocher, moleskin. Then there are the cruel-looking iron headrests and armrests that hold a body immobile for the long moments each exposure requires. The entire scene seems suggestive of death. "A trick of the light. It's no more than a trick of color and light," Crowther mutters as an assistant to M. Baptiste-Gourand escorts Dora to her place, leaning her delicate neck against a headrest, then pressing her temple against the cold metal and moving one hand to trail a nearby Corinthian column.

Dora's eyes, so habitually lively, grow dim with discomfort. She affixes a smile on her face, but the expression appears wan and tortured.

"The portrait lens is designed by Josef Petzval of Vienna," the parents are informed by another assistant, this one with an ingratiating and murmuring manner. "The Voigtländer lens is more famous, but is often counterfeited, having a forged facsimile of the Voigtländer signature engraved on the tubes. Naturally the forgery is of little consequence . . ."

Crowther doesn't reply; instead, he watches a stranger's hands manipulate his daughter's body. "Iodide of silver in order to coat the plate," the second assistant continues, "then vapor of mercury to develop the latent image, and immersion in a solution of sodium hyposulphite, which fixes the features. It is intended as a keepsake for Miss Crowther's fiancé, is it not?"

Harrison begins to answer but finds he's standing beside a series of horrifying pictures he hadn't noticed previously. They're quarter-plate memorial portraits of dead infants and children, set in ghostly white frames of mother-of-pearl. The daguerreotypes so upset him that he jerks backward in alarm.

"Oh, Papa, must you startle me?" Dora complains. "One would think you didn't want Percy to have his lovely gift. Please do keep still, or Mama and I will be forced to banish you from the room."

THE LOST PARASOL

THE DAY AFTER DORA'S VISIT to the daguerreian's studio, the neighborhood in which she dwells is visited by a force of nature unprecedented in the city. In an instant the afternoon sky above St. Peter's churchyard turns tarry black while the sun's gold rays are transformed into a spidery and threatening yellow. The pedestrians strolling along Pine or Fourth Street look upward in alarm, expecting an onslaught of thunderclouds and rain—or hail, as has been reported in the countryside. But not one drop of moisture falls. Instead, the air begins to crackle as though desiccated and sere; and a windspout springs to life on Lombard Street, whipping at the elms and the streetlamps as if trying to pluck them from the earth. The monstrous whirling thing grows in height and breadth until it's half as tall as a house and as wide as a heavyset man, then veers northward on Third, where it leaps over the brick wall encircling the church's memorial garden and begins playing havoc among the graves and Osage oranges and shaded brick paths.

Tree limbs as thick as human torsos are snapped in pieces, then hurled to the ground, toppling ancient marble headstones as they plummet. The noise of the spout is like the communal moan of a hundred voices; householders on the facing streets either hurry to their windows in order to witness the extraordinary event or scurry down toward their cellars, shooing their children before them.

Those who watch see three people huddling in terrified positions within the lee of the southern wall. They're an odd grouping: a woman who is obviously pregnant and whose elegant ensemble bespeaks wealth and a position in society, an older Negro man whom most recognize as the church's sexton, and another gentleman, shabbily clothed but bearing, despite the awkwardness of his pose, a proud and defiant bravado. The tall hat on his head may have seen better days, but it's clamped down tight as if the possessing of such an article were a mark of royalty. This unlikely trio touch hands with one another, then clasp their fingers together as though praying that the joined weight of three bodies will be enough to withstand the blast. Remarkably, the beaver hat remains in place.

Then the vicious gust hops away to torture other sections of the city, and the sun reappears, smiling down indifferently.

BECKY GREY—FOR SHE IS THE lady—finds she's weeping as she creeps away from the wall and stands. One side of her face is sore and scratched from the rough brick and mortar; the sleeve of her gown is rent; her parasol has been wrenched from her hand and tossed high into a tree; her bonnet is battered; the lace trimming her skirt hangs in strips as if the fingers that knotted it had forgotten the pattern. It's not from her ruined clothing or abraded skin that she cries, though, but from terror. She straightens her body and cannot stem her tears while the Negro man offers to bring her water and then hurries away, and the other man—after some shambling hesitation—supplies a threadbare handkerchief.

In former times, such ministrations would have brought her solace. Now, the efforts only make matters worse, and she continues to sniffle and cry as though she were a lost child rather than a woman six months pregnant. A woman who, by the strict rules of Philadelphia society, should not be venturing abroad without a serving maid or footman to await her wishes.

Becky doesn't care, for lost and frightened is precisely how she feels. Fearful for her physical safety, so recently threatened; and lost because the freak storm has proven once again how much she misses her homeland and all that was familiar and beloved. *Why did I settle in this provincial place?* her thoughts rail. *What did I imagine my life would be within the confines of such a narrow world? This is not London or Paris, after all. Why, oh why was I blinded by William Taitt's handsome face and his honeyed words!* " 'Nought's had, all's spent, where our desire is got without content,' " she mutters aloud. If she were alone, she would certainly add an oath.

"I'm guessing you're an actress," the man who offered the handkerchief states. The tone is rough, as though assessing the physical attributes of a horse.

If this had been last week or even yesterday, her response would have been very different. She would have drawn herself to her full height—and she is not a petite woman—and corrected the speaker with a disdainful "I am Mrs. William Taitt of Philadelphia and Charleston." Now she merely nods. "I was."

"If you was somebody once, you're that same somebody now," the man argues with a sudden frown; and Becky notices that his forehead is flinty with dirt, that his clothing gives off an unwashed odor, and that his linen is dingy and ill patched. "Who you be is who you be. No one can take that away from you," he continues with the same stolid inflection while Becky dangles the handkerchief from increasingly hesitant fingers. She would turn and depart from her insalubrious companion, but something warns her to take care. His manner and movements may seem bovine and dull, but it's the deceptive quiescence of a bull in an empty pasture.

"Thank you for your aid," she says instead, pressing the handkerchief upon him and opening her reticule in order to give him a coin.

"Do I look like a beggar to you, missus?"

He does, of course, but Becky shakes her head. Beneath his hat's low brim, his angry stare grows. "Because I'm not. I'm an honest man. As honest as any actress parading about on the stage."

Becky makes no answer. She wishes the sexton would return, or that some passerby would venture into the wind-whipped arena.

"More," he adds with a growl. "More."

Becky takes a step backward, then, with great relief, notices the sexton's reappearance. She calls out to him that she needs no further aid as she hurries off into the relative safety of Pine Street.

BECKY DOESN'T IMMEDIATELY JOURNEY HOME, however. The storm and its human aftermath have unsettled her, leaving her raw outside and in. So she pulls her mantilla tightly around her shoulders, trudging along as she weighs the words delivered in the churchyard. *If you was somebody once, you're that same somebody now.* She shakes her head, wishing the statements would vanish, but their echoes remain. *Who you be is who you be. No one can take that away from you.*

Except William Taitt, she reminds herself. *Except Taitt with his houses and servants and the luxuries he dangled in front of my eyes.*

And the willing bride who bartered her career and her future in exchange.

Her face full of distress, Becky plunges on until she comes to the boisterous open-air market appropriately known as the Shambles. As it's midafternoon, most of the shopkeepers have packed up their goods, leaving behind a malodorous assortment of ruined fruit, trampled vegetables, oyster shells, fish scales, and straw. Fresh and white-yellow this morning, the straw covering the long stone floor has become flaccid and gray; in the heat, it gives off a fetid odor of rot and horse dung.

Becky lifts her long skirts to avoid the mire; as she does, she notices a gypsy woman who has positioned herself beside a makeshift table where she's offering to prophesy the future. Such sights were so common in London that Becky's heart lifts and she rushes toward the woman, yanking off both gloves and thrusting forward her palms for the gypsy to read. "What is my past history, good dame? If your answer is true, I'll let you cast your cards and tell me what to expect in the future. Come. What was I once?"

The woman glances at Becky's hands, then snaps her fortune-teller's cards together, hiding them away in the bosom of her gown, a thing stitched of so many odds and ends that it looks like a cloth merchant's sample. "You are no mother" is all she says, but Becky responds with a wry laugh.

"You're correct, good lady. The role of maternal parent isn't one I've studied. However, I'm known to be diligent, so I warrant I'll learn my part in time. Now tell me who I once was—"

"Not in time. Or ever."

Becky continues smiling, although the severity of the gypsy's tone begins to disconcert her. "I have no choice but to learn. But let us leave this dull discussion of motherhood. Tell me who I was in the past. And how lauded—"

"You are no mother," the gypsy repeats, "and your small abode is filled with phantoms and apparitions."

Becky stifles an impatient sigh. "You've mistaken my existence for another's. I have several homes—large ones—and I am obviously great with child."

"You will have nothing" is the retort. "Now, cross my palm with a coin, missus, and then take yourself away."

"Oh!" Becky can no longer contain her ire. "You'll get no monies from me. You're nothing but a fraud." Despite these declarations, she reaches for her reticule. Too late, she remembers that pickpockets make a habit of circulating among crowds where gypsies and other street buskers perform.

"The man took it," the fortune-teller says while fixing Becky with a steady gaze. "The man creeping among them white graves."

IT'S BY HAPPENSTANCE THAT MARTHA doesn't encounter the now clearly agitated and homeward-bound Becky while she also walks along Third Street. Having left her father's former brokerage offices near the Merchants' Exchange, her first thought on hearing of the freak storm is to ascertain the condition of his memorial marker. Instead of the former actress, however, it's the lady's husband Martha spots as she enters the churchyard. Her steps cease, and she considers retreating because she finds William Taitt an unlikable person. Despite his outward cordiality and courtliness, despite his wide acquaintanceship and the position of respect he enjoys throughout the city, he strikes her as being intrinsically secretive and even sly.

But Taitt, ever vigilant and mindful of his aristocratic role, calls to her before she can escape. "Ah, Miss Beale, and looking as handsome as ever. Your sojourn in the countryside agreed with you." He smiles, but the expression goes no deeper than the surface of his skin. "I had heard you'd returned home. And the children you adopted, naturally. How fortunate for them that your paths crossed as they did, and they may now enjoy both the Beale name and estate." He rocks back on his high and fashionable heels, his well-formed, patrician features no more than a mask of empathy. Or so Martha decides.

"Yes. It is" is all she has time to answer before he dispenses with the subject of her wards and returns to studying the devastation that spreads about on each side. A blanket of yellow-green leaves covers everything: shorn tree limbs, broken monuments, hacked-apart shrubbery, and the splintered benches that line the paths. Small clusters of people wade through the debris, their bodies bent as though they were trudging through snow or a pounding surf.

"This will cost us a pretty penny to fix, but at least the church roof doesn't appear to be damaged. Let us hope that a majority of the stones are also untouched. The vestry cannot afford additional repairs."

"I came to ascertain whether my father's tablet was harmed," Martha tells him. "If so, I shall pay to have it replaced. And I'm certain other individuals whose family members are interred here will do likewise."

"Very good of you, Miss Beale. But it's not to our more recent markers that I refer, rather to those entrusted to us by history: the founders of our nation and so forth. I need not explain what an honor it is to serve on the governing body of a parish that played such a vital role in the birth of America." While he delivers this discourse, Taitt's glance roves up into the trees, which are almost wholly denuded and from which dangles an odd assortment of storm-tossed ornaments. A wheeled barrow hangs from a horse chestnut; a broom clings to a holly; a rope still bearing newly laundered table linens wraps around a crabapple; and finally the strangest addition: a lady's open parasol attached to the uppermost limb of a sycamore as if the tree were holding the handle because it desired protection from the sun.

"My wife has one like that," he remarks with what sounds like genuine astonishment. "Ivory, the handle is, with a nice bit of jade for ornamentation. Fancy there being another so similar." He frowns, but the expression rapidly transforms itself into sophisticated ennui. "If I'd known there were two, I might have argued over the price. Indeed, I might not have purchased it at all." Then he leaves off discussing jade-studded parasols and returns to his companion, gracing her with another flawless smile.

"As I was just saying, children do make a wonderful addition to a home, do they not? It's unfortunate your father didn't live to see his own house so happily encumbered. Such a tragedy, his untimely death. And the awful circumstances, too. How you must grieve for him."

Not one part of this speech seems sincere, but Martha's response is curtailed as Taitt's confident words roll forward:

"And what will become of his financial concerns now that he's no longer there to guide them?"

"I'm managing them, Mr. Taitt."

"You, Miss Beale? Surely you jest."

"Indeed, I do not." Despite an effort at civility, Martha is becoming increasingly vexed. "I admit I have no great love of numbers, and that my father's genius for foreign specie and his manipulation of bills of exchange on Germany and Ireland is still a new notion to me—"

"If it were not for that detestable Andrew Jackson, and his deregulation of the banking system—!" Taitt exclaims in a jovial shout, but Martha intervenes. The harangue is one she's heard too often.

"Yes, I know. If President Jackson had left the Bank of United States alone, the nation would not have been thrust into this crippling depression." The tone is more stringent than she intended, but her companion merely chortles at her discomfort.

"These are not subjects most ladies feel equipped to discuss, Miss Beale."

"I am not most ladies, sir. My father's demise may have forced me to embark upon studies that are normally the purview of men, but I'm determined to master them. Indeed, I've just informed a senior clerk that I wish to purchase some type of factory or manufacturing endeavor—"

"A factory! Oh, goodness me! And do you intend to work the ledger books, with your fine silk sleeves all covered in spotty ink guards—?"

"And employ people at decent wages," she continues in the same peremptory vein, "rather than keep them in semi-bondage."

"The master who embarks upon that foolhardy scheme will go bankrupt in jig time, Miss Beale." Taitt laughs again, an ample, condescending sound.

"So I was told" is the chilly reply. "But why should that be? And if the owner's profits are less than desired, what does it matter as long as there's employment? Or parents aren't forced to work for starving wages? Or consign their children to the mills and match factories?"

"Ah, my, my, my . . . You're as impassioned as my dear wife, Miss Beale. And, I venture to say, nearly as dramatic. But come, I see I've offended you. That was not my intent. There should always be kindly souls to weep over the plight of the suffering."

Martha turns to face him, her eyes so full of stubbornness and wounded pride that the color has turned a flat and stormy gray. She opens her mouth to speak but is saved from uttering words she might regret by the arrival of a second man.

"Mar— Miss Beale. I did not think to find you here." Thomas Kelman tips his hat, then nearly drops it on the ground. "You are only recently returned to the city, I understand . . ." The words trail away, leaving him to gaze hopelessly into her face. The stern stare that held young Findal Stokes in thrall is nowhere in evidence, while Martha also undergoes a metamorphosis.

"Yes. Two days past," she murmurs, then adds a more vigorous "Mr. Taitt, may I present Mr. Kelman. Thom— Mr. Kelman was of great service to me when my father died." Now Martha's cheeks are on fire, for she nearly committed the unpardonable sin of calling Thomas by his first name—which she *has* done, although never in company.

"Anyone would wish to be of service to you, Miss Beale" is Kelman's heartfelt answer. Then both fall silent. Taitt maintains his superior pose, studying the man and the woman before him as though probing their souls.

"I know you by reputation, Kelman. But I didn't realize how effortlessly you could tame this argumentative lady. She and I were discussing financial matters and so forth, and her desire to aid the poor and needy—"

"Miss Beale has expressed such opinions to me," Kelman states before again lapsing into silence.

"You're a fortunate man to be in her confidence, sir," Taitt says with another shrewd smile. "I wish you'd explain how you work these miracles with opinionated ladies, as I'm greatly in need of curbing my wife's lively wit. She was accustomed to a very different model before we wed." With that he bows. "Promise me you'll come visit my Becky one day soon, Miss Beale. She's sorely in need of a companion as iconoclastic as you. Who knows, you might become friends if you knew one another better." Then he saunters away, a man without a care in the world, although he does pause to glance at the lost parasol before continuing on his path.

Martha and Kelman watch him leave, but their awkwardness only increases, and Martha finds herself fanning her face as if the afternoon's heat rather than confusion were causing her discomfort.

"We should find you some shade, Mar— Miss Beale," Kelman says. "The sun is still high, and your costume is heavy."

"I would rather have you walk me home." She blanches at both the boldness of this request and that of her tone. "Or perhaps you have other business to attend to?"

"I would be glad to accompany you. Of course I would."

So begins the journey, although both avoid all physical contact with one another. If they were passing acquaintances, Kelman would offer his arm and Martha would accept the gesture; instead, they walk apart.

"Little Ella is well?" he asks after a moment.

"She is, thank you."

"And Cai?"

"He's exceedingly fit, too, although neither wanted to forsake the countryside and return to town. They . . . they enjoyed your sporadic visits to us, as I did also . . ."

"Your house is a refuge. I don't wonder at their sorrow at leaving. I would feel the same."

"You've become a great favorite with the children" is Martha's whispery reply.

"And they with me."

Words again fail them, although their footsteps roll automatically forward. What sights they see or whom they pass, neither could describe.

"I do hope your infrequent calls upon us weren't the result of your work with the police, Mr. Kelman. And that your labors haven't proven overly arduous."

"Not arduous. But disheartening, as is so often the case."

Hearing the despondency in his tone, she cannot help but spin toward him. "Oh, Thomas, I apologize! I should not have broached a painful subject."

He smiles gently down. "I'm glad to speak with you. I'm always happy to have your opinion and comments, but I'm sorry to say that the suicide of an unknown woman is all too common in our city."

"A suicide! How awful. And this is what you have been investigating?"

"It seems my skills are unnecessary. A newly delivered mother cast herself and her infant into the Schuylkill two days ago. A boy from Blockley House witnessed the incident and returned in order to report it. The baby was retrieved; the mother had placed him in a wicker-ware basket. She hasn't been found. Unfortunately, the boy was alone, and his retelling of the story is imprecise."

By now, Martha has stopped entirely. "That was the very day I returned to the city."

"Yes. I considered calling upon you, but—"

"I saw a blond woman wading in the river with a basket that I took to be full of laundry. But there wasn't only one boy on the cliffs above the river; there were many. And they seemed to know her."

WHAT FINDAL TOLD THEM

When Kelman recrosses the Schuylkill the next morning, he chooses the bridge rather than the ferry in order to spend additional time in thought. While his horse trots across the wooden planks, a paddle steamer chugs between its open wharfs, and several small schooners bearing goods transshipped from the Delaware beat against the current. Swifts wing past the vessels at a dizzying speed. When the birds sense themselves too close to the boats or each other, they spin and bank sideways, then sail away over the liquid expanse. In the space between one riverbank and the next, it seems to Kelman that the world is now no longer man's but nature's. Except for a few fellow travelers, gone is the noise of the city. Gone the carters' oaths, the vendors' cries, the pie men, soup sellers, the quacks purveying curative elixirs, the rag and bone men, the fancy ladies hawking their stale wares.

Hidden stream, he reflects, for this is how *schuylkill* translates: a Dutch word for a waterway discovered while those earliest settlers explored the greater Delaware. *Hidden stream,* his brain repeats, and the name takes on a sinister significance as if the river were capable of intrigue. Then the bridge is crossed, and Kelman turns his horse toward the lane leading to the almshouse.

"THE BOY'S GONE. DISAPPEARED WITHOUT so much as a ripple of warning. None of the others lodging with him seem to have been aware of his plans." As Blockley's director speaks, he turns away from Kelman and stares out the window. His body maintains the stance of a professional man receiving an official visit, but his tone suggests the fullness of his ire. That and the jittery motion of the hands clasped at his back. His fingers never cease twisting; they look as though they'd like to work their way around a deserving neck.

"He's run off before, of course. He may return. He may not. It's no great loss if he chooses to keep himself at large. Like his father, he's a schemer and as untrustworthy as the day is long. But then most of the children here are. The adults are just as bad. The elder Stokes is gone, too. Looking for work, or so he claimed. We shall see if he achieves his goals this time." The director pauses, either to take a breath or because he's considering the veracity of his remarks, and Kelman takes advantage of the silence.

"I'd like to interview the other inmates in the boy's ward, if I may."

"It won't do you any good. They fabricate lies as willingly as they eat their suppers."

"I understand." A "sir" is added to this effort, but the word sounds hastily considered rather than deferential. "But perhaps they can solve the mystery of why Findal insisted he was the sole witness to the suicide and the attempted murder of the infant."

"You're wasting your time." The inference is plain. The asylum's director believes that his own precious hours are being frittered away by a misguided investigation.

"That may be, but the time is mine to use as I see fit. I believe I've taken too much of your morning already. I'm comfortable proceeding on my own." Kelman awaits instructions, but the director doesn't turn to face him.

"I'll send for one of the warders to conduct you to the children's asylum." Then his voice completes this impolite dismissal with a querulous "The suicide was not a resident of Blockley."

"I understand, sir."

"See that you remember it. We have over fourteen hundred residents here, among them one hundred fifty-two syphilitics, twenty-four lunatics, and twenty-three epileptics. I'm sure you can appreciate that this is not an easy populace to control. There are too many malicious rumors in circulation, and I don't intend to have the citizens of our metropolis troubled by fraudulent tales when they might instead admire our chapel, or our medical library, or the excellence of our apothecary and obstetrical ward. The reports in the penny press concerning the beef contract were most unfortunate. We serve wholesome food here, and are at pains to make certain all of it is fresh and edible.

"As to the lugubrious whispers of body snatching and so forth, they are simply unconscionable. Why, our anatomical colleges must have subjects, mustn't they? For the betterment of mankind, our surgeons must learn their craft. And how else—?" The speech abruptly ceases. "We who labor here, Mr. Kelman, do our utmost to safeguard the poor wretches entrusted to our care."

"Naturally."

At that the director turns, uncertain as to his visitor's intent. Kelman's quiet gaze reveals nothing.

THE ASSEMBLED BOYS ARE A ragtag lot, of all ages and shapes and heights. Some have large heads supported by spindly frames; some heads are narrow and pinched; arms are long with wide and bony wrists or short with flapping hands. Their attire displays the same variety although the patches stitched to nearly every article are a constant, as is their pervading scrawniness.

If Kelman could use only one word to describe them, it would be "hungry." Hungry not only for food but for comfort, pleasure, safety, peace. In the barn-like room in which the boys sleep, these commodities are noticeably absent. Instead, daylight chinks in through sizable cracks in the board walls; the lumpy straw mattresses are bare of covering; no toy nor book is in sight; and the warders loom, sticks in hands and grimaces upon their faces like ogres in a fairy tale. In the heat the room stinks of piss pots and excrement; in the cold of winter, Kelman surmises, the bedclothes would certainly freeze upon the boys' backs.

"Why did Findal insist he was alone when he spotted the woman and her newborn child?" is the first question he asks. Pity and austerity war in his soul. He has no desire to harm these children, but he needs the truth.

"Oh, but he was alone, sir." This is one of the taller boys responding. He has a high white dome of a forehead poorly covered by sparse black thatch, and his chest looks as though it were caving in on itself. He stands, or rather hulks, at the rear of the clump of children but is such an odd specimen that he's easily distinguished. "None of us was up there on that embankment with him."

"I have information otherwise. A witness described a number of boys accompanying Stokes."

"Other lads than us here present," the same boy insists.

There's a murmur of hearty agreement at this statement, although Kelman is still regarded with apprehension.

"How did you know he was 'up' rather than closer to the river's surface?"

"He told us, sir."

"But he informed none of you where he was going when he ran away? Or even warned you beforehand?"

"Oh, no, sir. Not a word."

"Even if they knew Findal Stokes was planning to rob the mayor's house, they wouldn't say," one of the warders insists with a lazy grin. "He was by way of being their leader."

"Would young Stokes have explained his plans to his father?" Kelman asks and is rewarded by a communal snicker as though each child were affirming that parents are no more trustworthy or amiable than these paid keepers. Unlike the almshouse's director with his nervous hands, none of the boys make the smallest gesture as they laugh.

"Who was the woman?"

The boy with the prominent forehead and misshapen chest makes no response this time; instead, one of the shortest among them speaks up. "A lady having a baby. Findal said we must come quick if we wanted—" The words halt with a yelp of pain.

"If you wanted?" Kelman presses, but stubborn silence greets the question.

"I can get you an answer," another warder offers. He's an obese man with simian arms, and his exposed neck is covered with matted hair that looks like fur. "Like as not, it was mischief they had in mind. This lot always does." He swings his club into his open palm but is afforded no reaction from his charges. A beating will not pry loose whatever secrets they're keeping.

Kelman watches the scene and all at once experiences a leaden weariness. What does it matter what the children saw or did? The mother is assuredly drowned; the infant is already in an orphanage. And Findal Stokes, wherever he is, is probably better off without these harsh men to rule him. "No. I've learned enough."

"You should query Stokes senior," the ape guardian continues as if he were the soul of cooperation. "I can take you to him if you'd like."

"The director informed me that he was gone. Seeking employment."

"Seeking the bottom of a bottle, is more like it. Just as he does here. Stone-drunk Stokes. The boy will be the same. You wait."

Kelman stares. "Strong spirits are permitted at Blockley?"

"There's not much we can do to keep 'em out. And when we try, they make their own."

"I see." Kelman shakes his head and stifles a groan of frustration at a system so flawed.

"And, too, some of them poor wights is took so bad with the mania and deliriums when they come in, it's only a kindness to let them down easy. Envision all sorts of bogeymen, they do. Monsters with fifteen legs and the like. A tot or two can't do no harm, especially if it keeps folk in a gentle manner." The warder grins; the stumps of his teeth are black.

"Yes, I see." The tone is flat. Kelman turns to leave, but the shortest child speaks up again.

"If the baby dies, will the orphanage guardians cut off its skin and make it into a book?"

"Will they—?" He's not certain he's heard the bizarre question correctly.

"Will they tan the hide and bind a book with it?" For such a distressing query, the tone is as commonplace as if the child were asking whether cows ate grass.

"What would give you that horrible idea?"

"That's enough idle talk," another warder orders, but the little boy ignores the directive, chirping away in the same pragmatic manner.

"It's what they do here when someone dies. Or the person's carted off to the anatomical colleges—"

"Enough, I said!"

"They make us eat maggoty meat—when we get it—and when we die they make a handsome profit from our remains. Findal said so."

Kelman looks at the boy and then at his companions, who are now intently watching the visitor's reaction. Aware that the warders are also staring, and that it will go hard with the child if his pronouncements are accepted, he decides to treat them with disbelief. "Your Master Stokes must be a great personage for you to believe everything he says."

"His father made leather things. For horses. So Findal knew all about hides and such."

"A harness maker," Kelman says in the same false manner. "Well, that's certainly a fine trade."

None of the boys reply, although their eyes regard Kelman with another kind of hunger. The need for acceptance and approval haunts every face.

"That young Stokes was a one for trickery and deception," the fat man with the hairy neck growls, then laughs as though there were no more explanation necessary and escorts the visitor from the room, opening a calloused paw for a monetary reward that fails to materialize. "Mind how you go, sir," Kelman is told, and the words have the ring of a threat.

A QUESTION OF THIEVERY

Percy Vanlennep sits cross-legged in the Harrison Crowthers' withdrawing room and accepts a cup of chocolate from Dora's outstretched hand. Their fingers touch, providing both with such a physical thrill that they blush in consort, then slide guilty glances toward Miss Lydia, who's serving as chaperone, Theodora's parents being absent—attending a performance of Donizetti's *L'Elisir d'Amore*.

"You may kiss the girl, Percy," Lydia states in her overloud voice. "Goodness knows, you children are to be married soon enough. You should learn what lips are for."

Dora giggles and toys with her chocolate cup in order to conceal her embarrassment. Percy crosses his legs tighter and prays that the growing bulge in his trousers doesn't show.

"I have the greatest respect for Theodora, Miss Crowther," he says, which words the elderly lady inexplicably hears.

"Respect is a fine sentiment, but affection is better. And ardor, too." She leans back within a high-backed wing chair, which, like the room's other furnishings, harks from an earlier age when delicacy of shape was in vogue: a Chippendale chest-on-chest, a tea table with cabriole legs, an inlaid and japanned Hepplewhite sideboard, and two Sheraton settees positioned on either side of the mantel and covered in a rose madder shade that was popular thirty years prior. The only concession to the modern era is three vapor lamps, which burn with a muzzy glow, unsuccessfully illuminating the swagged *bleu de Saxe* draperies that are closed against the dark street outside.

"You view me as an antique personage, Mr. VanLennep," Lydia continues, "unwed, and therefore untried in matters of the flesh. But such is not the case—"

"Oh, Aunt!" Dora interjects, but her great-aunt appears not to have heard her.

"I was a great favorite of the general, Mr. VanLennep. Whenever he entertained at one of his *levées* or *soirées,* he always sought me out in order to offer a pleasant compliment on my attire or on a little frippery that had caught his eye. He was an exceedingly handsome man and always wore a uniform that fit him impeccably." Lydia Crowther sighs, momentarily lost in time, and Percy and Dora share a clandestine look, then start backward in their two seats when their chaperone resumes her speech.

"Do you know that Mrs. Washington came to visit me one day, Mr. VanLennep? My dear papa was away from home, and I was forced to entertain the august lady alone. Alone! And no older than Dora. The purpose of the visit, Mrs. Washington explained, was to view a portrait of the general that my father had recently acquired." Miss Lydia pauses; the mantel clock strikes the hour: nine chiming bells that echo through the still room and recall her from her reverie. "It was by the painter Gilbert Stuart and hung in a place of prominence in our withdrawing room. When Mrs. Washington spotted it, however, she declared it deficient. 'I have the original,' she told me, 'which I shall keep until I cease to draw breath!' A strange statement, don't you think, sir?"

But Percy has only been half listening, and so replies with a hasty "You must have many pleasant memories, Miss Crowther."

"Oh, I do. I do," Lydia croons while Dora, fearful that her great-aunt will lapse into another interminable tale, interjects a jubilant:

"Just imagine, Percy! We're to be married in less than one month's time! Just think of it! Husband and wife—"

But Lydia proceeds as though her great-niece hadn't opened her mouth. "I'm weary and must retire. You must excuse me, Mr. VanLennep. I've exhausted myself with my recollections."

"Oh, but Aunt, you're acting as our chaperone while Mama and Papa are at the Musical Fund Hall," Dora protests. "If you leave us now, then Percy must also depart, and we're so very happy in one another's company."

"You will have to speak louder, Theodora. I cannot hear a word you're saying. That is, if it's to me you're speaking and not to your swain."

"I said that Mama and Papa wouldn't permit Percy to remain in our home if we're left alone," Dora nearly shouts.

"Goodness, child! When you're wed you'll be alone, won't you? And no one to tell you how to behave. What you choose to do when I'm gone from the room is your concern, but I advise practicing for your wedding eve. Young couples nowadays are far too unschooled in the act of love."

Dora gasps, but Lydia has already turned her back upon the pair, walking daintily toward the darkened foyer as though she'd just noticed a person waiting there.

"Oh, Percy," Dora murmurs as she stands. "Now our pleasant evening is spoiled, and you must leave lest Mama and Papa return and find you here without a proper guardian."

But Percy doesn't quit the room; nor does he stand. Instead, he pats the silky seat beside him. "I'll go after you give me a kiss."

"You know I cannot." Despite the protestation, Dora tiptoes toward the settee.

"One little kiss. No one will know."

"I cannot, Mr. VanLennep" is the coy reply.

"Cannot or will not?" By now, Percy has taken both her hands, pulling her body into his until she stands between his knees. "Shouldn't we obey your great-aunt, Mistress Crowther, and do a little practicing?"

"Oh, but Papa and Mama would be so disappointed in me." The tone remains reluctant, but she doesn't pull away; rather, she giggles again, the sound airy and delighted.

"Then we won't tell them." He catches her with his knees while his hands draw her down until she sits in his lap. "I'm aching for you, Dora dear. Do have pity upon me. Just one small caress is all I ask."

Dora leans into him, clasping his neck with her hands as a sleepy child might. "My heart is all aflutter. I fear I'll cease to breathe if we continue thus."

"Then you must loosen your stays, dear." His fingers move to her bodice, and Dora gasps again.

"Oh, Percy, how do you know about ladies' garments? I certainly never told you."

"I must have seen an advertisement in the *Gazette*" is the hasty answer.

"How unseemly that a journal would mention such items," she

objects, then releases a tremulous sigh as her dress is unbuttoned and her stays unloosed. "Oh, Percy, this is so very wrong . . ."

All at once, Dora leaps to her feet. "A carriage! Stopping in front of our house! It must be Mama and Papa returning. Oh, stand up, dearheart, so that we don't seem so . . . so . . ." She glances down at his lap. "What on earth is that object?"

Poor Percy has no time to reply because Georgine Crowther sails into the room at that moment. "Theodora! Mr. VanLennep!" Her voice is thunder, rolling and crashing. Percy expects lightning to shoot from her mouth, as well. The bulge in his trousers disappears in a trice, but the fact is small consolation, because now Harrison Crowther strides into the arena, his opera cape hanging from his shoulders like a cavalry officer's pelisse. If his wife is irate, he appears apoplectic. His thick face is as purple as wine spilled on a white cloth; his jowls quiver.

"And to imagine we trusted you, Mr. VanLennep!"

"Oh, Papa! Aunt Lydia just now left the room," Dora whimpers. "Percy was merely saying a courteous good night."

"A 'courteous' gentleman does not take advantage of a young lady as though he were a thief, intent on stealing her virtue—"

"But he wasn't, Papa! And besides, we're to be wed—"

"Silence, Theodora! You have no notion what you're saying."

It's so rare that her father calls her by her full name that Dora's mouth falls open while her mother commences her own attack on her husband. "This is Miss Lydia's fault, Mr. Crowther. She has subverted this child's sensibilities—"

"Oh, no, Mama, Aunt Lydia didn't—!"

"Enough, Theodora. Your father and I know what is best. Now, go to your chamber."

"And you, Mr. VanLennep, sir," Harrison adds, "I will thank you to leave us at once. It's true that you're affianced to my daughter, but your obvious disregard for her person I find most disquieting. Most disquieting, indeed."

LEAVE THEM PERCY DOES. WHILE Dora sits weeping in her rooms, he stalks the streets, and his bland and boyish face alternatively turns ashen in shame or blazes with indignation as he considers how dreadful his forthcoming marriage will be. When will he and Dora be permitted to act as they choose? When will it not always be "Yes, Mama. Yes, Papa" and Miss Lydia telling her everlasting tales? When will he not feel like an ill-behaved child? And Dora, too! Or what if his sweet little wife eventually transforms herself into a replica of her mother: huge, redoubtable—and most probably frigid?

Percy grinds his teeth at this horrifying notion. He, who is so young and virile, should not have to suffer this dreadful fate! *I should postpone the marriage. No, I must cancel rather than postpone. I'll own up to my mistake. And if Dora is unhappy for a time, well, she'll survive.*

By now his footsteps have taken him to the corner of Lombard and Sixth streets. A number of fancy houses are found here and farther west toward Tenth and south along Bainbridge. Many of the establishments are of the lesser sort and not frequented by gentlemen of his pedigree, yet they serve his purpose and have been doing so since the day Theodora accepted his proposal of marriage. Custom dictates he keep himself pure for his nuptial eve; and Percy knows that no one in these shabby places will report his wayward ways.

Here again he rails at destiny. *Why do I need this lowly house when my companions disport themselves in finer surroundings with more comely girls? If my engagement to Dora is finished, why should I care what people say? Let her father and mother suffer for the wrongful situation they've created and the anguish of their only child!*

Duty and habit, however, are difficult traits to conquer. Percy was no more reared to a life of rebellion than he was to be a soldier or explore an unknown world. He was bred to be precisely who he is: a young man accustomed to comfort, privilege, and self-indulgence. He turns his path toward the nearest bawdy house.

Dutch Kat's is the name, the madam being a plump, resourceful Hollander with a saucy tongue and an instinct for what her customers enjoy. Percy couldn't say whether the woman's given name is Katya or Katarine, nor does he care. At the moment, he's preoccupied with pillowy breasts and broad hips and dimples found in hidden places.

In his absorption, he nearly stumbles over a boy perched on the lowest stair leading to Dutch Kat's front door. The boy holds out his hand as though extracting tribute.

"Please, sir, are you seeking the good lady within?"

Startled, Percy draws back. He doesn't recall the child, although he feels that he should, for the boy's ears are oddly pointed.

"I can call her if you'd like," the urchin repeats.

"No. No," Percy stutters. Without another word, he passes up the steps, wondering whether to supply a copper or two, then decides against such an extravagant act. Besides, he doesn't wish to be remembered.

WHEN PERCY WALKS BACK DOWN the same stairs an hour later, the boy is gone. The surrounding alleys remain busy with potential patrons, however, causing Percy to creep away as if his guilt were attached to him like a cheap-Jack's sign, visible for all to read.

Clear of the area, he hurries north toward home but then

pauses in front of William Taitt's somber mansion, where he notes with surprise that lamps are still burning in several upper windows. *Oh,* he thinks, *if I had a wife like Becky Grey, I'd be awake at all hours of the night, too! And abed as much as we wished during daylight hours.*

Hoping to get a glimpse of the fortunate couple—in what he believes might be a compromising position—he crosses the road and stands on tiptoe. But no one appears, and so he trundles glumly on his way, comparing every woman he has known or met to Dora. *Why don't I have the courage to marry an actress like Becky Grey, someone sultry and provocative, a lady with a knowing air and experienced lips?* For a moment, he considers returning to Dutch Kat's, but fear overcomes his need, and he marches along.

IF BECKY HAD LOOKED OUT her window and spotted VanLennep's dejected figure, she might have been amused to imagine herself the subject of his amorous attention. And she's in dire need of such a distraction; for despite her invisible admirer's assumption, her husband isn't romantically sequestered in her rooms but away for the evening, leaving her to the exile of expectant motherhood.

"Damnation," she swears aloud. "Hell and eternal damnation!" *En déshabillé* she drifts through her second-floor chambers, taking up her needlework and immediately flinging it aside, reading a page from a newly purchased novel, then letting the book slip from her fingers. She glances at a collection of Mr. Browning's poems, only to forsake it and resume her restive wandering. She sighs and sighs again until the activity becomes as regular as yawning. "Damnation . . . Damn . . . damn!"

It doesn't occur to her to go downstairs and walk through other rooms rather than these three, or ring for one of the sleeping servants and inquire if her husband has sent word when he would be home. Instead, she keeps to her own suite because she finds it more appealing than the remainder of the house with its ponderous furnishings and its portraits of tight-lipped Quaker Taitts staring disapprovingly down.

At length, she sits at her *escritoire* to write some grumbling remarks in her journal, but then tires of the activity, pushing away the leather-bound volume in order to riffle through the latest offering from *Godey's Lady's Book.* She peruses the frontispiece and the editors' names: Mrs. Sarah J. Hale, Mrs. Lydia H. Sigourney, Morton M'Michael, Louis A. Godey, and the address, which is Publishers' Hall, Philadelphia, 101 Chestnut Street. *Those two ladies are permitted to work and have their names displayed on the printed page,* she argues. *They're allowed to write poems and stories and commentary. Is that not also rash behavior? As audacious as treading the boards?*

Thoroughly irked, Becky studies the monthly fashion plate, analyzing the words printed beneath the models and their costumes as if she intends to memorize them: *Dress of India muslin over a pale yellow underdress. Corsage half high. Tight sleeves. A fichu of lace. A drawn capote of sulfur color crepe trimmed with lilac ribbon and ornamented with a plume of feathers, which droop gracefully to the left.*

One delicately colored figure holds a dainty parasol—which causes Becky to sigh loud and long. She turns the page only to be confronted by a mezzotint entitled "Family Devotions" that depicts a humble wife sitting in rapt attention as her husband reads aloud from the Bible. Exasperated by the self-righteous sentiment, Becky flips the page to a story titled "Civility Is Never Lost," then to another mezzotint melodramatically named "The Elopement Prevented."

Nothing but insipid instruction! Becky thinks as she releases a groan and prepares to cast the publication aside. But a ballad penned by a J. Philip Knight catches her eye; she follows the scored notes and begins to sing:

"'I've trod the festive halls of light/ When music filled the air—'"

The melody dies in her throat. "Oh," she wails. Then her cry, accustomed to carrying to the balcony, grows in force until it takes on an operatic pitch.

She throws the book from her hands, thrusts out her arms as though in supplication—but when she opens her eyes again it's not a stage that greets her, merely her own circumscribed Philadelphia quarters. The ceiling with its crystal chandelier and the walls hung with their myriad gilded frames seem as claustrophobic as a cave.

Your small abode, she recalls the gypsy woman saying. *Your small abode is filled with phantoms and apparitions.* Becky bites her lip until the color drains.

Then a noise breaks in upon this private storm. In the chamber below, which serves as her husband's personal receiving room and where he displays his collection of curios and antiquities, something like a large book or a small bronze statue thuds to the floor. She listens, her face now darkening in wrath rather than self-pity.

So William has returned home and failed to come upstairs to my rooms and ask how I've fared in his absence. He has been disporting himself and drinking champagne while I've been forced to keep my own tedious company. Well, I will not endure this situation a moment longer. Either he permits me to accompany him on his rounds of fetes and musicale evenings, or he must remain sequestered with me until this child of ours is born!

Becky's feet bear her out through her door and down the staircase before she can consider the consequences of her actions. When she reaches the closed door to his study, she doesn't pause a second but presses the latch and throws open the heavy wood. "William, I must—!"

It's not Taitt who gazes defiantly back at her, however, but a boy who appears no more than six or seven. His face and clothes are covered in soot, which also bemires the carpet; and the hearth, dormant in the summery heat, looks as though a wind had rushed down the chimney bearing with it the detritus of every fire that had burned within it. In the child's hands is clutched one of William's precious leather-bound folios.

Another woman might have screamed or even fainted; most would certainly have fled the place, but not Becky Grey.

"You! Put that down!" The loud rebuke almost makes the boy obey. He wavers for a second. "Sneak down the chimney, will you? And enter my house! I think not!"

She grabs for him, but the child shimmies away, his eyes owlish in amazement that this cumbersome woman would attempt to catch him. "We had thieves like you in London. Nests, they were called. And I won't have a nest of such odious individuals sneaking in here." Becky notices that the boy is stealthily regarding the door through which she entered and angles her body to prevent his escape. Every ounce of indignation enkindled during the previous hour energizes her. "I've got you now."

The boy is too wily for her however. With a deft thrust, he hurls the pilfered book at her, hitting her square in her swollen belly, then flies toward a window. Too late, she realizes the sash is open. Despite the knifing pain in her abdomen she hurries after the fleeing urchin, then peers into the night. As much as she looks or listens, there's no sight or sound of human life. The boy has vanished, leaving only smudged black footprints upon the windowsill and trampled earth below it.

Becky turns back to her husband's room and gasps at the

scene of chaos that greets her. Surprising the small thief, she was so focused upon capturing him that she didn't realize how thoroughly he'd performed his task. Every drawer is open; every cabinet door hangs ajar. What remains of William Taitt's library is scattered across the floor; the other costly objects he displayed with such pride appear to be gone. Certainly all the silver is.

"Oh," she groans, then sinks down upon a settee. *If I hadn't been engaged in histrionics I would have heard the noise earlier. This couldn't have been the work of one boy, but of a gang: the smallest child to enter through the chimney, the others to wait until the window was unlatched—just as they did in London. Oh, how outraged William will be when he returns home. As he should be . . .* As she justifies her husband's anger, she realizes that her former fame will be to blame; she will have brought undue attention upon the house, or consorted with unsavory characters.

Then she remembers her lost reticule and the man in St. Peter's churchyard. She groans again, shutting her eyes until she becomes aware of another unpleasant sensation. There's a stickiness between her legs that she instantly recognizes as blood. With no practical knowledge of birthing babies, Becky intuitively understands that this is a dangerous sign. She cradles her heavy belly and forces herself to her feet. *I'll ring for my maid and have her send for the accoucheur. Surely my time is not yet come.*

With determined steps she crosses the carpet. Her shoulders are straight, her neck held high; she feels she's acting the part of a queen sentenced to death. *There must be a remedy I can consume to set things aright.* She strides to the bell pull in order to alert the sleeping staff. Not once does she consider what else the gypsy foretold: that she would be no mother.

BUT WORSE IS TO COME

THEY SAY THE ACCOUCHEUR WAS summoned in the dead of night, and that despite her ministrations, Mrs. Taitt and her unborn child remain in precarious health. When the husband returned home, there was such a commotion—what with the servants running about, and the night watch and constable surveying every window—that Mr. Taitt imagined he'd entered the wrong house. Imagine that, Miss Beale, not knowing your own home!"

Martha makes no reply to the voluble commentary, nor has she for the past seven minutes. Instead, she sips her morning tea, nibbles another piece of now-cold toast, and allows her glance to return to one of the office ledgers she's been perusing while taking her morning meal. All the while, Miss Pettiman stands before her, as inflexible as a soldier at attention—if a soldier were clad in wide black skirts and a starched apron that reaches from shoulder to shoes. Clasped in the woman's right hand is a book, which is purportedly the reason for this interview, although she has yet to refer to it, so anxious is she to discuss the spectacular tale of the previous night.

"But imagine a nest of burglars! Like vipers! And climbing down the chimney to make their mischief! They say that when Mr. Taitt examined the scene his wrath was so great that his reaction was to blame his—"

Martha, at last, interrupts. All morning she's been subjected to the same gossip; her lady's maid was full of the story—who had it from the cook, who, in turn, had it from the egg man, who'd sworn he'd visited the Taitt household himself. "Miss Pettiman, I would rather not discuss these intimate details. I'm heartily sorry the couple has been thus afflicted, but we do them a disservice by bandying about rumor and conjecture."

"Oh!" is the tight-lipped reply. "I would never engage in spreading rumors, Miss Beale. I simply mention the robbery as a warning. If the Taitts are targets of such an invasion, then imagine what might befall the daughter of a financier as famed as Lemuel Beale—"

"Do you suggest we block up each of our chimney flues?" Martha almost smiles at the notion but stifles the impulse.

"I fear, Miss Beale, that you are not sufficiently concerned about this matter."

"I assure you I am. But a city as populous as ours will always have thieves—"

"If you're not worried about your own safety, madam, you might think of Ella and little Caspar. Anything could happen to them. It's not uncommon for the children of the prosperous to be—"

"Thank you, Miss Pettiman, I will consider everything you've told me. Now, you wished to discuss a certain lesson book? Let us examine it, for I would like to conclude this conversation before I leave the house." Martha settles her face into a reasonable expression, but the effort isn't easy. It won't be enough for Cai or Ella to envision ghosts spiraling through the chimneys; now the flues will be inhabited by real boys with ropes and grappling hooks and souls as black as their sooty faces. "It's Mr. McGuffey's *Reader,* perhaps?"

"Yes. *McGuffey's Rhetorical Guide,*" the nursery maid corrects in her loftiest manner. If the mistress finds her servant's character flawed, Miss Pettiman also believes her employer is imperfect. She refuses to conform to the norm, is careless in her choice of friendships, and, worse, insists on entering the business affairs of men. In Miss Pettiman's view, women like Martha Beale do not wed because no true gentlemen will have them.

"What is it about the *Rhetorical Guide* that troubles you?" Martha pushes aside the ledger and her lukewarm tea.

"It's too eclectic. Young minds need rigor and moral guidance, not poetry and fanciful tales—"

"Ella read one of the stories to me: 'Little Victories.' I found it exceedingly—"

"The children should have the primers popular in New England, as well as Noah Webster's *History*. They should be studying pious observations and fact, rather than—"

"Thank you," Martha interrupts as she stands. "I will review your suggestions."

But Miss Pettiman isn't easily dismissed. "The present generation is too indulgent when guiding children. Such laxity cannot help but cultivate crime. You and I won't be safe in our beds—"

"That may be, but let us take care not to express those fears to the children. Their youngest days weren't easy. I want them to feel they live in a safe and loving place now."

The nursery maid accepts the rebuke with eyes grown as frosty as her graying hair. "I've taken too much of your time, madam." She places the offending book on the table, curtsies, and prepares to leave the room, but Martha calls her back.

"Miss Pettiman, I must caution you not to mention the Taitt

burglary to Ella or Cai. The best of intentions, which I know you have, can be misunderstood. And if you overhear other servants discussing it when the children are present, please remind them of my wishes. Cai, especially, is harmed by overstimulation of his imagination."

AS THE DAY PASSES, HOWEVER, and the next and the one following that, it begins to appear that Miss Pettiman's fears are justified. The Washington Square home of Professor Ilsley and his wife is robbed, as are two neighboring residences. Every penny paper and broadsheet trumpets the reports, sparing no detail of stricken family members, or the value of each lost object. Even the staid *Philadelphia Gazette and Commercial Intelligencer* devotes two full inches of editorial space to warning its readers about a "dangerous nest of burglars at work in the city."

But worse news is to come, for the traffic in stolen goods suddenly takes on a human face when Dora Crowther is found to be missing from her home.

"AND NO ONE IN THE household was aware until this morning that your daughter wasn't in her rooms?" Thomas Kelman sits in the Crowthers' withdrawing room, ignoring the tea he's been served as he seeks to understand the calamity that has befallen the family. "What hour was that?"

"It was her maid who alerted us," Georgine tells him. Her eyes are so swollen they're nearly shut, and her ruddy face has turned a splotchy, unhealthy white. "She took up the hot water for Theodora's morning ablutions at half past seven as she always does, and found her mistress gone and a number of her possessions also missing. It wasn't until later that we discovered this room had been ransacked, as well." A sob attacks Georgine, but she does nothing to suppress it. Instead, she moans afresh, shifting her considerable weight on the divan, which creaks in protest. Opposite her, on the matching settee, Crowther and his aunt watch in immutable silence, like painted statues of themselves.

"At the risk of posing an insensitive question, is it possible that Miss Crowther decided to leave your house of her own volition—"

"Her own?" Georgine echoes while her husband interjects a nearly inaudible:

"You're asking if she ran away from her home?"

"Yes, sir, that's my meaning."

"Why would she do such a thing?" Georgine demands. "She's engaged to be married, and to a most eligible young man. A gentleman of her own choosing. A VanLennep, in fact. Percy VanLennep." Dora's mother's voice is verging on the shrill.

Kelman turns back to the husband. "Has her betrothed been informed of the situation?"

"I sent word to his residence, but our footman was told he wasn't at home. Naturally, I didn't wish to impart disquieting news in a letter."

Kelman accepts the information and nods. "That was considerate of you, sir, although I'm afraid the story's already in circulation. Your servants may be discreet, but your neighbors are probably less so. Additionally, any tradespeople with business near your residence would have queried this morning's presence of the constabulary." Then he adds a hesitant "And none in Mr. VanLennep's household had seen your daughter? Either last night or early this morning?"

"Dora didn't run away!" Georgine fairly shrieks. "She would

never shame us like that! She's been stolen, sir! Stolen just like the objects that were in her rooms! And this chamber, too!"

"My dear, let us allow Mr. Kelman to proceed with his inquiry. He's the professional in this matter, not we."

"But why would Dora run off to join Percy when they're about to be properly wed? Why would she do such a silly thing? Or are you going to declare that she left our house and also robbed us?" Then Georgine's head sinks toward her chest. "These people must be stopped," she murmurs at length.

"I intend to do everything in my power to achieve that goal, Mrs. Crowther" is Kelman's steady reply. "As will the day and night watches, and our city constables and sheriffs."

No one speaks for several more moments. The tea service continues untouched; the normal sounds that resonate through a household—the footsteps of upstairs maids, the opening and closing of windows, the airing of bedclothes, the dull hum of the kitchen and butler's pantry signaling the beginning of luncheon preparations—are absent, as if those homely chores were also left untouched and unattended.

"I'd like to examine your daughter's chambers, if I might," Kelman eventually requests, "and speak to the maid who discovered her mistress gone." He looks to Harrison Crowther for permission, but the man merely gazes dumbly back while his wife, lips curled in disgust, responds:

"That girl is as dull-witted as a newborn calf. She'll tell you no more than we have already. Mr. Crowther and I have described Dora's rooms. You need only consider the damage the thieves wrought in this space to imagine what vile work they carried out upstairs." As Georgine concludes this rant, her husband seems to recall himself.

"I'm sure Mr. Kelman makes the request in order to aid his investigation—"

"I don't want strangers entering Theodora's chambers, Harrison!" she cries out, and Kelman marks the dismay the improper use of her husband's given name causes her. "Mr. Crowther, please. It would be altogether wrong. A young lady, unwed—"

"My dear, if we wish to solve this mystery we must submit to Mr. Kelman's request. After all, it's the mayor of our metropolis who dispatched him."

"But shouldn't we . . . shouldn't we be ordering Dora's rooms tidied for her return rather than permitting inappropriate people to wander about and 'examine' them? Think how upset our daughter would be at the intrusion!"

"All in good time, my dear. And Mr. Kelman is hardly ill suited for the task." Harrison stands while his wife, his domineering wife, regards him with the meekness of a child, letting her gaze linger upon his boxy form as if she cannot bear to be parted from him for a moment. "Mr. Kelman, sir. If you'll follow me, I'll escort you upstairs. My wife and aunt will remain below."

THE CHAMBERS TO WHICH HARRISON Crowther conducts Kelman are not what he expected, and he has visited a great many places where crimes have been committed. True, there's some disarray: Several drawers in the chest-on-chest jut out at disconcerting angles as if hastily searched; and the doors to the armoire hang open, revealing the airy pastels and laces a young lady like Theodora would favor. The remainder of the scene, though, is calm. Save for the bed the maid apparently prepared the previous evening but that her mistress merely sat upon—and impatiently, too, Kelman surmises, for the bedclothes bear the print of scurrying fingers—the other furnishings appear untouched.

The *escritoire* with its inkwell and a nicked wooden ruler that must have been a schoolday tool seems ready to receive Dora's latest correspondence. The washstand with its porcelain bowl painted with pink posies seems to await a pitcher of hot water. The marble mantel is still hung with bits of ribbons, a showy feather from a peacock's tail, several *cartes de visite,* and two elegantly penned invitations that are clearly cherished possessions.

Tears begin wetting Harrison Crowther's cheeks as he stands at Kelman's side. He does nothing to dab them away.

"It's not necessary for you to remain with me, sir," Kelman tells him.

"No, no . . . I need to be here. Dora would wish it—" The effort at speech fails.

Kelman studies the surface of the chest-on-chest, cataloging what the thieves left behind: a silver hairbrush, but no comb and mirror; an enamel portrait of a young woman who he expects must be Lydia Crowther in her prime, but the armature that held the picture is gone, as are the contents of what must have been a small box of jewelry. Despite the apparent thefts, there's an orderliness to the apartment that Kelman finds odd. *Wouldn't Dora have fought her abductor?* he wonders. *Shouldn't there be a trace of a struggle? Was she simply surprised and overwhelmed, or is there another conclusion I'm missing?*

"Miss Crowther's maid found the room exactly as it is now?"

"Exactly. At least, I believe this is how she found it. When she summoned my wife and me to Dora's chambers, this was the picture that greeted us."

Kelman nods in thought, then pauses, measuring his words.

"Mr. Crowther, there's a matter I didn't wish to mention when we were with the ladies as I felt they would find it too distasteful."

When the father makes no reply, Kelman continues. "If your daughter has indeed been abducted, sir, rather than perhaps eloping—"

"Not our Dora. She would never—"

"Hear me out, sir, please. We'll need to return to the ladies soon, and this subject must be broached. Now, if this is a criminal offense, and your daughter was taken against her will, you should expect a message from her captors stating as much. As well as a demand for remuneration."

"Remuneration," Harrison echoes.

"Yes, sir. You'll be instructed to provide monies in payment for your daughter's return—"

"Oh," Crowther gasps, but Kelman perseveres as if there had been no interruption.

"You'll also be warned to keep information regarding the directive private; however, I urge you to contact me at once."

"Contact you?" The question reveals both skepticism and disbelief.

"Yes, sir. The moment you receive any missive that mentions your daughter."

"Money for my child," Harrison repeats in the same dull tone. "Who would be so base as to embark on such a diabolical scheme?"

"Crimes are not committed by godly men, I'm afraid, Mr. Crowther."

The father falls silent, and Kelman continues his investigation. "Miss Lydia Crowther's rooms are below these?"

"Yes, directly below." Harrison stares at his feet, and his face bears an expression of such intense sorrow that Kelman wonders whether the man is wishing his aunt had been the victim rather than his daughter. "The house is really two joined into one. This rear section is older, which accounts for its varying levels and the quaintness of the rooms. My wife and I reside in the newer space."

"And your aunt heard nothing untoward?"

"Her acoustical skills are severely impaired" is the leaden response.

"Not always, nephew," the lady herself says as she enters the apartment. She gives Kelman a placid smile, albeit one tinged with sadness. "I left your wife with the smelling salts and the servants," she tells Harrison as she brushes past him. "I did hear Dora, nephew. Some parts of these floorboards creak a good deal. I know because the chambers were mine when I was Theodora's age and a great favorite of the—"

"Aunt, I beg to interrupt, but we're all aware of the difficulty you've been experiencing with your—"

"You needn't shout, Harrison. I can hear perfectly well. You and Georgine make a grave mistake treating me as though I were a useless person. My father lived until he was ninety, and no one questioned his abilities. As doubtless you recall." She returns to Kelman and gives him another smile. "Theodora was worried about Percy, you see. She hadn't received a single word from him since he was driven from the house four days ago. It was my great-niece's and her betrothed's practice to—"

"Aunt, please—"

Lydia continues as if her nephew hadn't spoken. "It was their practice to communicate with one another: she by looking for him from this window; and he by passing below in order that she might see him. Last night I knew she was awake and had positioned herself here, because of the telltale noises. I was also aware that she must have been reading, since light from her lamp slips through the floor. It provides the most picturesque shadows when my own lamps are extinguished. One can imagine all types of wondrous—"

"Aunt Lydia—"

"When I heard her whisper Percy's name, I sat up directly in my bed. I thought Mr. VanLennep had come to spirit our Theodora away. They're very much in love, you know, but sometimes my nephew and niece—"

"Oh, Aunt!" Harrison again interjects. "Your brain is creating fabrications—"

"What are you attempting to say to me, nephew? I do loathe it when people mumble. When I was a girl, I was taught to speak with clarity and purpose."

Harrison Crowther gives Kelman a beleaguered glance. "If you could hear Dora whispering, why weren't you aware that she was being taken from the premises? Surely Dora must have cried out in protest—"

"Of course, I wouldn't interfere if Theodora and Percy were meeting clandestinely, Harrison. Love should be our dearest hope for one another, should it not? Isn't that the message our preachers repeat? 'He that loveth not, knoweth not God; for God is love.' "

Then she dispenses with her nephew and Kelman and walks toward the door. "When I fell back asleep I was so happy. Dora left the lamp lit, so I had many pretty pictures to keep me company. And then, too, Mr. VanLennep is such a handsome man that he couldn't help but make any lady happy. And I did hear her cry out, Harrison. You're quite wrong when you suggest I didn't. But it wasn't in protest. Her dear little voice was agitated, but not afraid." With that she quits the room as if her nephew and Kelman were no longer of interest.

"I apologize," Dora's father states after an embarrassed moment. "My aunt doesn't always have full use of her faculties. She can be a trial sometimes, I'm afraid."

"I understand, sir. She's remarkably fit for her years, however."

"Yes. Yes, she is." Again the tone is ambivalent, as if Harrison isn't convinced his aunt's physical health is a boon.

Kelman takes note of the nephew's attitude as he studies the floor beneath the window. On the pretext of gazing at the scene below, he walks across the wooden planks and is rewarded by the creaking Miss Lydia described. "Was this lamp still lighted when you and your wife arrived upon the scene?"

Harrison thinks. "I cannot recall."

"Would the maid remember?"

"You're welcome to ask her, although as my wife stated, the girl's not a clever lass; she was greatly distressed to find her mistress gone." His shoulders slump; his head droops. "As we all were. As we continue to be."

MOLES AND BATS

INSPIRED BY REPORTS IN THE penny press and daily gazettes, the tale whips around the city, dividing the populace into two distinct camps. One comprises citizens who react in horrified disbelief to the notion of a young woman abducted from her home—and therefore redouble their efforts to remember to bolt their doors, avoid strangers, and bar admittance to the beggars routinely clustered beside the service entries to their houses. The other group displays both covert and overt satisfaction at the misfortune of the elite.

Among this voluble crowd, exaggerated descriptions of the Crowthers' wealth and station are quoted over and over until quite another family emerges. One scandalmongering journalist decrees that Harrison Crowther has amassed more money in his coffers than the government in Washington, while another itemizes the extent of his possessions: gold plate intended for the most casual use; enough crystal goblets to serve one hundred guests; silver tureens and ice bowls, and ormolu candelabra; the rarest silks and embroidered satins tossed aside because the garments are no longer in vogue. Then, tired of reading and reciting the long list of luxuries, the talk on the street turns toward hearsay that Georgine has always been hard on her servants, as well as on her aunt and her husband. She's ridiculed for her exacting measures; it's even bruited about that her husband has been seen taking his pleasure among the city's fancy houses. Finally, Miss Lydia is scorned for her addled brain and romantic memories, which then become the brunt of coarse jests and coarser gestures.

Then the gossip alters course, for Percy VanLennep is rumored to have also disappeared.

"'ENTER INTO THE ROCK, AND hide thee in the dust, for fear of the Lord, and for the glory of his majesty.

'The lofty looks of man shall be humbled, and the haughtiness of men shall be bowed down, and the Lord alone shall be exalted in that day.

'For the day of the Lord of hosts shall be upon every one that is proud and lofty, and upon every one that is lifted up; and he shall be brought low.'" The voice of Amor Alsberg, the itinerant evangelical preacher, roars out these last words while his eyes, hot as live coals, burn into those congregated at the southwest street corner behind the State House. This open-air pulpit is Alsberg's favorite. Kelman would have avoided the place if he'd remembered; as it is, he can't help but be drawn into the fevered speech and equally fervent response.

"Amen!" a man cries out in a voice choked with ardor.

"The Holy Prophet Isaiah, my brothers and sisters. Listen to him. Heed him. Believe, and be reconciled unto your God." For a moment the tone is coaxing; then it booms out again, crescendoing with each phrase:

"'And the loftiness of man shall be bowed down, and the haughtiness of men shall be made low; and the Lord alone shall be exalted in that day—'"

Another communal "Amen" interrupts, but Alsberg is far from finished, and his words stride over the response.

"'And the idols he shall utterly abolish'!" The preacher repeats the phrase twice more before pounding toward his conclusion. "'In that day a man shall cast his idols of silver, and his idols of gold, which they made each one for himself to worship, to the moles and to the bats.'"

A moan circulates through the growing crowd. "Moles and bats," many mutter aloud, and Alsberg takes up their cry:

"Are not the thieves who prey upon our city no better than the filthy bats and moles that cleave to the insalubrious places? Are not those haughty rich now brought low, and their pride repaid with loss? Is not this the hour when the Lord 'ariseth to shake terribly the earth'? My friends, abandon the ways of those who store up treasures upon earth, who allow their daughters and sons to fornicate evilly—"

Kelman turns aside. He's certain that any moment he will hear Theodora Crowther and her family being vilified, and he's afraid of what his reaction to such callousness of heart might be.

He pushes past the throng toward Chestnut Street, and all at once decides to walk west to Martha Beale's house.

BUT AS HE'S ADMITTED INTO her parlor, every reason for the visit suddenly appears so contrived, so ill considered and self-serving, that he wishes he could turn on his heel and leave. At the same time, Martha, who has risen from the bombé desk where she was working, finds her welcoming steps arrested by the fierce ambivalence of his gaze. "Thomas, how kind of you to call," she exclaims by rote.

"I did not intend to do so," he states, then lapses into a shamed silence.

"Ah . . . But you're here, nonetheless." She ventures a smile as she motions him toward a chair, but Kelman remains standing; and so she clasps her hands together and also waits in awkward limbo. "I assume you've uncovered information on the woman I saw the day I returned to the city?"

"The . . . ?"

"When we last met. Following the windstorm . . . You said you were investigating the case of a suicide."

Kelman's face flushes with hot agitation. "No. No, I came to see you because I hoped you might help me in my conversations with the Crowther family."

"With the Crowthers? What possible aid can I give you there? A priest, perhaps, but not—"

"But I see I was deluding myself. I was seeking an excuse to spend time in your presence—"

"Surely that's not such a terrible misdeed." Martha gives him a brighter smile and again urges him to sit, but Kelman's cheerless speech rolls on:

"You're a wealthy woman, Miss Beale, and I am . . . I am not of your station and class. You should be free to choose other suitors."

"This is what you came to tell me?" The hurt in her voice is evident, but there's also indignation. "That you have decided the future of my marital status?"

"No, that's not my meaning. Or, yes, perhaps it is. Oh, Martha, I want you to have a happy life! But I cannot make it so. You must understand that."

"No. I don't" is her simple reply. "I know we enjoy one another's company, and that you're kind and compassionate."

"So is a priest." The bitterness in his tone is unmistakable.

Martha studies his face, her expression equally firm. "Shouldn't I determine what's appropriate? Rather than society, or you? Haven't we discussed this matter?"

Instead of responding directly, Kelman looks at the laden desk where Martha was recently working. "I've disturbed you at some important labor."

"Ah, yes . . . mathematical calculations on the exchange of one currency into another" is her acerbic reply. "However, I doubt that analyzing foreign specie and banking establishments in Havana, La Guaira, and Puerto Cabello is as vital as discussing a young lady who has been abducted from her home. Or whatever issue brought you to my door."

Kelman makes no answer. If he were alone, he would pace across the carpet, pounding his feet in frustration. *Leave this house,* his brain admonishes. *Relinquish the sham purpose of your visit. You're here because you're in love with this woman, although you know very well you can never ask her hand in marriage.*

Of course, Martha hears none of this battle. "I cannot assist you if you don't explain what you wish. Now, come. Let us sit together and talk in a convivial manner. Because you *are* kind and compassionate, Thomas, and you cannot convince me otherwise." So saying, she walks to the bell pull in order to summon a servant and request tea and cakes. Then she seats herself, gathering her skirts to make room for him on the settee, but he continues to stand, his legs locked, his dusty boots planted upon the carpet.

"Have you heard of the preacher Amor Alsberg?" is what he asks.

"Whose followers believe that the Day of Judgment is at

hand?" Martha shakes her head in rueful acknowledgment. She has heard Alsberg's street-corner rantings and gives them as little credence as she does the charlatans who purvey their questionable nostrums and patent medicines. "What has Theodora Crowther's disappearance to do with the man's misguided prophesies, or his devotees' equally perturbed inclinations?"

In reply, Kelman poses a question of his own. "Do you feel your household is well enough protected?"

"From the burglars plaguing our city, do you mean?"

"From anyone who wishes you harm. And yes, let me mention Alsberg in this context. In listening to him, I was struck by the depth of his disciples' discontent. True, they're anticipating the rewards of the kingdom of Heaven and revel in quoting Scripture and invoking God's protective care. But they're also a resentful people who cling to every reference to Hell and eternal damnation. In their minds, the rich are venal and deserving of destruction. If the leap from burglary to Amor Alsberg seems extreme, I assure you it isn't. At least to my mind."

"You and Miss Pettiman must be in collusion," Martha answers in a brief attempt at levity, then adds a more serious "Yes. I've discussed the need for vigilance with my staff. So you needn't worry, Thomas. We're quite safe."

"But I do worry! I worry about you all the time—" That declaration is interrupted by the arrival of a footman bearing a silver tray laden with two gold-rimmed cups, two saucers, a silver teapot fashioned in the Adam style, and an additional silver pot containing hot water, as well as a small epergne displaying candied fruits and sweet biscuits.

Martha watches the man's white gloves arranging the gleaming display, extends her thanks, and then pays not one particle of attention to the food and drink arrayed before her. So the tea remains unpoured and the delicacies left untouched while Martha and Kelman gaze at each other across the vast expanse of mahogany table and Turkey carpet and damask-covered seats, tapestry footstools and the small and large pieces of statuary that litter every available space.

"Oh, Thomas!" she finally declares while he blurts out a jagged:

"You've won my heart, Martha Beale! What can I do but consider your well-being every moment of every day?"

In the silence that follows these wondrous words, Martha is aware of the dull throb of noise in the street, then the small creaks, tip-taps of feet, and swinging of doors as unseen bodies move through the house. Mostly she hears the beating of her own heart.

Instead of proposing marriage, however, Kelman flings himself down on a facing chair. "Forgive me. Please forgive me. My outburst was inexcusable. I told you I had no intention of standing in your way. What I said was beneath contempt. I apologize. I hope and pray that you'll accept my apology. I will be a friend to you. I'll be a friend to you all my days, but I can't allow myself to prevent you from seeking a better and more deserving companion."

Martha regards him, her eyes filling with tears, which she blinks away in irritation. Her mouth opens in reply, then immediately clamps tight while Kelman leans forward. "Let us speak about the Crowthers, Martha."

"Is that what you wish? To discuss Dora's disappearance? Is that the sole purpose of your visit? Or to confer on the odious Amor Alsberg?"

"Yes," he lies.

"What if my choice is another subject? Two people who have reached a certain understanding and ease of companionship, for instance?"

"Then I must beg your forgiveness and take my leave."

"You seem very certain how I should conduct my life, Mr. Kelman"

"Martha . . . Listen to me. You state we've reached an 'ease of companionship,' and you're correct in the assessment. We've entered a level of friendship that's more than ease; it's a deep level of trust. But there are other gentlemen with whom you could experience the same harmony—"

"What if I don't choose to seek them out?"

"That decision is yours."

Martha stands. So abrupt is her movement that the table with its plethora of dainty objects jumps, setting in dangerous motion the porcelain cups and silver spoons and gilded cake knives and fluted forks. She glares at this discordant array, then moves the same commanding gaze to Kelman. "What is it you wished to ask me about the Crowther family?" she asks. Her voice is flat and harsh.

Kelman watches her for a moment, as she also regards him. It would take nothing for them to sweep aside the tea tray and table, but neither moves. Instead, he begins to speak in a brisk and competent tone, although his agitated expression belies this seeming detachment.

"I wish you to meet with the Crowthers. As my mouth and ears. You're of their social sphere. I'm not. And I believe they don't fully trust my motives; the mother, especially. I'm sure you plan to call upon them to express your hopes for their daughter's safe return, but endeavor when you do to detect whether the family has an enemy—"

"An enemy."

"The notion came upon me when I was listening to Alsberg preach. Two days is a long period for the culprit to remain uncommunicative—if profit is the sole motive."

"Couldn't the young couple have simply eloped? Uncaring as that action may be."

Kelman apparently doesn't hear the suggestion. "I'll also add that the robbery of the Crowther household struck me as being different than those I encountered at the Taitts' and Ilsleys' and so forth—"

"I have no idea how to conduct such a conversation. I haven't any training in the art of interrogation—"

"What you have, Martha, is an innate understanding of the working of the human heart. You listen. You watch. You examine. I've seen you do it."

"That's habit only. The result of a childhood spent in solitary pursuits."

He smiles at her, the first such happy expression since he entered the room. "Those are precisely the gifts I require: your humanity, your sense of wonder, your compassion and loving heart." Before she can answer, he continues with a rapid "Query Miss Lydia Crowther first. She'll be an easier subject; and I believe she has information concerning VanLennep and Theodora that the parents don't. And yes, as you suggest, an elopement isn't out of the realm of possibility. Although if that's the case, I'm perturbed by the callousness of the act."

Martha makes no immediate reply, though her eyes continue to search his face. "And my remuneration? May I name what I wish?"

"You'll have my undying gratitude."

"We bankers drive harder bargains than that, Thomas. Surely you're aware of the formidable reputation of the Beales." Then she suddenly wearies of the game. "Yes. I'll be glad to help in any fashion I can. Whether you're a 'suitable' companion for me or not."

In answer, Kelman stands and walks to a window, then pulls

back the lace undercurtain and stares into the haze-heated street beyond. "I wish this weather would break," he states in a hollow voice. "Man and beast alike are suffering. If this isn't God's judgment, what is it?"

MR. ERASMUS UNGER'S BANK

TRUE TO HER WORD, MARTHA makes a formal call on the Crowther household the following morning. As she approaches the marble steps that lead from the brick walk and street, she's struck by the stillness of the house. In other circumstances, these early hours would be bustling with energy: the stone risers scoured with a paste of turpentine, pipe clay, and bullock's gall; the brasses polished with fresh lime; the wrought-iron railings treated with Brunswick black. But it's not the lack of servants and enterprise that arrests her; rather, it's the building's air of sorrow. Longing seems to emanate from it as though the stone and brick, the wood and mortar were yearning for Dora's return.

Martha must summon all of her fortitude in order to proceed. She feels not only like an interloper in this private space but like a spy—which is precisely what she is. She steels her heart for the encounter, ascends the steps, and knocks upon the door. *Query Miss Lydia first,* she hears Thomas cautioning, but the phrase is no sooner in her brain than the portal swings open and she's swept inside.

"Madam will receive you in the withdrawing room," she's informed a mere minute or two after having handed the footman her *carte de visite.* It's as if the lady of the house had been waiting for this call.

"MISS BEALE, HOW GOOD OF you to call." Georgine Crowther, so habitually aloof, nearly rushes through the room's double doors in order to greet her guest. "You're so kind, so kind . . ."

The words trail away as she clasps Martha's hands and draws her toward a settee, then all but forces her to sit. "You're friendly with my Theodora?" There's disbelief as well as pleasure in this question. Martha, older, wiser, and heir to Lemuel Beale's fortune, is the sort of companion the mother would greatly desire for her daughter.

Martha avoids the question, responding instead with a tender "Mrs. Crowther, please accept my sympathies. Your distress is shared by all residents of this city."

Georgine's staunch shoulders sag. Her mouth contorts, her eyes pinch, but she makes no immediate reply. Instead, she continues to hold Martha's gloved fingers in her own lace-mittened ones while tears spill down her cheeks. "It's been three days, Miss Beale. Three days . . . We were assured we would hear some word of our darling one's circumstances before now."

Martha doesn't speak, although she squeezes Georgine's fingers. Beneath the lace, the older lady's flesh feels spongy and infirm.

"My only child to survive past infancy . . . My dearest, dearest daughter. Oh, how difficult I believed those earlier losses were: three little babies snatched away one after another. How I wept and grieved and railed at fate. But I knew nothing. Nothing!"

Georgine falls silent; her breathing slows until it all but vanishes. "Forgive me. I'm forgetting myself. I should ask if you'll take some libation."

"Oh, no, thank you, Mrs. Crowther. I don't wish to cause an imposition."

"In truth, I think the staff would welcome a task. My husband and his aunt and I have been disinclined to take much sustenance since Dora—" Again Georgine stops speaking. "But perhaps you have another engagement and cannot remain." There's both appeal and diffidence in the statement, and Martha can't help but mark how greatly her hostess has changed. The woman is merely an outward manifestation of herself, as if her numerous whalebone corset stays and petticoat wires were keeping her together.

"I would like very much to stay, Mrs. Crowther, if I may be of comfort to you."

"Oh, comfort!" is the harsh rejoinder. "Why should I be permitted such ease of mind? Indeed, I'm beginning to despise the word! The only relief I have is imagining Mrs. Taitt during her struggle with the burglar who invaded her home. If I'd encountered the thieving creature who took my child, I would have laid heavy blows upon his head. More than heavy blows; I would have become a veritable demon."

"Then you heard an intruder?" Martha asks.

"No. I did not." The tone is so dejected that the words are scarcely audible. "My chambers and my husband's chambers are in this newer section of the house. I heard nothing."

That bleak testimony delivered, Georgine forces herself to her feet and then tramps slowly toward the bell pull in order to summon a footman and send for tea and biscuits. Meanwhile Martha considers her response. Emotion calls for a soothing demeanor, even a prayer for Dora's return; the awareness that she's acting on Kelman's behalf decrees a more premeditated approach.

"So no one in the household was aware of what had transpired until morning? How extremely difficult that knowledge must be to bear."

"My husband's aunt claims to have heard various sounds, but she's elderly and has an overvivid imagination." Georgine sits again, or rather nearly collapses into the settee. "If Miss Lydia guessed that a stranger, or even an acquaintance, had entered our home, I fail to understand why she raised no alarm." There's venom in this declaration, but more is to come:

"We had an official representative of the mayor here, Miss Beale. A Mr. Kelman, who gave too much credence to Miss Lydia's ill-advised remarks. I cannot imagine what he hoped to gain by interviewing her, unless it was to add to gossip already in circulation."

Martha can't help but draw a protesting breath. It's hard indeed to hear Thomas spoken of in such a critical vein. But Georgine mistakes the response for assent and continues in the same severe manner:

"Such gentlemen are quite abominable, if the term *gentleman* can be employed in such instances. Policing the city is a trade that apparently attracts those of questionable repute."

"Those men keep us safe, Mrs. Crowther," Martha counters in a sterner tone than she intended, then adds a conciliatory "We do wrong to malign them, I think."

Georgine will have none of the suggestion however. "Then why was my Dora stolen from her own home?"

Martha has no answer. She knows she can't acknowledge her admiration for Thomas without jeopardizing the work he entrusted to her. Instead, she must proceed as the innocent visitor, although her jaw tenses and her teeth clench into a disingenuous smile. "I'd hoped to extend my personal condolences to Mr. Crowther and to his aunt."

Georgine's response is a sigh. "I'll be certain to convey your thoughts, Miss Beale. And I thank you. From the depths of my soul, I thank you. My husband is not at home, or he would also extend his gratitude. As for Miss Crowther, she's indisposed. In fact, she has hardly left her rooms since Theodora vanished." This last statement is so full of wrath it seems as though Miss Lydia had never done one good deed in all her days.

"Ah . . ." is all Martha can think to respond. Then tea and cakes arrive, providing her a brief respite from her mission while the libation is poured by Georgine, then handed ceremoniously to a footman, who conveys it to the Crowthers' guest.

"Do you know what I find especially terrible, Miss Beale?" Georgine asks after placing a slice of Savoy cake on a plate and giving it to the footman to place within her guest's reach. "The thief who robbed me of Theodora also stole various objects from her chambers. Among them was a gift Mr. Crowther and I purchased for Dora's betrothed: a daguerreotype—" The mother releases a small sob, and then another and another, while Martha watches in helpless silence. "Who would steal something that's only important to those who love her, Miss Beale? And why take the portrait when they have carried off the original!"

As Georgine gives vent to her grief, and the footman becomes suitably mute and stationary, the doors to the room open and Harrison Crowther enters. The effects of the past three days are as prominent on him as they are on his wife. His skin is gray; his flesh seems to have withered, and his spine is bowed as though bearing a mighty weight. "Oh, my dear." He moves toward Georgine, but she turns her head away. "The loss of that object was purely coincidental—"

"And should that upset me less, sir?"

"But Mr. Kelman's theory is—"

"Mr. Kelman! Mr. Kelman! That's your continual litany. What does he care! A picture of Dora, or Dora herself. They're one and the same to him!"

"Georgine, you're suggesting the man has no heart—"

"*Suggesting*, sir! Is it a *suggestion* that our daughter's gone? Is my brain creating illusions? Have I also invented the fact that Percy has failed to appear, despite repeated appeals to his household—?"

"You know the reason, Georgine—"

"I know what you and this Thomas Kelman continue to tell me. That Percy went on a journey and neglected to disclose his destination. But why would he go a-visiting and fail to inform Dora, or us, or even his servants of his—?"

"It's an honest mistake. And VanLennep never could have conceived what would transpire when he—"

"But he departed the very morning we discovered Theodora was—!"

"I've explained that peculiar happenstance, Georgine. Repeatedly."

Seated, she draws her spine to its full height and glares at her husband. "Then you must also explain that your aunt is mistaken, Mr. Crowther, and that she in no wise heard Dora calling out Percy's name. You and I both know our daughter would never have—"

"Georgine! Have done!"

"I will not, sir. Either Percy VanLennep was in this house, or my daughter fell victim to a stranger's hands. Which is it, sir? Which is it?" Georgine is almost shouting now; her body surges upward, interposing itself between her husband and her guest. "I'm told by our physician, Miss Beale, that my thoughts are becoming dangerously morbid, that it's unhealthy for me to surrender to what he and my husband refer to as 'despairing'—"

"Georgine, this is not a matter a guest would—"

"But why shouldn't I despair, Miss Beale? The greatest treasure in my life has been ripped from my arms. And we have not received one word as to how she fares, or how we can restore her to our home!" Then Georgine Crowther covers her face with her hands and half stumbles and half rushes from the room.

Martha remains frozen in place, as does the unlucky footman, while Harrison also stays planted in one spot, although his sagging body appears to wilt further. "Please forgive us, Miss Beale. My wife is not herself."

"Your apologies are unnecessary, sir. These are dreadful times. I came to express my condolences, but I fear I've made matters worse."

"It's not you, Miss Beale. When my wife is not lucid, she blames me for this catastrophe."

Martha can't think of an appropriate expression of surprise or solace and so keeps silent until Crowther decides to continue. "Unfortunate and misguided as her opinions may be, I'm powerless to alter them. The problem is my position at Mr. Erasmus Unger's bank, you see." He pauses to draw a worried breath. "I'm a new member of the board there, although Georgine was against my accepting the honor as the gentleman has certain moral precepts she finds offensive. However, Unger is a brilliant financier, and his institution has weathered the monetary storm that continues to shake our nation." Again Harrison Crowther pauses, this time as though struck by an idea he hadn't previously considered. "What do you know of the practice of making astute investments, Miss Beale? I don't refer to your father's specific activities but to the method itself."

Martha considers her reply. Rather, she considers the response Kelman would make. "As a director of Mr. Unger's institution, you would know more than I."

The answer seems to satisfy Dora's father. "Unger's approach is simple and can best be described as a two-pronged technique. One involves large investments such as many thousands of acres of anthracite coal lands in Schuylkill County, two railways to carry the commodity to market, a shipbuilding concern, a substantial merchant fleet, and so forth. The second comprises small loans to minor borrowers: coopers, cord winders, shopmen, and the like. Naturally, the rates are high and the borrowers are needy men. The slightest slip in the exchange rate of paper currencies can—"

Martha waits for the speech to advance, but instead, Harrison Crowther stares at the mantelpiece and groans. "I must bid you good day, Miss Beale. I should attend to my poor wife. On behalf of us both, I thank you for your charitable concern."

A CHANCE ENCOUNTER

WHILE MARTHA VISITS THE CROWTHER household, Ella embarks on her own mission. She escapes from school. The act doesn't require scaling a wall or dropping from an upper-story window, but it does take planning and a certain watchful slyness that she learned when she was a child of the streets.

Once her decision was made (the day prior), the notion wouldn't leave her alone. Returning home with Miss Pettiman on the afternoon before the bold deed, Ella plotted; at supper with Cai, she schemed in silence; in her bed that night, she revisited each room of the schoolhouse, counting the minutes she and the other pupils were left alone, and measuring how long it would take to descend the stairs from her second-floor classroom, cross the foyer, and skip out the front door.

In the end, though, her plans miscarry. Teachers walk back and forth with alarming irregularity; her schoolmates profess a need to spend every moment in her company; and the minutes relentlessly tick past. Then she recalls the privy in the building's rear garden and how well it lies concealed by the ground's sheltering trees; and success is assured.

Ella complains about a pain in her stomach, apologizes for disrupting the class, and rushes downstairs and outside as though speed were essential. From there, she snakes through the meandering shrubbery and fruit trees until she reaches the door to the alley. One quick glance at the upper windows confirms that none of the teachers have grown suspicious. In the next second, Ella unlatches the garden gate and steps into the midst of a busy city thoroughfare.

BUT THEN WHAT? STANDING ALONE at the corner of Eighth and Locust streets, she realizes her scheme has a vital flaw. For it isn't freedom and a chancy escapade she seeks, but its opposite. Despite every luxury Martha Beale's household offers, what Ella wants is her long-vanished mother.

However, she has no notion how to begin this quest. Her recollection of the woman who allowed her daughter to be sold is dim, as it is of the place—or places—in which they dwelled. There was a sister and a tiny brother who fell into the fire until half his face was scorched; there was constant hunger and sorrow, as well as blows and oaths from a man who must have been her father. None of those fractured memories are useful, though. Ella looks at the school's wall but finds no aid in its stolid bricks. She watches the passersby; no one gives more than a cursory glance to a hatless child in a pinafore—unless it's to frown in disapproval.

She begins to walk. For a moment, she worries about the punishment that will be meted out for this act of disobedience, for she has every intention of returning home in time for the evening meal; and her spirits flag and her footsteps drag. She considers creeping back to the schoolyard gate, but then bravado and a depthless ache take hold, and she sets her mouth and soldiers forward.

The city she encounters is no longer the pleasant town she's come to know while in Martha's care. All at once, beggars seem to be everywhere; starving dogs cringe near each kitchen door; the dray horses pulling the workmen's wagons are scrawny and ill kept, and their masters no better. They and their apprentice boys regard her with cunning eyes that reveal envy, contempt, and hopelessness. Ella tries to return their stares but finds she's lost the habit of confrontation, so averts her gaze.

Unwittingly, her feet travel south and east into the seamier areas of the city she once trod. Then her progress is arrested, for she finds herself on Lombard Street and so close to the fancy house from which she fled that she jerks backward as though slapped.

"Never seen an enterprise like this before, I'll warrant," a nearby voice sneers.

"What?" is Ella's uncertain reply while she eyes the door and the three stone steps, recalling every second of her flight into the icy cobbles of the road.

"A fancy house. For fancy ladies. Them that sell theirselves for profit. It's an easy life if you're pretty." The tone has a swagger, although wistfulness pokes holes in the edges.

Ella turns to find a raggedy boy. "I'm known hereabouts," he boasts. "I do odd jobs for the ladies at Dutch Kat's up the street a ways. It's a finer establishment than this miserable shop here, and some of those lovely creatures like to favor me with their wares in gratitude." He winks as he speaks, and his ears, which are curiously pointed and which Ella hadn't observed before, wiggle as if they belong to an animal rather than a human.

"I doubt that" is her trenchant reply. Then she returns to studying the terrible place that was once her home.

Ella's disregard obviously wounds the boy. "Why?"

"You are both dirty and a child."

"A child, am I? That I am not, Miss Priss! Besides, you don't even know what a fancy lady is!"

Ella casts a dismissive glance at her unwelcome companion. "I do, in fact. Now leave me alone."

"Then what are they?"

"You just told me, didn't you?"

The logic of these words only irks the boy further. "You're a fine one, you are, to be wrinkling up your snooty nose at me."

"Go away," Ella tells him.

"I have as much right to stand here as you."

"Not near me, you don't."

"I have. It's a free country. Or that's what the toffs say. Someone like your da or mam would spout a stupid thing like that. Freedom for who, that's what I want to know."

Ella releases a noisy sigh. For the first time she notices that the boy smells. "You should bathe," she says, although she doesn't move away.

"I'll do as I see fit."

"Well, no lady will 'favor' you with her 'wares' if you stink. Which is why I doubt the truth of your claim."

"Ain't you the grand one! With your smart speech and your elegant costume, ain't you just a sight! 'Doubt the truth of your claim.' Who are you to doubt me? And if I'm a 'child,' then you're one, too!"

"At least I'm not a thief" is the lordly retort.

"And who says I am?" the boy hisses.

"I used to know boys like you. That's how you work. You rob gentlemen of their wallets when their attention is distracted. You reach into ladies' reticules while they're gazing into a shop window or walking through the Shambles. You even steal from drunken beggars."

"That, I would never do!" The words are loud; the boy stands to his full height, which is taller than Ella by several inches.

"Hah!" is her victorious answer. "I caught you."

Despite this heated exchange, neither moves away. Ella, because she recognizes the kind of rough-and-tumble companion of her previous existence, the type of person long since replaced by well-born, well-scrubbed girls; the boy, from loneliness. But something else pricks at his brain, a memory from some distant, happy time his thoughts can't fully recapture.

"You've got pretty hair," he mutters under his breath, then adds a more assertive "I would never rob a drunken man, nor woman, neither. As for you, I could have picked your pockets in a second if I'd wanted."

"And been rewarded by a single stick of chalk," Ella scoffs. "For that's all I'm carrying about my person."

For all his bluster, the boy is instantly protective. "What sort of family lets you walk abroad without so much as a coin in your pocket?"

"Never you mind about that!" In spite of this injunction, Ella's eyes puddle with tears. "Never you mind about my family."

The boy studies her. "You rich people whimper and wail for no reason, don't you? I'm tougher than that. A lot."

"You don't know the first thing about me!" Ella fights back.

"I know you don't belong on this street."

"No . . ." is the halting answer, "but I did once. I lived here."

The boy cocks his head to one side, looking her up and down as he calculates every article of clothing, the scent of expensive soap, Ella's obvious health, her rosy complexion and lovely, lustrous hair.

"So, your mam labored hereabouts, did she, until she made good and repaired to nicer digs?"

"No" is the still-hesitant reply. "No, she didn't work in a bawdy house." Even as Ella speaks the words, she's not certain if they're true. "I don't know where she lived." By now, Ella's weeping openly and sniffling into her sleeve, which would certainly irk Miss Pettiman. "I wanted to find her. I ran away from school so I could hunt for her." Ella's chest heaves while the boy's greasy face crumples in empathy.

He reaches into his pocket, but the cloth he produces is no longer clean enough to masquerade as a handkerchief, and he quickly replaces it. "I made an escape, too," he offers instead. "But I never returned. And never will. So since I'm on my own I could help you. With your hunt for your mam, I mean. I keep my ears to the ground, I do."

Ella stifles a hiccoughing sob. "Is that why they're so oddly shaped?"

The boy laughs. "There, now. I never thought of that. That's a good one."

Ella returns a small and grateful smile. "Will whoever you ran away from catch you?"

"Not if I see them coming first." A knowing wink accompanies this statement, then builds to something bolder. He lifts himself up on his toes, momentarily towering over Ella. "I've got a daguerreian picture of a lady with pale curls like yours back in the hidey-hole where I sleep at night."

"Lying's a mortal sin" is Ella's sole reply to this clearly bogus claim.

"Who says it's a lie?"

"Boys who keep themselves in hidey-holes don't own ladies' portraits."

"I do, too! And if you come here again tomorrow, I'll prove it to you. A pretty lady, like an angel—" The words cease; and Ella turns to see what caused her companion's sudden silence. At the corner is a uniformed member of the day watch making his regular patrol. When she glances back at the boy, the spot where he stood is empty.

"You there, miss," the day watch addresses her. "Where's your parents at? Not in one of these dismal places, are they? And leaving you here by your lonesome?"

"No, sir," Ella tells him.

The watch regards her. His face is broad and bewhiskered, and Ella decides he looks like a big dog: small eyes, thick snout, and hair. "Then how did you come to be in these unsavory parts?"

"I don't know, sir," Ella says almost truthfully. "I suppose I got lost."

"And who was that urchin bothering you?"

"Urchin, sir?"

"The beggar lad."

Ella shakes her head. "A boy, is all."

"Well, miss, you must take care. Them boys have got sticky fingers, and don't mind who they rob. And they can be dangerous. I'd best take you home."

This, however, is the last thing Ella wishes. "Oh, no, sir. I can find my way."

"No, miss. If you got lost before, you'll get lost again. And I won't have Mr. Thomas Kelman swearing at me if I should let a girl in nice clothes like yourself fall in harm's way."

At this name, Ella brightens considerably. "But I know Mr. Kelman. He wouldn't swear at anybody."

"I doubt it's the same gentleman we're discussing" is the blunt reply. "Now come along. You tell me where your parents live, and I'll walk you home."

"YOU FOUND MY WARD WHERE?" Martha asks again, while the day watch provides the same answer he gave only a moment before. He might be misled into thinking the lady's hard of hearing, but he knows it's both disbelief and fright she's experiencing. As well she should. If criminals can snatch a young person from her house in the middle of the night, how much easier to steal a child off roving alone?

"The lass told me she got lost," the watch concludes equably.

"Yes" is all Martha answers, although she suspects the statement is untrue. Instead of voicing this opinion, she graces the watch with a grateful smile. "I'm indebted to you for your conscientiousness, sir."

"It were nothing, madam. Duty is all. And besides, I have a certain rigorous master who'd have my hide if another girl vanished."

"Well, your 'rigorous master' shall have my thanks if you mention his name to my footman before you leave. And for your pains, you'll also be provided with a monetary token of my appreciation."

"Oh, madam, I cannot accept such a present."

"Will you take the gift to your family, then?"

The watch considers the suggestion. "For the missus and little ones, madam, I would cart home Heaven and earth if they was offered."

"Good. Then it's a gift from me to them. You are simply the messenger."

With the watch gone, Martha turns to Ella, but the child is now diligently examining an invisible object on the floor beside her shoes. The defeated line of her shoulders and her hunched stillness make her the picture of doom. "That was a naughty and thoughtless thing you did, Ella. And potentially dangerous, too. The school was in an uproar when they discovered you gone. One of your teachers came here hoping against hope she'd find you." As Martha speaks, she keeps her gaze fixed on the child, but Ella scrupulously avoids this steady observation.

"Weren't *you* worried?" she finally asks; the tone is so quiet that it takes Martha a moment to decipher the words.

"Of course I was! Do you think I wouldn't be frightened for your safety?"

Again silence is the answer; although Martha is beginning to recognize that it's not sullenness dictating her ward's recalcitrant behavior but distress.

"Why did you run away from school, Ella? Are you unhappy there? Is a classmate teasing you, perhaps?"

The response is a gloomy sigh.

"Sometimes girls—and boys, too—can make remarks they don't fully intend, or completely understand. But that doesn't mean those schoolmates dislike you—"

"I didn't escape because I was sad." Ella looks up only as long as it takes to deliver this declaration, then instantly returns her focus to the floor.

"Perhaps you can explain what your reason was, then."

"I don't know," Ella states in a breathy rush. "I don't. I just decided to go. And then I did."

"For an adventure?"

Ella shakes her bent head. "No . . ."

Martha stifles her rising frustration. "So, your motive wasn't adventure, nor was it because you felt a classmate snubbed you. Let me list other excuses you may have had—"

"I didn't have an excuse. I just wanted to go out."

Rather than react in irritation, Martha walks across the room and gazes into the street. As she peruses the scene, a disquieting sight catches her attention. A boy dressed in rags loiters near one of the trees on the opposite side of the road as if he were scrutinizing the house. Her heart beats faster, and she begins to wish she hadn't been so quick to dispatch the day watch. "Did you happen to meet a street child during your excursion, Ella?"

"I saw a lot of people coming and going."

"But none that you remember, in particular?" Martha prods, for she's all but certain her ward is concealing a secret.

"No." Ella pauses just a moment too long before answering, which increases Martha's skepticism.

"Are you certain?"

"Yes. I am. I'm certain."

There's a newfound stubbornness in the tone; and Martha forsakes her sentry post in order to better scrutinize the child. "Ella, unpleasant things are afoot in our city. Not the usual pickpockets and cutpurses. I don't wish to frighten you, but we must be vigilant. Now, I promise I won't be upset by what you're hiding from me. But I will be upset—and angry, too—if I find you've lied."

Ella looks up, although her expression remains stony. "I ran away because I wanted an adventure. I'm sorry for the trouble I caused. I won't do it again. And I didn't meet anyone. Except for the gentleman who brought me home."

It's several moments before Martha responds. "You may go to your room. When you decide you can be honest with me, we'll continue our conversation." Then she returns to the window and looks at the street, but the beggar boy is gone.

OH, WHAT DREAMS TORTURE MARTHA that night! She envisions Ella when she first met her: freezing, nearly naked, hideously abused. Then she sees the beggar child dodging behind the tree. Another, smaller boy joins him, and another and another until the street fills with tense, gray bodies whose eyes burn yellow with malice. Martha must run to each window in order to bolt them against the onslaught of this small army. But as she rushes through the house, a boy slithers down one chimney while a second gains access through another flue, and a third appears in her upstairs chambers. Soot and dirt cling to these invaders, making them look as though they were covered in fur.

Then the nightmare transports her to a cavernous interior space where a young woman calling herself Theodora Crowther beckons from the shadows. On approaching, however, Martha finds that it's not blond and delicate Dora but a girl whose skin is black and chalky. The girl opens her mouth and it's full of blood.

Awakening, Martha sits bolt upright in bed, staring at the dusky room and the shapes of its familiar objects: the satinwood tables, the chaise and chairs, the armoire, the mantel with its china figurines and candelabra. Instead of solace what she feels is fear, as if the entire purpose of her interrupted sleep was to rise in terror.

Then she becomes aware of raindrops spattering the windowpanes. She throws aside the bedclothes and hurries across the room, closing the sashes against a storm that appears to be flying nearly sideways. Thoroughly wet, she gazes down at the deserted street and the rivulets of black water swelling over the cobbled stones. Her thoughts race with them: her visit to the Crowther household, Georgine's grief and rage, the ambiguities of what Miss Lydia had or had not heard, Harrison's connection to Erasmus Unger's bank.

Finally, she circles back to her awful dream, and to the boy she's certain followed Ella home.

A REQUEST

Despite Miss Pettiman's protests that misbehavior should be rewarded with punishment rather than prizes, Martha decides that the best recourse for Ella's transgression is love—and a guarantee that it will never, ever be lacking. To this end, rather than being consigned to school the morning after her misadventure, Ella and Martha embark on an excursion whose purpose is solely pleasure.

After considering expeditions that would appeal to an eleven-year-old—the exhibition of Hindoo Miracles performed by the Fakir of Ava at the Masonic Hall (over Miss Pettiman's stringent objections), a visit to the natural history museum where the bones of a great mastodon are displayed, or even having a daguerreian portrait made—Martha chooses the recently opened Traveling Diorama of Monsieur Moissenet of Paris. After examining the diorama, they'll have the opportunity to venture into Parkinson's Ice Cream Palace, also new and the height of fashion and excitement, and sitting conveniently across the road on High Street.

However, this happy project isn't as easily accomplished as

Martha envisioned. The diorama is an extraordinarily popular attraction. Outside the building, which resembles a circus house rather than a gallery of art, the demand for tickets is intense. Having purchased them, Martha and Ella must wait in a long line that inches slowly forward into the exhibition hall itself. After a full half hour spent in this fashion, they're next forced to climb stairs so laden with legs and feet that it's nearly impossible to move. When the pair eventually reaches the circular platform that replicates an open-air teahouse set atop the terraced steps of Montmartre, Martha finds that Ella is too short to see past the crowd oohing and aahing its astonishment.

It does little good to say, "Oh, look, Ella, that must be the River Seine, and those caparisoned horses prancing through the park and the soldiers in their plumed helmets, they must be the cavalry" or "See the lady reading by the window, and the washerwoman hefting her basket, and the faraway church dome bathed in gold. Doesn't it look as though genuine sunlight were striking it?" No, Martha must lift the child, which causes both discomfort in the tight space. Then she forces her way to the front of the platform in order to enable Ella to appreciate the wonders that surround them.

Instead of rhapsodizing on the life-like birds lofting through the canvas sky, or the wooden steps wobbling down the hillside, or the barges bobbing along the painted quays, Ella's reaction is a perturbed "It's a trick, isn't it? The straw hat on the park bench and the hoe and barrow and mound of earth: Those are real . . . But the little boy and the lady who holds his hand, and the gardener trimming vines, they're merely picture people, aren't they?"

"Well," Martha replies slowly, for she's still enthralled with the artist's illusion, "it's not a trick as much as a fantasy. You and I are supposed to believe we're in Paris while we stand here, just as we're meant to envision ourselves in other circumstances when we read a book or a tale in Mr. McGuffey's *Reader*. But you're correct, this isn't really a French hillside. When we step outside of the enclosure, we'll be back in Philadelphia."

"We're in Philadelphia now," Ella persists, and her face, so close to Martha's, clouds in disappointment.

"Would you like your ice cream?" Martha asks as she regards the unhappy girl.

Ella nods, although her eyes remain fixed on the painted child and his beaming mother.

Martha follows her ward's longing glance. "Then you shall have it. And sugar biscuits, too. As many as you wish. And as much ice cream as you can hold. Now, I'll set you back on the floor, but you must hold my hand like that boy in the diorama so we don't become separated."

SO, IT WAS ON TO Parkinson's ice cream palace with its floor inlaid with mosaic tiles, its ceiling painted by the famed Monachesi, depicting Roman gods and goddesses that appear to swoop down from above, its numerous divans and private alcoves, its air of Continental abandon. In a city where diners are accustomed to sup in cramped oyster cellars or at indifferent *tables d'hôte,* Parkinson's is a palace, indeed.

A waiter in a swallowtail coat escorts the pair to a table, then flourishes menus bordered in crimson and rose. Ella says not a word except to mumble her desire for currant ice cream and preserved morello cherries; nor does she speak when the sweet is delivered in a silver dish and tasted with a golden spoon. Instead, she stares at the elegant crowd: the ladies in their feather-tipped bonnets and silk mantillas, the gentlemen in cravats of Italian blue or solferino. Martha, in turn, studies the child.

"I'm not going to ask you again why you ran away yesterday," she begins at length, "because I know you'll tell me your reasons eventually. But I will repeat that it was a very dangerous thing you did—"

"Miss Pettiman said I could have been abducted and hidden in an evil place without room enough to breathe. And nothing wholesome to eat," Ella announces before inserting a spoonful of currant and cherry into her mouth. She's become the picture of unconcern, as if the girl who challenged Martha yesterday or displayed such woe an hour past weren't the same child sitting in Parkinson's Palace. "Like Miss Theodora Crowther, she said. Stolen away right under her parents' noses."

Martha's jaw tightens. How like the nursery maid to attempt to terrify her charge with melodrama rather than setting forth simple rules. Instead of arguing against Miss Pettiman's assertion, though, Martha answers with an even "Hopefully not the same as Miss Crowther, but these are not wise times for well-dressed young people to be out walking alone. Which is precisely the reason I and Miss Pettiman and Mr. Kelman and the gentleman who brought you home are so concerned—"

"The day watch is scared of Mr. Kelman," Ella states in the same nonchalant fashion.

"Is he?"

"When I told him I knew Mr. Kelman, he didn't believe me. He said it must have been a different person, but that couldn't be, could it?"

"No . . ."

Ella helps herself to more ice cream, holding the spoon between her lips as if savoring all the syrupy fruits in the world while Martha suppresses a sigh of frustration. *Who is this girl who can manifest defiance and sorrow one moment, and innocence the next? Or is it the way of all children?* Martha tries to recall her own youthful behavior but can only attest that she never sat eating ice cream with her father.

"If you wish to visit Lombard Street, Ella, I'll take you there. But I want you to understand that your history is no longer your future. My home—my homes—are yours. Yours to enjoy for all time. No one can alter that fact."

"No one?" The voice posing the question is so quiet that Martha misinterprets the query as a need for reassurance.

"You'll remain Ella Beale until the day you marry. And even after you're wed you'll still be my daughter."

In answer, Ella frowns into her half-empty dish.

"Would you like more ice cream?"

"No. Thank you." Despite the careful tone, Ella's expression is full of yearning. "Did you have a mother?"

"Of course I did. But she died when I was very young, so I was raised by my father."

"How young were you?"

"Five."

"That's how old Cai was when you adopted him."

"That's right."

"And did your father beat you?"

Martha frowns a little as she weighs her words. "No. But he didn't really love me, either."

"He must have if he didn't beat you. Or sell you." This last is said in the faintest of whispers.

"Ella, you've experienced many, many hardships in your eleven years, more than enough for an entire lifetime, but I promise you'll never endure those misfortunes again. I want you to be as happy as humanly possible, and to recognize that you're free to speak to me, to express your worries and fears, what you most deeply desire, what hurts and angers you. Like the boy yesterday who I believe must have followed you home—"

"There wasn't a boy."

"Oh, Ella!"

If Martha had asked outright why her adoptive daughter was concealing the truth, Ella couldn't have told her. The superficial answer would be that he offered to help find her real mother, although she realizes Martha would never permit such an association. The deeper motive is that the boy with the strange ears now belongs to some secret part of Ella's heart and brain. Cunning and conniving though his ilk might be—and she knows precisely what sort he comes from—she inherently trusts him. "There wasn't anyone!"

"Street children aren't safe companions for you, Ella dear."

"I know that, Mother."

"If you spoke to a pauper child during your adventure yesterday, I'm afraid he may have designs upon you. Try to rob you when you're outside playing, perhaps." Martha hesitates. Not for the world does she wish to sound an alarmist like Miss Pettiman. "Or Cai."

"He wouldn't do that."

"Ah, so there was a boy."

"No." Ella's lips clamp shut, and she looks away as though to examine some distant part of the room while Martha continues to regard her.

"I want there to be trust between us, dear. As well as love."

Ella maintains her faraway gaze.

"Are you listening to me?"

The response to this is a brief nod but no words.

"You may keep your mystery for now. However, I will reiterate that such acquaintances can be harmful. If not the boy himself, then perhaps some adult with whom he dwells. Beggar lads often work in unison with older children or men."

Ella says nothing. The boy with the odd ears told her he lived alone in a private hidey-hole, and she has no reason to doubt him.

"Promise me you'll tell me if you spot the lad again."

Ella's reply to this request is an indifferent shrug as if she's forgotten both the encounter and her escape from school. "Why did your mother die?" she says instead, and Martha, taken by surprise, drops the previous topic.

"I don't know the answer to that, I'm afraid."

"Lots of mothers die when they're having babies. Maybe you had an infant sister or brother, and that's what killed her."

Martha remains silent for a moment. Her eyes search Ella's face as the child now turns her full concentration on her adoptive parent. "What I recall is a dark room and a number of people in it. I could only see the top of the bedclothes on my mother's bed and one of her hands lying on the sheet. Her face was invisible, but her fingers were a bluish white. And chilly. I touched them, so I remember."

"Who were the people?"

"I don't know. I wish I did."

"Did you hear ghosts at night afterwards? Her ghost wandering up and down through the chimney flue like Miss Pettiman says?"

"That story's a fabrication, Ella. What we hear is the wind and nothing more."

The girl sits back, skepticism stamped across her brow. "It sounds like ghosts. Howling and crying."

"That's your imagination at work. If we let our thoughts escape the real world, which we do when we're dreaming or daydreaming, then we can invent a multitude of circumstances. The figures at the diorama, which you rightly identified as being painted, can become living people in our thoughts."

Ella's eyes survey the silver dish, the gold spoon, the immaculate white of the tablecloth, but Martha spots tears clinging to her lashes.

"Does that notion trouble you?"

The reply to the question is so subdued that Martha isn't certain she's heard correctly. "Can we find my mother? My real one?"

"Your—?"

"Can we ask Mr. Kelman? That's his job, isn't it? To find people who've been stolen like Miss Crowther, or escaped from prison, or committed a dangerous act."

Whatever Martha is about to respond dies in her throat when Becky Grey enters the establishment. Heads turn as the former actress passes among the tables, the ladies' lips pursing in dismay and the men's eyes narrowing with covetous curiosity. "I thought she was under supervised care following her indisposition," one woman confides to a companion, who answers a snide "The lower classes must be hard to kill. And their offspring, also."

Either oblivious to the malicious chatter or stubbornly ignoring it, Becky proceeds into the space, but not a single table is available and no one seems to be awaiting her arrival. She pauses while the elite of Philadelphia close ranks, bending over their dishes or volubly talking with one another. Martha's reaction to this communal show of reproof is immediate ire.

"Mrs. Taitt!" she calls with such forced pleasure that the same faces that had assiduously gazed into their ice cream bowls now swivel in her direction. "Join our table. Please do. I'm simply delighted to find you in improved health. You suffered a dreadful trial, I know."

"Thank you" is the resolute reply. Despite a dangerously pale complexion and eyes that bear a feverish glint, Becky forces herself to stand erect.

"We can attest that the fruit creams are not only a novelty but delicious," Martha continues in the same bright and artificial tone.

"So I surmise by your empty dishes, Miss Beale." Becky drops heavily into the chair. "Parkinson's is a popular spot, is it not?"

Here the effort at camaraderie grinds to a halt. The women have held no private conversation before this one. Martha can't help but feel provincial and dowdy when she considers her companion's illustrious former career, while Becky ponders how marvelous it would be to find herself an heiress. An heiress of such stature that society's approval or disapproval would be of no importance.

"You're quite well?" Martha asks after an awkward silence. "I had heard—"

"That the accoucheur confined me to my quarters" is the overloud response. "I've now regained my strength, however. I simply couldn't linger in an invalid state. I'm not a person intended to exist in a cocoon." Like Ella's eyes before, Becky's swell with tears. "As you see, I'm still great with child. I'm told that I should be exceedingly thankful." She sounds anything but, which inspires another gush of half-heard comments. Becky looks at the speakers; she appears to be about to rebuke them but instead returns her attention to the table. Sweat stands out on her brow; her lips are ashy. "Who is your delightful young companion?"

"Ella is my ward. My adoptive child."

"We're going to find my birth mother," Ella offers. "Mr. Kelman will help us."

"Ah" is the sole response. Becky appears to have already lost interest in the girl beside her.

Then the waiter presents himself, and the pregnant woman orders almost as many sweets as the menu affords. "Iced apple pudding," she insists, "and preserved mulberries and nectarines, and tipsy cake, and French plums. Oh, and almond flowers and *puits d'amour,* and let us have a few gooseberry tartlets, as well, if you have them."

Martha makes no attempt to reduce the extensive list. She intuits desperation in every syllable in her companion's voice.

Thus the much-touted excursion to Parkinson's limps forward: Ella consumed with her visions of lost and found parents, and Becky speaking only for the sake of being seen in animated conversation.

It's only when the various desserts have been either enjoyed or dispensed with and the threesome is preparing to depart that the situation changes. For neither woman has money with which to pay.

"Oh, dear," says Becky, and she releases a ragged laugh because she's always been accustomed to having gentlemen pay her bills.

Martha's reaction is the opposite. She scowls in indignation, for she suddenly realizes she's been robbed. "I had my reticule with me when we visited the diorama—"

"Then, my dear Miss Beale, you're the victim of a clever cutpurse who found you an ideal target." Becky inclines her handsome head; some of her famed verve begins to return. "I was deprived of my pocketbook in the same manner, which led me to believe that Philadelphia is as dangerous as London. Perhaps one day the city will have equally compelling entertainments."

Despite Becky's growing smile, Martha's expression remains aggrieved. "You're very lighthearted considering everything you've experienced at the hands of criminals, Mrs. Taitt."

"Such risks are the result of dwelling in a metropolis, are they not, Miss Beale? If we wish to avoid pickpockets, we should take ourselves away from these crowded streets and retire to the country with the oxen and sheep. I'm certain Mr. Parkinson will permit us to sign a chit or some such thing. It's not as though the names Taitt and Beale were unknown in the town."

"I should have kept my wits about me in that crowd—"

"Oh, bosh! Should have. Could have. Would have. What an odious trio. When I was forced to keep to my rooms these past days, I made a promise to ignore those gloomy villains. I suggest you do the same. And call me Becky. Please do. It was how I was known back in London."

Becky Grey, even a weakened version, is a tonic; and Martha finally smiles in earnest, reaching across the table as though meeting her for the first time. "And I'm Martha." There's so much warmth in the exchange that the women's fingers remain locked while Becky continues her breezy remarks:

"You're a fortunate girl, Ella. You'll have the world at your feet—even if your adoptive parent loses her purse on occasion. Better that than her heart, however." Then she turns to the waiter, instructing him that they wish to sign for their meal.

"Oh, if we're dining on credit, let me be the host and you the guest—"

But the jesting words are interrupted by a gentleman neither lady knows. "Excuse me, Miss Beale. I couldn't help but overhear. It would be my pleasure to cover your small expenses."

Martha looks up in surprise. She sees a man of medium height with soft brown eyes and hair that curls abundantly, like a portrait of a Renaissance prince. "I'm Nathan Weil," he tells her. "I hope you'll forgive the intrusion."

"The publisher?" Becky interjects.

"The same." The answer is addressed to Martha rather than to her companion, and Becky's expression registers the slight.

"Mr. Weil is famous among literary circles," she states in a tone that doesn't disguise her pique. "He brought the works of our English *artistes* to an American audience."

"My efforts are of a mechanical nature only. The creation of poetry and other masterpieces, I leave to those with gifts greater than mine. My vocation is to serve. Please, Miss Beale, say that I may help you."

Unlike Becky, Martha finds the attention of unfamiliar gentlemen such a rare occurrence that she acquiesces without considering whether the decision is appropriate or not. "You may, Mr. Weil. If we agree to a loan rather than a gift."

He smiles. It's a relaxed and confident expression, and she can't help but compare it to Thomas Kelman's brooding gaze. "I'm not certain I should lend money to the Beale brokerage concern. I'm afraid you'll have my few coins transferred into notes of credit and I'll discover myself in debt rather than being a creditor."

"Oh, you'll find I'm not as exacting a financier as my father was, Mr. Weil."

"And I'm not my brother." As the reference eludes her, Weil continues. "My brother is chief director of Mr. Erasmus Unger's bank. He was acquainted with your father. Zechariah is older than I by a decade, and most would agree he's a good deal more consistent and solid."

"Ah, consistency," Becky announces. "Gardeners praise soil for that property, but it's the roses we enjoy."

Weil acknowledges the sally with a courteous nod but keeps his focus on Martha. "What say you, Miss Beale?"

"I accept, sir, and I thank you for your kindness."

"Mine is the gratitude."

As he walks away to settle the bill, Becky leans across the table. "Well, you've certainly made yourself a conquest."

"Nonsense" is the reply, but Martha blushes all the same, then experiences immediate remorse, and her cheeks grow even pinker.

"And one of the city's most desirable bachelors," Becky blithely continues.

"He's certainly polite."

Becky laughs again. "If he were, he wouldn't have spoken to you without a proper introduction, Mistress Beale."

As the foursome of Nathan Weil, Becky Grey, Ella, and Martha depart the ice cream palace and enter into a circuitous conversation about who should escort whom home and how delighted Weil would be to accompany both ladies in turn, Ella shouts an elated "There's Mr. Kelman." Her voice rings out as if she'd magically conjured him up, but Martha's reaction is something akin to shame.

"Thom—Mr. Kelman. What an unexpected surprise. May I introduce—"

"I called at your house and was informed you were here or visiting the diorama." His black eyes bore into hers as though unaware of being in the company of strangers.

Becky glances at Martha, then not so covertly pinches her arm as proof that she recognizes the intimacy of the relationship. "My dear, you must share your handsome acquaintance with all of us."

"This is Mr. Kelman" is Ella's boastful reply. "He's going to find my mother."

Kelman receives the statement with the same pained astonishment that Martha did. He studies her face for a sign that perhaps he hasn't heard correctly, but her response is a level "Ella believes you can find anyone."

Kelman's countenance darkens. In contrast with the gilded manner of Nathan Weil, he looks dour and forbidding. "I can try." At these slow words, Ella takes his hand, swinging it as if she owned the man himself.

"Miss Pettiman says you're capable of solving crimes because you're so relentless in your pursuit, and that—"

"Ella! Mr. Kelman doesn't wish to hear Miss Pettiman's opinions at the moment."

He smiles for the first time, but the pleased expression immediately disappears. "Can you come with me to the Crowthers', Miss Beale? That is, as soon as Ella is safely delivered to Miss Pettiman? They've received a message regarding their daughter."

IF YOU WISH TO SEE YOUR DAUGHTER

Harrison Crowther's hands are shaking so vigorously that he can scarcely hold the letter. At Kelman's silent urging, Martha reaches for it. "May I, Mr. Crowther?"

The man's fingers can't or won't release the missive, and so Kelman walks to Crowther's side, lifting a lamp in order to better study the sheet of paper. "You found this on your doorstep?" The tone in which the question is posed is firm, too harsh in Martha's opinion, although she's unfamiliar with the protocol demanded by such situations.

However, the authoritative manner seems to recall Theodora's father from his trembling state. He places the letter on the table, then thrusts his hands into his pockets. "One of the under-housemaids did. When she went outside to polish the brass door-appurtenances. My wife had noticed marks upon them, you see, and insisted they be eradicated immediately. Mrs. Crowther and I and my aunt had just assembled for our luncheon when the missive was carried in to me."

"This under-housemaid saw no one loitering nearby? A boy

who delivered this, perhaps?" Kelman asks, although his focus remains on the document.

"What makes you suspect a child is involved?" Crowther glowers as if he suddenly finds Kelman's presence not only abrasive but superfluous. "Theodora may possess a delicate and graceful frame, but a mere boy couldn't have abducted her."

"It was a boy who robbed the Taitt household, nephew." It's Miss Lydia who makes this pronouncement from her place at the center of one of the settees. An ear trumpet rests on her lap, and her fingers play across its surface as if it were a little dog. "A boy who slithered down the chimney flue and then opened a window that couldn't be seen from the street."

"Aunt, please—"

"May I not say my piece, nephew? You posed a question. I choose to reply."

"It was Mr. Kelman I was addressing, Aunt Lydia. Not you." Crowther's resentment builds until the veins on his face turn purple-red. "We waste precious moments fretting needlessly over nests of burglars and children who enter houses in the dead of night. Whoever stole my daughter from her home is an adult."

At this exclamation, Dora's mother finally stirs. From the moment Martha and Kelman entered the room she has remained as still as death, propped up in a wing chair whose upholstery replicates the color of her Persian blue gown. True, her eyes open and close, and her chest rises and falls; but her conscious mind, dosed with laudanum—or so Martha suspects—is distant from these mechanical activities. "My Theodora . . . my baby girl . . ." she mutters before again nodding into silence.

"My wife took a turn for the worse when the missive arrived," Harrison explains, "and as our physician had prescribed—"

"What Georgine requires is exercise, nephew, not elixirs

which cause her to become insensate. A constitutional such as I make it my habit to engage in—"

"Aunt, desist, I beg you! It's my daughter we discuss. Not you. Nor Georgine. Nor idle saunters round the park, or mystery boys who—"

"Am I forbidden from having an opinion? Just like Theodora?"

"Aunt!"

"Don't shout at me, Harrison! It's very ungentlemanly of you."

"I'm not shouting." As proof of this fact, Crowther lowers his voice, but his fists are clenched.

"Nor are you employing a conversational tone." Undefeated, Lydia Crowther fluffs at her *peau de soie* skirts and repositions her petite shoes on the stool at her feet. "I find it puzzling that young Percy cannot be found," she states while Martha shares a look with Kelman.

"And you still have had no word from Mr. VanLennep?" she asks in a soft voice. "How distressing that must be to you and your wife, sir. In this worrisome time, it would be beneficial to have a friend help shoulder your burdens."

"Well, that thoughtful person would never be Percy VanLennep." Crowther's irate words fly out, and he quickly tries to reclaim them. "He's young, you see, Miss Beale. And impetuous—"

"Impetuosity should be prized, nephew, rather than trounced in the mud."

"Aunt!"

"If you find Percy unsuitable, you shouldn't have permitted their betrothal."

"Aunt, please." Crowther's hands now join together in a gesture of reconciliation while his eyes shift first to Martha and then to Kelman as if seeking their indulgence for the old lady and her meddling ways. "I fear that Mr. VanLennep's great love for my daughter might cause him to be a hindrance rather than an aid. Hopefully, by the time he returns, this frightful interval will be no more than memory."

"Let us pray fervently for that joyous event, Mr. Crowther," Martha concludes, then looks again at Kelman, who maintains his watchful pose beside the table.

"What can you tell me about this message, sir?" he asks, and Martha is relieved to note that his tone has grown friendlier.

"No more than I've said. A housemaid found it and gave it to a footman who in turn presented the missive to me. I immediately sent word to you—as you requested."

Kelman regards Harrison Crowther; then his glance shifts to the nearly stupified Georgine and then to Miss Lydia, who maintains her alert posture, raising and lowering the ear trumpet while her face beams cheerful concern.

"I must be honest with you, sir. I find the wording of the message—" But Kelman has no sooner begun than Crowther interrupts. His voice is sharp.

"What is there to understand other than that the writer demands money, and that my daughter will not be released until the sum of one thousand dollars is delivered?"

"That's the intended interpretation, I admit. But I believe this missive is fraudulent."

"Fraudulent! How can you claim such a ludicrous thing?" Crowther grabs back the letter and reads aloud. "*If you wish to see your daughter, I require a payment of one thousand dollars.* What could be clearer than that?"

"On the surface, nothing. However, I find the simplicity of the demand perplexing. Despite an attempt at disguise, the handwriting clearly belongs to an educated person—"

Again Crowther starts to challenge the statement, but Kelman overrides him. "I'm also concerned that there's no mention of Miss Theodora's welfare, or how or when you might expect to be reunited with her . . . And although the sum is high, it seems insufficient given your family's status—"

"This palaver of yours brings us no results, sir! What do I care about the amount as long as I get her back? And quickly, too! You state this demand may be a fraud. Then my question for you is: Where is my Dora, and why can't you find her? It has been four days since she vanished. Four days! Even the most lethargic of our city's journalists are trumpeting that disturbing news. Surely this town is not so large that it has swallowed my daughter whole. Furthermore: If this missive isn't a ransom letter, what is it?"

Despite the barrage of words, Kelman remains calm. "I'm beginning to wonder, Mr. Crowther, whether it might have been composed by a stranger hoping for a chance at easy money. As you just mentioned, every journal and gazette has been full of the story—"

"Easy money, sir! Is it *ease* with which Dora's mother and I wait out each day hoping for our child's return? Is it a *chance* of finding her that we expect? No! It's a suitable investigation. It's dedication and police work, sir, rather than guesswork and hypothesis!"

The loudness of Harrison's voice has again startled Georgine. Her body jolts within the chair's supporting wings, and her eyes open wide as though waking from a sleep. She stares at Kelman; for a moment, she seems not to recognize him; when she does her mouth turns downward in mistrust. Then she looks at her husband's irate face, and her skeptical gaze dissolves in sorrow. "Mr. Crowther, sir, please be so kind as to escort me to my rooms. I fear I am unwell."

Immediately solicitous, he hurries to his wife's side, jamming the ransom letter into his pocket as he does. "Of course, my dear. Of course."

Hefting the large woman to her feet isn't easily done, however, and Crowther requires both Kelman's and Martha's aid in order to raise the woozy lady and set her traveling in the correct direction. As the pair moves unsteadily toward the door, Crowther lands a parting shot. "I have it in mind to hire a secret service agent, sir. Someone for whom our case would be of the highest priority."

Kelman receives this latest insult with dismay. "Mr. Luther Irwin's Bureau of Secret Service, is that your intention?"

"It is. I've already spoken with Mr. Irwin in person. He assures me that he can guarantee results, and that he will personally handle the affair."

Kelman nods once, although his face remains set. "So he will. But if this missive is the hoax I intuit it to be, you'd be advised to tread more lightly than Luther Irwin will recommend. To my knowledge, he has never handled anything of this nature before. You don't wish to jeopardize your daughter's safety—"

"What safety do you speak of?" Crowther cries out. "If Theodora is not under her own roof, what protection is she assured?"

"You're correct, sir, but an agency like Irwin's can do more harm than good—"

But Harrison Crowther and his wife are past the door and treading uncertainly across the foyer by the time this final warning is uttered.

"He won't listen," Miss Lydia now states with the trumpet held firmly to her ear. "He never has. He was stubborn as a child, Lord knows, and the bane of his mother's existence. He's stubborn yet, and will be until the day he meets his Maker. But then my nephew is of a short and ungainly build. A tall, imposing stature is more appealing in a gentleman. More impressive, too. The general stood head and shoulders above his peers; and look what he accomplished." Then the ear trumpet is returned to her lap while she closes her eyes as if shutting out every trouble the modern world offers.

"COULD DORA AND PERCY HAVE eloped, do you think?" These are the first words Martha utters as Kelman walks her home. So intent are they on their interview that they've unconsciously assumed the appearance of husband and wife. Martha's hand is tucked into the crook of Kelman's arm; his own fingers caress hers in return. A stranger could easily mistake them for the most comfortable of couples.

"With Miss Lydia's connivance? Is that your supposition?"

Martha nods, her gaze fixed on the street before her. "She claims to have heard her great-niece whisper Percy's name the night she vanished. And if Crowther dislikes his future son-in-law as much as he appears, then perhaps—"

"Dislike is a strong word, Martha."

"Is it? An only child and a daughter. Clearly a father would want a suitor of the highest caliber. Missing the mark by even a small amount might cause the candidate's status to plummet."

"Was your own father so exacting?"

"He never permitted me a suitor." This bitter confession is out before Martha has time to stop it. She pinches her lips as if to prevent the escape of further awkward disclosures while Kelman's jaw tightens in self-reproach.

"Forgive me, Martha. My question was insensitive."

"It was honest, Thomas; so there's nothing to forgive."

"I would rather my nature were more naturally thoughtful and considerate—"

"And replace truth with good manners?" She smiles as she speaks. "I'd rather have you as you are." Then her eyes crease with worry as her thoughts return to Dora Crowther. "When I originally visited the household, I found the behavior between husband and wife perplexing. Georgine displayed a good deal of anger. I had the impression she was harboring a secret grievance."

"Given her present state, it's difficult to know what she believes."

"It is. I must admit, I find such liberal use of calmative potions troubling." Martha's pensive frown deepens. "Explain to me again why you feel the Crowthers' letter is fraudulent."

"If this were the second missive they'd received, I would have few questions other than those I already posed. But the writer makes no mention of Dora, nor does he enclose a snippet of her hair or a memento the parents would recognize. There's only the statement that money must change hands if the Crowthers wish to 'see' their daughter—although the directive curiously fails to provide a means by which that payment can be made. So, does the author, in fact, possess the young lady? And why did he wait so long before approaching the family? I also remain baffled by the differences in the robbery the Crowthers suffered and those perpetrated on other families. In short, these queries lead me to believe that things are not as they seem."

Martha thinks for several long moments. "Could the missive have been written by Percy—with Dora's collusion?"

Kelman shakes his head. "What sort of daughter would inflict this kind of misery on her parents?"

"An angry one? Or a young lady so deeply in love that she can think only of herself and her swain? If Miss Lydia is correct in inferring that Dora and Percy were denied each other's company—perhaps even conclusively—then I imagine the girl's ardor could turn ruthless."

"But Georgine has stated repeatedly that Dora is soon to be wed."

"And Crowther? Does he seem to you to share his wife's positive attitude about the marriage, or its date?"

"I believed so. I continue to believe it. In my opinion, Dora's father is simply a choleric man facing a situation he can't control. Stubborn, too, as his aunt suggests. Yes, he referred to VanLennep as thoughtless and impetuous; and yes, there were other innuendoes regarding his displeasure with the match, but he also mentioned Percy's 'great love' for Dora, which leads me to believe that a state of helplessness is the sole cause of his immoderate speech. Gentlemen like him who are accustomed to wielding influence are sometimes easily provoked."

Martha inclines her head, pondering what Kelman has said. "What of this Luther Irwin? You warned Crowther to step lightly. Are the secret agent's methods overly harsh, then?"

"Severe or brutal might be a more fitting word. I realize that much of police investigative work relies upon cowing the criminal classes, but Irwin doesn't mind breaking heads to get results. In the case of a kidnapping, when a human life is at stake, such measures may prove counterproductive. There, the guilty persons are more apt to be attacked by fear and doubt, and therefore fight amongst themselves. It's not unknown for the victim to be found murdered—" Kelman interrupts himself as Martha lets out a frightened gasp. "I apologize. We shouldn't be discussing such eventualities. You may be perfectly correct. Dora and Percy may have eloped."

Martha isn't soothed by the statement, however. "Oh, Thomas, let us hope that my theory is accurate. Dora must be found. Alive and well, too!"

He makes no immediate reply. When he speaks again, his voice is resolute and his eyes bear a distant glint. "With or without Irwin and his rowdies, I'll maintain my investigation. Theodora Crowther will be reunited with her parents."

With that they fall silent as they continue their journey, their footsteps falling side by side, their bodies linked, their minds consumed by similar concerns. "Is Ella serious about wishing to find her true mother?" Kelman asks at length, and his tone, although steady, sounds like the saddest of songs.

"Yes. She is."

"Is that what you want, too? Because such a search can be set aside. False leads, or none, might be unearthed. Of course, the deception may be necessary. Children like Ella usually enter the world without anyone recording pertinent information."

Martha is silent for a moment. When she does reply, her words are philosophical. "I will do as Ella requests, and therefore earnestly ask you for your help."

"If, and it is an uncertainty, mother and child can be reunited, you may be compelled to relinquish your own role."

"I'm aware of the consequences." Martha allows herself a fleeting smile. "This isn't to suggest that I'm pleased—just that I'm aware of what the future may hold."

"And if I discover the father who sold her?"

"Let us ponder that problem when and if it arises."

They cross the street to the greensward leading to the State House. Amor Alsberg and his flock are encamped there, and Kelman mutters his dismay. "How stupid of me. I should have chosen another route." The confession is drowned by the itinerant preacher's ferocious rant:

"And what does the Prophet Isaiah say about the haughty daughters of Zion, my brothers and sisters? Does he not state that the Lord will afflict them, smiting their heads with scabs and laying bare their secret parts? Is that not the third chapter of Isaiah, beginning at verse sixteen, wherein the Lord deprives those heartless women of all that they hold dear? 'Woe unto them that call evil good, and good evil . . . Their children also shall be dashed to pieces before their eyes'!"

"Oh," Martha murmurs, pulling back. "Is this the same message you heard the other day?"

"Not the same, but similar." As Kelman answers, it becomes clear to Martha that his focus is fixed on a man standing several paces away. Despite a poorly patched coat and dirty linen, he has a boastful stance as if poverty were a source of pride. Feeling Kelman's eyes upon him, he turns and glowers while his lips curl back from his teeth like an angry dog's. Martha notices that the man's ears have turned very red and that they are pointed at the tips. Beneath the tall hat he wears squashed on his head, the ears escape like leathery wings.

"Do you know that person?" she asks.

"I'm not certain" is the quiet reply. Then Kelman extricates his arm from hers and asks if she would be comfortable strolling off a little distance, away from Alsberg's congregation.

"I can take myself home, Thomas."

"No. I would rather you wait for me. You're dressed too finely not to be noticed and perhaps followed." So saying, he moves toward the man with the ugly stare, who steps away from the crowd as if he's been awaiting this confrontation.

"Are you Mr. Findal Stokes senior, by any chance?"

"Who is it wants to know, *by any chance*?" Martha hears sarcasm drip through the words, then realizes to her dismay that the man, Stokes, has spotted her. He touches his hat and gives a private leer that Kelman fortunately doesn't see. "I may be. I may not. It depends on what's on offer."

"And your son is young Findal Stokes?"

"If that's my name, it would make sense I'd pass it along, wouldn't it? I believe that's what you fine gents and ladies do. Or is there a rule saying us lesser folk haven't the right to emulate our superiors?"

If Kelman notes the heckling tone, he doesn't show it. "Where's your son now, Mr. Stokes?"

"I haven't said that's my name yet, have I, guv?"

"A boy called Findal Stokes has information concerning a mother who attempted to murder her baby and is herself believed to be a suicide. He and his father were kept at Blockley—"

At the name of the institution, Stokes's fists fly upward, and his mouth opens in a roar that doesn't come. "What should I know about that place?" he demands, but his tone is choked as if fingers grasped his neck. "Do I look like a pauper to you? Do I look like a bankrupt, to be consigned to the almshouse—?"

"Are you a recent resident of Blockley?" Kelman persists.

"What if I was? And what if I wasn't? It's a free country, ain't it? The last I heard it wasn't a crime for a man to move about the city, no matter how full or empty his pockets." He makes to turn away, but Kelman lays a cautionary hand upon his arm.

"I'm asking if you know the boy—"

"What do I care about a boy? I've enough trouble as it is. And I know no blond female, neither. Not living and not dead. So I'll kindly ask you to leave me alone—"

"I didn't say that the woman in question was fair-haired, Stokes."

The response is a snarl. "Don't you try to trap me with your fancy words, Constable, or whatever you are. I'm an honest man, I am. A harness maker who—"

"How did you know the woman was blond?" Kelman persists, but the reply is a dogmatic continuation of the previous recitation:

"A harness maker who never stole from his master. Me and him, we never cheated, nor sold shoddy. We did an honest day's work. Not like you people with your cheating trades. Your snatch-and-grab bankers, and Erasmus Ungers, may he rot in Hell eternal. He couldn't build a set of reins, or—"

"What do you know about this suicide, Stokes?"

"You didn't hear Preacher Alsberg warning those foul schemers? 'Their children shall be dashed to pieces—' "

"The dead woman, Stokes!" Kelman tightens his grip on the smaller man, but he shakes himself free, then dodges into the crowd and out the other side, running faster than his legs seem capable of carrying him while Kelman shouts for the day watch and whatever constable is near.

"I WILL NOT MARRY DORA"

MARTHA SITS ON HER BED, not in it but upon it, although she's dressed in her nightclothes and her lady's maid has long ago brushed out her hair, put away her gown, her underskirts and pantelettes and corset, her earrings and bracelets, and then just as methodically prepared the chamber for sleeping. Martha can't consider the placid refuge of repose; her mind is too full, her thoughts too turbulent.

Did Dora elope with Percy? Or has she been abducted by someone seeking financial gain, or else who's so full of loathing for the parents that he would harm the daughter? Is Crowther the overbearing parent Miss Lydia insinuates? If so, why did he permit the engagement if he opposed it? Or has his aunt invented a tale because it suits her to gossip and meddle . . . ? But if the father approved the matrimony, and Dora had the blessing of both parents, why would she and Percy run away?

Martha shakes her head. There are no answers to be found, only questions that coil back into one another. Then her thoughts veer to the elder Stokes and his denunciation of the rich, and in particular Erasmus Unger. She recalls the shouted oaths, and her shoulders hunch forward in perplexity. *Could it be happenstance that Thomas attempted to question Stokes concerning the other matter—only to discover he's involved with Dora's disappearance? Or is my brain playing tricks on me?*

Martha sighs aloud, then rises and walks to a table near her chaise, taking up her Bible and immediately putting it down in order to light the lamp. When the flame burns clean, she opens to the Book of the Prophet Isaiah. "*Amor,*" she mutters under her breath, "the Latin word meaning love. So, let us see if we can find this *Amor* Alsberg's message of compassion." She reads the passages the preacher chose, then skips ahead until she comes to the close of chapter fifty-five: " 'For ye shall go out with joy, and be led forth with peace: the mountains and the hills shall break forth before you into singing, and all the trees of the field shall clap their hands.' "

Why couldn't he have recited that verse, instead of urging his followers toward hatred and censure? she wonders while her mind envisions Becky Grey clapping her hands with joy. The image promptly produces an accompanying vision of Nathan Weil, which casts Martha into confusion again. She can recall each glance he gave her, every word he spoke, the boldness of his smile, his probing eyes. The memory makes her groan. *You don't deserve a solid, high-minded man like Thomas. Indeed, you don't. Not if a raft of pretty phrases can seduce you. Why, Weil may have no more substance than the paper upon which his books are printed.*

Thus feuding with herself, Martha tosses the Bible aside, and tosses her head and shoulders, as well, then glares at her room as if the place were the cause of her consternation. Finally, she takes up another book, a recently published collection of Tennyson's poetry. She leafs through works she's already read, *The Miller's Daughter, Mariana,* and *The Two Voices,* until she comes to pages as yet uncut, and slits them with a vengeance. Then she draws in a quick, astonished breath at the title, *Dora,* and commences to read aloud.

> "'*I cannot marry Dora; by my life,*
> *I will not marry Dora . . .*'"

Martha slams the book shut, but not before the title page flips past her eyes. The publisher is Weil and Harte of Philadelphia. She drops the volume as though her fingers were on fire.

IN ANOTHER PART OF THE house, up another staircase and down a narrower hall that fronts the children's bedrooms and day-rooms and Miss Pettiman's chambers, Cai hears a ghost. A ghost clanking and muttering in the chimney, moving down and down and down.

He freezes in his bed; his eyes against the darkness grow very large and white, and his mouth opens in a wide O of fright. Despite his adoptive mother's adamant disclaimer, he knows that Miss Pettiman is correct. Ghosts are everywhere, and they especially enjoy spiriting through cold chimneys and terrorizing small, defenseless boys. If Cai were less afraid, he'd leap from his bed, fly across the room, out the door leading to the day nursery, and so into Ella's private chamber; but he's too alarmed to move.

Instead, he stares at the hearth and watches glinting shards of chimney stone tumble down amidst the velvety soot. Then two black boots appear, and two legs and a body, which wriggles free, bending into a crouch as a dark and streaky head ducks forth, and two arms and two hands slink down to untie a rope tied to the apparition's chest. Spotting the small body that is Caspar Beale, the ghost puts a warning finger to its mouth, but the child gazes numbly back. He couldn't scream if he wanted to. Besides, who can offer protection against a spirit from the netherworld? Not a living person, surely. Not even Miss Pettiman in her forbidding apartment across the passageway.

"Where's the girl?" the creature demands while Cai begins to tremble all over.

"Cat got your tongue?"

Cai only quivers in his sheets, so the specter walks to the child's bed and peers into his face.

"A Negro child, eh? Or mulatto, is a better guess. How did you come to own such a fine setup, then? Living like a little prince while the rest of us scrabble and starve . . . You're not a bastard son of the lady's, are you? Or her skinflint old dad? I heard all about him. Rich as Croesus, he was. They talk about him in a place where I do an odd job or two. So, yes, I guess you could be old moneybags's love child. If he fancied one of the fancy ladies in the Negro houses." The ghost chortles at his own play on words while Cai's shivering intensifies.

"What's wrong with you? Got the falling sickness, is that it?" The ghoul bends closer. "Here now. You'd better stop your jouncing and jiggling. You'll hurt yourself otherwise, and I won't be held responsible if you do."

Despite the stern words, the tone is kindly. The wraith touches Cai's face. "There was a little lad like you at Blockley. We learned how to bring him round when he got the palsy. Here, you keep your eyes open and you look at me. I won't harm you. I'm your friend." The ghost continues to stroke Cai's rigid cheek. "There now . . . there now. You'll be right as rain in a minute or two. Keep your eyes glued to me. There you go . . ."

The fit begins to pass, but not before Cai does something unbearably shameful. He wets his bed, and not just a little. He soaks the entire horsehair mattress. The smell of this egregious accident fills the air, and Cai, now returning to cognizance, yelps out his distress, to which the ghost hisses a vehement:

"Shut your mouth!"

But Cai's whimpering moans increase, which causes the specter to grab him by the shoulders.

"Hush, I tell you! I mean you no harm." The ghost stops speaking and listens, then flies back to the hearth, where he hurries to bind the rope around his chest before shooting his arms up into the chimney. "Tell the girl to take care," he hisses. "Tell her I came to warn her that a bad man has evil designs on her. I'm the boy she met when she ran away from school. She'll remember. I'm the fellow who keeps his ears to the ground. But she must tell no one I was here, and neither should you. Dangerous things will happen, otherwise."

IS IT THE DEVIL?

Cai's story is such a garble of fright and mortification that Ella can scarcely understand what he's trying to say. Sitting on the floor beside her bed, his nightclothes still drenched and sticky, he sniffles and hiccoughs as he describes the ghoul who dropped into his room.

"Is it the devil?" he asks as soon as he finishes his narration. "Is that who has designs upon you? Miss Pettiman says he's powerfully evil."

"No. It's a real person." Ella clambers out of bed, pulls a blanket from the cedar-lined chest beneath the window, and drapes it over Caspar's shoulders before perching on the edge of her mattress. "We must change your clothes—"

"Do ghosts speak to living people often?" Cai interrupts.

"It wasn't a ghost that climbed down your chimney—"

"It was! I saw it!"

"No, Cai. It was a living boy. Like a chimney sweep."

"Sweeps don't work at night."

Ella sighs. "I didn't mean he was a true sweep. Only that he crept inside the chimney in a similar fashion: first securing a rope, and then—"

"Ghouls and specters don't creep. They fly and howl. Miss Pettiman says—"

"Didn't the boy say he'd met me the day I ran away from school?"

Cai considers this. He's of a more fanciful nature than Ella and is loath to relinquish his association with a dead person—no matter how hideous the encounter. When he responds, his words are cagey. "Miss Pettiman says that spirits from the netherworld—"

"Cai, listen to me. That was a real boy who found his way into your hearth, and the man he spoke of is more terrible than any airy spirit . . . Do you remember Miss Pettiman warning us about a nest of burglars? And do you remember how upset Mother was when the day watch brought me home?" Ella eliminates any reference to Theodora Crowther; she's certain Cai is missing this piece of information, for if he knew it, the story would be his sole subject of conversation. "And how she said that Mr. Kelman was worried about burglars, too?"

Cai nods.

"Well, that's because they're extremely bad people. And they work their crimes by climbing down chimneys. Boys slither through the flues—just like this one did—then they roam about the houses they've entered, and take things and pass them to other boys who wait outside in the dark near a window or door on the ground floor. Their master also waits, in order to make certain no one steals from him."

"But he's stealing, too, isn't he? The master, I mean."

"Yes. He's taught the boys what is valuable and what is not."

Cai frowns in thought. "Well, if my ghost was just an ordinary thief, he didn't take anything from me."

"You don't have any possessions important enough."

"I do, too" is the staunch reply. "I have my stuffed dog with the genuine hair, and the lead cavalry, and—"

"They want silver, Cai, and jewels." *And people,* Ella thinks but doesn't say.

"Is the master like a pirate, then? Like the pirates Miss Pettiman said used to sail their ships up the Delaware River and dock near Front Street, and swagger around the town and hit people they didn't like?"

"Yes." If Ella weren't so engrossed in wondering what Cai's peculiar visitation means, she would find this conversation vexing. As it is, her concentration is only half on her adoptive brother's words. "Exactly like a pirate."

Cai considers her answer. The adjustment from spectral terror to flesh-and-blood danger was difficult to make, but having accomplished it, he's now absorbed in the new menace. "We must tell Mother and Miss Pettiman," he announces.

"No" is Ella's swift response. "The boy said to confide in no one, or it would be dangerous."

"We'll explain that, too—"

"No, Cai. We must keep what happened our secret for a while."

"But Mother—"

"Mother and Miss Pettiman will only worry further, and perhaps not allow us to play in the park or go for walks. You wouldn't wish that, would you?"

"But—"

"Cai," a now exasperated Ella declares, "surely you don't want that dirty creature coming back into your room and warning you again."

The maneuver works admirably. Cai shakes his head in abject

silence while Ella rises and walks with measured steps across the floor. "We must get you some dry nightclothes. Then you may curl up with me so long as you don't kick or suck your thumb. Or go into one of your funny fits."

"The ghost told me he knew a lad who—"

"Never mind about your ghouls and wraiths now, Cai."

"He stopped my shaking sickness. I wet my bed anyway."

"Yes. Now, let's get you changed."

Returned to bed, Ella squints in concentration at the dusky walls while Cai immediately falls into an exhausted and grateful slumber. *She'll remember me. I'm the fellow who keeps his ears to the ground. A bad man. Evil designs.* The nameless boy's pronouncements repeat and repeat themselves until they join his previous boastings and form a litany in her drifting mind: *Help you hunt for your mam. I've got a scheme . . . Tell her . . . Mam . . . Remember . . . Bad man . . .*

DAWN BREAKS. THE LIGHT OF a new day sifts in through the nursery windows, illuminating the children's sleeping faces as if it were merely checking to make certain they are well and happy. In parts of the house unprotected by curtains and shutters, the sunlight grows more insistent, waking the maids, the footmen, and the cook, while the sounds of the egg man pushing his cart and the bread seller beginning his rounds issue a louder warning.

Soon those who serve the household are stirring, as are those in other households across the city. Fires are lit in stoves; water is heated and biscuits set to rise; coffee is ground, veal and ham pies prepared; collared and potted fishes are removed from the larder; cheeses are unwrapped from their cloths, and grape branches artfully piled in cut-glass bowls.

And at the Crowthers' residence another under-housemaid tiptoes through the front hall in order to sweep the outside steps before her mistress or the majordomo can find fault. When the girl opens the door, she spots a letter wrapped around an object she instantly recognizes.

It's the missing daguerreotype of Miss Dora.

AMONG THE TALL PINES

As Luther Irwin of Irwin's Secret Service is summoned to the Crowthers' house; as Martha finishes breakfast and ponders her sleepless night; and as Ella and Cai keep their pact of silence, another scene plays out far south of the city where the Delaware courses its fifty-one meandering miles toward the Atlantic Ocean.

Now wide and undulant, now narrowing and reedy, dotted with uninhabited islands, or broken into coves that splinter apart into marsh grasses, the river is bordered on both banks by thousands of acres of land, most of which remain primitive and pristine. Some carry the names supplied by the original inhabitants, the Unami tribe of the Lenni-Lenape who gave Philadelphia its own distinctive labels: Shackamaxon, "Place of Eels"; Passyunk, "In the Valley"; Pennypack, "Still Water."

As it was before the advent of the earliest European settlers who hewed the first farms and fisheries in what would eventually become the states of Pennsylvania and Delaware, the area is rife with animal life: bald eagles, saw-whet owls, quail, downy woodpeckers, opossums, deer, bear, and elk. Red maple, white ash, black oak and black walnut, sweet birch, blue-water birch, hop hornbeam, linden, and pawpaw serve as the creatures' homes. The area is a garden of Eden, still.

It's to this natural paradise that Percy VanLennep has chosen to journey, and where he rests at the precise moment Luther Irwin begins reading the letter that accompanied Dora's portrait.

Percy's voyage to the spot was more headlong flight than intentional design. The seeds of his hasty decision were sown on the night of his ignominious dismissal from his betrothed's home. Naturally, he meant to inform Dora of his intentions, but being young and callow and more concerned whether his boots and newest Canton flannel coat were brushed, he forgot. He also intended to provide his servants with an itinerary, but as he hadn't a clear one, he let that effort pass, as well.

Instead, he embarked on a schooner lying at the foot of the Chestnut Street Wharf on September sixteenth, the very morning his betrothed was discovered missing. He was careful not to supply the captain with his name, not because he was trying to conceal his travels, but because he didn't wish to cause Theodora undue embarrassment should some unkind gossip impugn the motives for his sojourn, and thereby suggest he was running away from his duties. Percy told himself he would be absent four or five days, certainly no longer than a week; he reasoned that an unmarried man—or even a married one—should be accorded that much privacy.

His aim in sailing south along the river was to seek out the counsel of his reclusive friend Nicholas Howe at his plantation house in the state of Delaware some forty miles south of Philadelphia. By late afternoon of the same day, and a little north of Pea Patch Island, he found himself in a sailing skiff being maneuvered up Hamburg Cove toward Howe's secluded estate. The man at the helm was a tenant of Nicholas's who, by luck, had come down with goods to trade. Percy finally felt safely removed enough from the ogre Mother Crowther and her equally ferocious husband to confide his true name and the nature of his visit.

NICHOLAS, HOWEVER, ALTHOUGH A FELLOW graduate of Princeton, was less interested in Percy's travails than in the health of his sheep and cattle. In the years since their classroom friendship, Percy had become an urbane gentleman, and Nicholas the owner and manager of his family's ancestral residence. Country ways suited him; silence pleased him; simple fare and ample opportunity for rumination and meditation were his necessities.

Percy, with his persistent questions about his future and his preference in brides, with his prattling on about the other young women of his acquaintance—even those of easy virtue—Nicholas quickly found as pesky and tiresome as a bluebottle fly. How could someone who found the ways of elk and bear and fox endlessly fascinating provide advice about which course to follow? Whether to recommend Percy wed Theodora Crowther or not? Or how to break off the engagement if he wished? And what fate would befall VanLennep if "society" deemed he'd acted dishonorably? Nicholas knew livestock, not the hearts and minds of ladies and their parents.

As a result of these mismatched temperaments, not thirty-six hours following Percy's arrival in Hamburg Cove, he was urged to set forth on another journey: this time toward the wilder inland terrain where Nicholas promised spectacular scenery and abundant wild game to substitute for his friend's many worries. When the thought of the giantess Georgine proved too terrible to tolerate, Nicholas suggested, Percy need only point a borrowed percussion rifle into the air, and an excellent supper would fall from the sky.

Unaccustomed to such rustic ways, but inspired by the romantic notion of manly and rugged tramping, and provided with a bedroll and basic cookery utensils, Percy left the cultivated fields and pastures of the Howe farm and entered the woods. Coaquannock, the locals called it: the "Grove of Tall Pines." He reasoned his marriage date was many days hence, and he would have ample time to make a decision whether to wed or not, and return without Dora or her parents being aware of his escapade.

NOW, ON THE THIRD DAY into this solitary retreat, Percy is ensconced among the pines and buttonwoods and hickory, and as far from the news of urban life as anyone can be. Purple grackles swoop and argue above him; weasels and foxes scurry through the dense thickets; deer freeze and then cautiously walk on. Glimpsed through the overshadowing trees, the morning sky is blue and clear and high; the scent of earth and wildflower and honeysuckle revives the soul. There are bees; there is birdsong, and the breeze's lullaby in the uppermost branches of the leafy boughs.

Percy hears none of this lyrical melody, however, for Percy has been badly wounded. A bullet has shattered his shoulder, spraying out so much blood and gristle and bone that his head and upper back are soaked in gore. He breathes, but the breaths are labored; he opens his eyes and sees ants and beetles scrabbling through the wet red soil. He mutters aloud; then even that whispered plea falls silent while the tall pines moan.

I CAN TELL YOU MANY A TALE

"A WORD WITH YOU, SIR." KELMAN'S voice is peremptory; it brooks no refusal or delay. Not that he imagines Luther Irwin would dare snub him, but the man is audacious and cocksure, a contentious new breed spawned by the nation's financial crisis. He and his ilk remind Kelman less of humans than of dogs chasing after a flock of recalcitrant sheep; they're all dodges and feints and sly nips to vulnerable places.

"Mr. Kelman." Irwin neither tips his tall hat nor doffs it; instead, he retains the impudent air with which he departed the Crowther household not one minute past. "Were you strolling by, or did one of your spies inform you that Mr. Crowther had sent for me?"

Kelman makes no reply to the snide remark, although it's difficult for him to conceal his irritation. "I think you and I had better work hand in hand in this matter, Irwin. A young lady's life is at stake."

"And has been for some time, Kelman. However, I must inform you that Mr. and Mrs. Crowther aren't impressed with your efforts, so a partnership between us isn't possible. In fact, Mrs. Crowther was just telling me she believed you've been both remiss and tardy in your hunt for their daughter, and she had no intention of contacting you—"

"Mrs. Crowther said all that?"

"The lady does have a tongue, sir. Surely she's allowed to use it."

"Yes, of course." Kelman isn't focused on Georgine Crowther's complaints but on the fact that her drug-addled state has apparently been lifted. "The lady has been under a physician's care; combined with her worried frame of mind, it has made her less than verbose."

"She was talkative enough with me. But then I pride myself on having a way with the ladies. It's one of the secrets of my trade. Please the wife, and you'll secure the husband's business. Now, tell me what you want of me, sir, for I've work to do."

This time Kelman doesn't disguise his ire. "You're very sure of yourself, aren't you, Irwin? I needn't remind you that an unkind word from me could end your practice."

"With no centralized police force, I hardly believe that's possible" is the derisive retort. "Read the penny presses if you want the truth of the matter. According to their allegations—and everyone else's, too—the city's gotten too big for its paltry constabulary, and the mayor needs every bit of help he can find. I needn't remind *you,* sir, that our elected officials and their minions serve at the citizens' behest. One vote could put your friends out on the street; and a man like me could occupy your office."

Kelman studies Luther Irwin: his creaking new boots, the bold weave of his coat, its bright brass buttons, and the damnable hat tilted to one side as if its owner were either defying it to fall or feigning the studied ease of a gentleman. For a second, Kelman imagines knocking the ridiculously shiny thing to the ground, and Luther Irwin with it, but he suppresses the impulse. "A man like you, sir, cannot rise without successful outcomes to your endeavors. I propose we join forces in this instance—"

"I don't need the aid of an inadequate—"

"If Miss Theodora Crowther is harmed, Irwin, and your agency is the sole enterprise responsible for finding her, you'll never work again. Never. Do you understand?"

The secret service agent glares while his lips turn upward in a sneer that then quivers with a measure of doubt. "What's your interest in this affair?" he demands in order to cover his unease. "Are you sweet on the young lady, perhaps? I'd heard tell you'd set your sights on more lucre than old man Crowther has salted away. Miss Martha Beale is who folks are saying—"

This time Kelman can't help himself. He grabs Irwin's shoulder. For such a long and elegant hand, it's surprisingly strong, and Irwin winces under the pressure. "Do not mention that name again. I also advise you to speak well of your erstwhile patrons and their daughter. Now, what arrangement will you have? Do we work together? Or do I allow you to proceed with your dubious practices and risk adding to the problem—?"

"What do you mean by 'dubious practices'?" Irwin demands as he struggles unsuccessfully to free himself.

Kelman watches the man squirm. "How do you intend to find Miss Crowther? Threaten your informers if they can't discover where she is? Threaten their families? Cut a wide swath among your felonious friends? Spread largesse and drop hints there is more of Crowther's 'lucre' to come? Or are you in on this scheme in some fashion?"

"I'm a respected businessman, sir. I'll ask you to remember it."

"You're a businessman, Irwin, but 'respect' is not the term I would have chosen. Now, what will you have: a joint effort, or certain failure on your part?"

For all his bravado, all his swagger and jeering, Luther turns sulky and defensive in a moment. "I have nothing to do with Dora's disappearance," he mumbles.

"Good. Then we'll work in unison. I suggest you learn to refer to the young lady as Miss Theodora. You may believe you've won the mother's heart, but she doesn't take kindly to inappropriate intimacies. She can be a veritable tiger when she wishes. Now, tell me what you have."

Luther Irwin then proceeds to do so, recounting, albeit sourly, how the under-maid found the daguerreotype wrapped in a letter, how Crowther summoned him, and how he discussed the case with the young woman's parents—although not Miss Lydia, who remained "secluded in her chambers upstairs"—and finally producing the same missive for Kelman to peruse. "Georg—Mrs. Crowther wanted to keep the portrait."

"Naturally" is Kelman's terse reply before he examines the message . . . *ten thousand dollars to be concealed within a basket of discarded ladies' linen, and left on the front steps of a house at the southwest corner of Sixth and Lombard Streets at seven tomorrow morning. No earlier, and no later. The note attached must read: A gift to be distributed among the poor.* Kelman looks up. "I know the address. It's a fancy house belonging to a madam by the name of Dutch Kat."

"That's right," Irwin says, but the tone remains bitter.

"I wonder what her connection to this situation is, because the address can't be a random choice."

"My opinion exactly. Though I can't see Kat getting involved in any traffic as illicit and complex as this. She's no longer a young woman—and a fairly simpleminded one at that. I used to believe she was dim-witted on account of her being a Dutchie and not having a perfect grasp of our lingo. Now I'm not sure. She may be as cunning as they come. These Dutchmen are hard to judge, aren't they? They pinch their pennies and grow jealous of each one you stash away in your own pockets."

Kelman considers the assessment. It's clear he's of a similar opinion regarding Kat's character, if not of her fellow countrymen's. "I think it would behoove me to make a visit there."

"Crowther was insistent that I involve no one" is the hurried answer. "None of my men. Just me. You'll notice those are the letter's instructions. '*No person is to observe said house, nor linger close at hand. To do so will risk your daughter's life. Be forewarned, or you will not see her alive again.*'" Irwin recites the concluding directives from memory, then, surprisingly, waits for Kelman to speak as if hoping that the tall, grave man can supply advice.

Instead, Kelman doesn't reply for a minute or two. "Ten thousand dollars is a goodly sum to raise in a single day," he eventually offers. "Or in a lifetime for most men in our city. And I'm perplexed that the number has escalated so rapidly. Yesterday, the price was one thousand dollars. Too little for someone of Crowther's station. But this is a fortune."

Irwin ignores this observation. "I'm ordered to return to the house this afternoon and accompany Mr. Crowther to Unger's bank, where he'll withdraw the money—as per a letter he wrote and dispatched in my presence. Then I'll escort him home to make certain no common thief robs him. Crowther and his wife will assemble the contents of the basket themselves, and the husband will bear it to the address indicated tomorrow—"

"Alone?"

"He was emphatic about being viewed as a solitary figure. In truth, there's scant likelihood that footpads or cutpurses will be abroad at such an early hour. The only company Mr. Crowther may encounter is farmers bringing their produce to market, or the rounds made by other comestible purveyors."

"I'll make certain that the most senior members of the watch are laid on," Kelman says, "but I'll instruct them to keep their distance."

"I'm afraid if Crowther spots them, he'll be exceedingly angry. He told me several times that his only wish was to have his daughter alive and well and residing in her home again. The money, he said, was nothing compared to that desire."

Kelman releases an uneasy sigh. "He's playing into their hands," he states at length. "I fear for the remainder of the populace if such crimes are so easily worked." After another heavy silence, he adds a pensive "Mr. and Mrs. Crowther have had no news of Percy VanLennep yet, have they?"

"None. I called at VanLennep's home yesterday and was told by his manservant that he had no notion where his master had gone. The fellow was downright disrespectful. I put him in his place."

Kelman doesn't comment on this news, although he made an identical inquiry of the same person and was willingly supplied with a list of VanLennep's gentlemen acquaintances. These men, Kelman proceeded to write to. Three have yet to respond, but one—a Nicholas Howe—lives in such seclusion that it's uncertain how often he receives his correspondence. The servant also stated that his master seemed "distracted and not himself" when he departed from his home.

None of this information does Kelman impart. Nor does he tell Irwin that he believes the Crowthers' second letter had a different author than the first. Instead, he asks an oblique "Did you see the initial missive, by any chance?"

"No, but from the looks of the writing on this one, I'd say our man is a learned fellow."

"Or a hired scribe—of which the city has plenty."

"Ah, yes . . . That could be. That could be." To cover his gaffe, Irwin poses another question. This time his voice is full of forced conviviality. "So, what do you make of young VanLennep's disappearing act, Kelman?"

"I'm afraid I don't know."

"Well, Crowther's dead set against him, it would seem. Not the missus, however. Odd as it may sound, it occurred to me that our Percy could be involved in this peculiar plot—that maybe the young couple ran away to wed in secret because Papa had changed his mind. But it would be a mighty cruel prank they're playing. Writing the parents while pretending to be someone else."

"It would be, yes" is the somber reply, and Irwin continues with a blustery:

"I decided my notion was faulty, though. The family was robbed, after all; and in the exact same manner as the other burglaries. So I'm guessing it's a straightforward matter. The criminals were caught in the act by Dora—"

"Miss Theodora."

"Yes. By Miss Theodora, who then—"

Kelman interrupts again. "Very interesting, sir, but I must bid you good day. As you previously stated, you have work to do. And I have my own matters to attend to."

"DON'T KNOW A THING ABOUT her except what our daily gazettes and such like have been reporting. And the fact that she disappeared down a rabbit hole." Dutch Kat laughs at what she believes is a saucy jest while continuing to regard Thomas Kelman with a professional leer. The practiced expression sags in places, though, just as her full face does. As Luther Irwin stated, the madam of Dutch Kat's House for Ladies of Pleasure is past her prime.

"I've no information on any wayward laundry basket overflowing with lucre, neither. Unless you're suggesting I look like a laundress—which I sincerely hope you're not." Kat chortles heartily again, wriggling her thick shoulders for emphasis. Rice powder clots upon the exposed skin above her bosom, and the smell that envelops her is the cloying scent of too much patchouli applied to little-washed flesh. Kelman is reminded of her earlier boast that a "French gentleman" had told her she was as "ripe as a Holland cheese." It was obvious she'd taken the words as a compliment and hadn't considered that cheese can have an offensive aroma.

"But I can tell you many a tale about the great and lesser men in this city, Mr. Kelman," she continues with a stagy wink. "Many a tale, and not all of them pretty. Or polite and dignified, neither."

"About Harrison Crowther, do you mean?"

At the name, Dutch Kat turns stiff as a carpenter's board. The unwitting reaction takes a moment to undo, and unexpected color fills her face—true color, not the painted vermilion spots on her doughy cheeks. "About Percy VanLennep. That's the gent I meant."

When Kelman makes no reply, Kat sashays away from his side and calls out to someone hidden behind the heavy drapery that conceals a door leading to the house's kitchen and larder. "Boy! Bring some refreshment for my guest and me. A little fortified wine. Some preserved fruit, too. The sugared plums. And that box of elegant confections one of last night's gentlemen presented to our Chloe."

"Nothing for me, thank you, madam," Kelman tells her, which produces a cackle before Kat shouts again for the unseen servant and rescinds the order.

"Madam! I do admire how you say the word. You make me sound like a regular gentlewoman. I'll have to hire me a carriage and footman next, and order up some of them *cartes de visites* so I can go a-calling upon my elegant friends—"

"What can you tell me about Percy VanLennep?"

Her gap-toothed grin is replaced by a businesswoman's level appraisal. "He likes his ladies young but experienced. Appreciative, too, if you get my meaning—"

"So he's one of your customers?"

"Why else would I know about him if he weren't?" Kat tilts her head; her once-yellow curls that are now a thatch of gray, citrine yellow, and henna pink clump together like a dusty mop. "You're thinking he could aim higher, are you, Mr. Kelman? So he could. There are more exclusive properties: Madame Sylvester's on Wood Street, or Mrs. Jennie Nettleton in that discreet little manse she keeps on Pine. But then he'd be encountering his acquaintances, wouldn't he? And the fathers of his peers."

"Like Crowther."

Again the name works a miracle on Kat. "I wouldn't know nothing about him. Aside from what I've read."

These statements Kelman recognizes as lies. "Is that a fact?"

"Young VanLennep notwithstanding, my girls don't service every rich gent in the city. No matter how much I like to boast about their winning charms and graces." Following this declaration, the madam clamps her lips shut, placing her arms akimbo and planting her feet as if daring Kelman to prise further information from her.

"If I find you're involved in this affair, madam, it will go hard with you. You understand that, don't you? Conspiring with kidnappers is no better than committing the act."

"I'm no fool, sir" is her contemptuous reply. "You can be certain I'm not. In future, I suggest you supply facts to bolster your unsavory theories. You may believe my house is a lowly one, but I assure you I have a number of clients from the cream of society. The thickest and best part of the cream. None of them enjoys being stirred up with the rest of the milk."

YOUNG FINDAL STOKES HEARS EVERY word of this conversation, because he's the boy Dutch Kat summoned. In the modified butler's pantry that's really a catch-all larder for every bottle, punch bowl, earthenware jug, and claret cup Kat doesn't want displayed in the parlor nor left cluttering the already crowded kitchen annex, he's not only eavesdropping but also thanking his lucky stars that he doesn't have to produce the requested refreshments. He remembers Thomas Kelman only too well, and doesn't want to come face-to-face with him again.

But what to do with the information he now possesses? Ransom monies, the man said! And to be sequestered in a mere laundry basket! Ten thousand dollars! The figure dances in Findal's brain, almost too astounding to grasp. Can this Miss Theodora Crowther be worth as much as that? Surely a fine mansion might be purchased for that enormous price. Then his eyes draw into a squint, for he sees not only the flaw in the plan but the person whose addled mind created it.

A CERTAIN POSSESSION, RETURNED

WHILE FINDAL PLOTS AND SCHEMES as he slips unnoticed through the city streets, Martha and Kelman enjoy a private if somber luncheon. The fare is excellent, because Martha's cook is masterful. There is a clear oxtail soup, a savory pigeon pie, ragout of lobster, a saddle of mutton, fruit jelly, a warm plum tart, and cabinet pudding; the table is set with a tall epergene bedecked with flowers and candied fruit, giving the room a festive appearance neither Martha nor Kelman feels. They attempt to converse about matters in the city—matters other than Dora or the proposed hunt for Ella's mother—but the words have the shallow sound of memorization. None of their gambits concerning the celebrated actor Junius Brutus Booth in the role of King John at the American Theater, or the popular trotting races out in Nicetown's Hunting Park, or the rumors regarding the future of Joseph Bonaparte's palatial estate at Point Breeze, or the former emperor's brother's predilection for shocking his lady guests draw more than cursory notice. The interruption of a messenger bearing an urgent request from Harrison Crowther is a welcome relief to them both.

Kelman immediately rises, then finds it impossible to proceed to the Crowther household without Martha. "Surely you'll need me there, Thomas," she states as she folds her serviette, pushes it aside, and rises from her chair. "If only for Georgine's sake." She crosses the room and calls for her mantilla and bonnet. It's of little use when Kelman protests that the brevity of the message probably indicates an unhappy turn of events and that he wishes to spare her feelings, since her response is an airy:

"I understand as much, Thomas, and I thank you for your concern. However, not so long ago you requested my aid in this matter, and I've come to have great empathy for the afflicted parents. Now, shall we proceed?" Then she ties the long ribbons of her bonnet, pulls on her walking gloves, and allows the footman to open the front door.

WHAT AWAITS THEM AT THE Crowthers' is a situation that requires some untangling, because Dora's father spends as much time berating himself as he does explaining what transpired.

"Why didn't I have the footmen scour the streets as soon as the parcel was delivered? Wouldn't whoever left it have waited to make certain his task was accomplished rather than worry about an unknown person stealing the bundle from the steps?"

"What bundle is that, sir?" Kelman asks.

"Why, this one! This one." Crowther waves an irritable hand toward a twine-wrapped piece of sacking lying on the floor. Valuable objects peek out of it as though the package had been hastily tied. "It was too dirty to put on the furniture, so I told the footman to set it down there—"

"Oh, Mr. Crowther, what do we care for such niceties now—?" his wife begins to protest, but he rudely shushes her, then also glowers at his aunt and at Luther Irwin, who has preceded Kelman there, but who wisely keeps silent while his employer drops down beside the mysterious delivery and begins unraveling the hempen knots. "These are our missing candlesticks" is all he says at first. With nervous fingers, he stands them on their bases and sets them on the floor. "And these three leather-bound volumes. And this ivory figurine. And these two porcelain snuffboxes—"

"But what of Dora's own possessions, Harrison?" Georgine interrupts, so far forgetting herself as to use her husband's Christian name.

"How should I know?" is the brusque reply.

"Oh, but—"

"Let me attend to this in my own fashion, wife! We must remove the contents of this receptacle in an orderly manner."

"May I, sir?" Kelman takes his place at Crowther's side. "No message was attached to the sacking's exterior?"

"None, damnation! Why didn't I order that the person who brought us this be caught? What was I thinking to allow the fiend to slip away?" He swears again, then pounds the floor with his fist.

Both his wife and aunt protest the oath, but Crowther only repeats the word in a more stringent tone, lashing at the gilded candlesticks and knocking them over. In the quiet room, they clatter on the wood, causing the three ladies to jump.

Kelman continues to sort through the collection. There's a silk fan, an inlaid camphor-wood box, and a lady's reticule that makes Crowther leap backward. "That's not Dora's."

"Isn't it?" Martha asks as she picks it up, for it's a very showy article and she can imagine it appealing to a young woman of Dora's exuberant tastes.

"Goodness, no," the mother answers. "I would never have permitted my child anything so vulgar."

Then Kelman pulls out a separate sack in which reside a silver buttonhook, a comb, and a mirror; each is engraved with a willowy *T*. Harrison's body sags while his wife cries out, "Her toilette set!"

Kelman reaches inside the small sack, but finds no letter, while Crowther attacks the camphor-wood box and yanks open the books. "Who is doing this, Kelman? Who's so intent on torturing us—?" The words disappear in a sob that swells from his chest. One inconsolable cry follows another and another.

No one speaks. Harrison remains in his bent and defeated position; his wife reaches down and takes the buttonhook, turning it over and over in her palm while her eyes dull with misery. For once, Miss Lydia keeps her own counsel.

Martha searches for words of comfort. Finding none, she toys absently with the reticule until the small button securing it falls off and the thing opens. Inside is a folded scrap of brown paper and an engraved *carte de visite* belonging to Becky Grey. In silence she hands the coarse paper to Kelman, who studies it, but says nothing.

"Well, Kelman?" Crowther at last demands. "Does that have some bearing on the case, or not?"

"It purports to, sir."

"What do you mean, man? Speak plainly."

"The message is brief; the scribe uneducated, and probably—"

"What the devil difference does it make whether the person has schooling? I assume the villain isn't some lofty professor—"

"Hear me out, Mr. Crowther. You've received two previous missives. The first was penned by an accomplished hand; the second by a lesser man—"

Without waiting for Kelman to finish, Crowther bursts to his feet, grabs the note, and thrusts it into Luther Irwin's hands. "Read it, Mr. Irwin! I want action, not palaver."

The secret service agent does as he's commanded. "'*Don't trust uther messige*,'" he quotes.

"Which last two words are misspelled," Kelman adds.

"For God's sake! What difference are these niceties of language? The fiend has my daughter—"

"*A* fiend, sir, indeed" is the calm reply. "But this directive, together with your stolen articles, makes me wonder whether the person you're intending to pay is the same one holding Miss Theodora."

"Don't we have my daughter's daguerreotype to prove it?"

"Yes, sir. But why were these objects not delivered with them?"

"That's for you to tell me, Kelman, not I you!"

"Then I propose to you, sir, that you may be dealing with several different entities—"

Irwin scoffs. "We nab one of them blackguards—if more than one it is—we nab them all. A nest of burglars isn't made up of a solitary person, *Mr.* Kelman."

"No, it's not. But you know as well as I do that thieves often turn against one another. In which case, trouble is certain—"

A roar erupts from Crowther. "Stop this cant at once, and find me my child."

LEAVING THE CROWTHERS' HOME, NEITHER Martha nor Kelman speaks, but by tacit consent their feet turn toward the Taitt home: Martha to return the reticule, Kelman to question its loss and strange reappearance. Both are relieved to find the mistress of the house alone, although Becky appears the most grateful at her husband's absence.

"You won't tell Taitt, will you?" she begs. "It was so careless of me to allow that man in the churchyard to steal this little purse of mine; and William doesn't appreciate thoughtless behavior. Then, too, it may have precipitated our own burglary."

Kelman presses Becky for an account of the thief, and as she describes a man who sounds very much like Findal Stokes senior, her husband strides into the room.

"How now, wife; I see we have unexpected company." He bows to Kelman and then to Martha, but the gesture is perfunctory. It's clear his attention is on Becky, but she makes no reply. Rather, she withdraws into herself. Martha observes the behavior with puzzlement. This is not the woman who sauntered so intrepidly into Parkinson's Ice Cream Palace.

"We've just come from the Crowther household, sir," Kelman explains. "Some valuable possessions were delivered to them that may, in fact, belong to you."

"Did you bring them with you?" is the drawled response.

"No, sir."

"Then may I ask to what we owe the pleasure of your company?"

"I was hoping to have a further conversation about the child who robbed your house, sir, as the connection between the crime that occurred here and the abduction of Theodora appears certain."

"And did my Becky provide the necessary information?"

"I believe so, sir."

Throughout this conversation, Martha has noticed Becky secreting the reticule within the broad sleeves of her gown. She looks at Martha in appeal, and Martha covertly answers, but Taitt is oblivious to this wordless exchange. Instead, he makes another half bow to his guests. "Mr. Kelman, Miss Beale, our thanks for this visit. I've no doubt you have pressing obligations, and I'm certain you won't feel we're inconsiderate hosts if we excuse ourselves. My wife hasn't been herself since the night we were robbed."

MARTHA AND KELMAN ARE NO sooner escorted out the door than she commences a barrage of questions. "Why would Becky's reticule have been used to deliver this latest message to the Crowthers, and what is the significance of the writer's warning? You mentioned that thieves often turn against one another, and I sensed there was some urgency in the statement. What is it, Thomas?"

They are passing along the brick walk fronting the Taitt house, Martha's high brow creased as she considers these quandaries. She seems unconscious of her surroundings: the trees dropping their dappled shade, the carriage wheels grinding over the cobbles, a lone horseman, her fellow pedestrians, even Kelman at her side. "And why did Becky conceal her purse? What's she frightened of? Not Taitt, I hope."

"That, I can't answer," Kelman says, then smiles as he notes Martha's look of concentration that increases by the moment rather than diminishes. "The complexities of the marriage pact are alien to me—"

"What would cause a woman who experienced autonomy in her career and private life to grow so cowed?" Martha's strides stretch out, the soles of her shoes slapping at the pavement, her face turning fierce as if it were Taitt rather than Kelman she was addressing.

"Do you believe her vocation was hers to control?" His tone is mild and inquiring, but Martha remains vehement.

"Yes, I do. Of course I do."

"Rather than being limited by the fickle whims of the public? Or the theater managers? You feel your friend had that much freedom?"

"She was Becky Grey!" is the indignant rejoinder. "And she still is."

"She's also Mrs. William Taitt."

At this Martha sighs anew, the sound angrier this time. "I don't like that man. I don't mind admitting it. I find him manipulative. Manipulative, despotic, and sly."

"It's fortunate it's your friend who married him rather than you, then, isn't it?" Kelman's voice is gentle, although a hint of humor has begun to color it.

Martha draws back in order to study his face. "I would never submit to such a domineering spouse."

"No, you wouldn't. Nor should you. Nor should anyone who can avoid such a choice. The lady may have been guided by other considerations. I can't claim to understand what makes a person select one path over another, but I recognize that an uncertain livelihood is a cruel companion." He pauses; this time Martha makes no attempt to challenge him. "You believe she lived an independent existence, but that's an invention most performers cultivate: their daring and temerity."

Martha thinks. "What you propose is reasonable, but I'm loath to ascribe that incentive to a person who was as lauded as she."

"Fear is a heartless master, Martha. It can drive men and women to commit acts they could never have imagined."

She nods, but remains silent while their twin footsteps continue on their journey. "What course will you follow now?"

"I'm going to see you home. After which I plan another excursion to Blockley. If Stokes is our man, and it certainly seems as though he is, then the officials and staff must be warned. And, too, I may be able to encounter some comrade of his who'll be willing to supply information for a price—"

"And tomorrow?"

"Unless I can persuade Crowther otherwise, I'm afraid he'll deliver the ransom money as planned."

"Could I talk to Georgine about your fears, do you think, Thomas? Perhaps a frank conversation between two women would be helpful."

Kelman shakes his head. "The man is exceedingly stubborn. And equally—and understandably—upset."

"Yes," Martha agrees, then falls into gloomy silence until: "Tell me more about this notion of thieves turning against one another. How would that affect Dora?"

Kelman pauses before he speaks. "This isn't a subject I feel happy sharing with you."

"Because you feel I won't understand its complexities, or because it's a sorrowful one?"

"The latter, Martha. You have a brain as apt as anyone I know—or know of."

She allows herself a brief smile at the compliment. "Well, then, proceed. I'm not a stranger to grief, as you know."

"Yes. I do know . . . So, let us suppose that Dora's been hidden somewhere in the city—"

"By the person or persons who abducted her from her home."

"And that there's a master of the criminal band who committed the act. In this case, we'll call him Stokes."

"Yes . . ."

"Now, Stokes has others working with him: boys, certainly, but perhaps older ruffians as well. What if one of them decides to act on his own recognizance and send a fraudulent missive? Or perhaps becomes too anxious to continue the ruse? What happens to Dora then?"

Martha shakes her head. "Nothing worse than what's befallen her already, I would imagine. She's a valuable commodity for those who keep her."

"Unless they lose their nerve. In which case, Dora becomes a liability."

"A liability?"

"I'll say no more. This is hypothesis only."

"But Thomas—"

"What I've explained is conjecture, and I'll pray it remains so."

"But what's to be done?"

"We must wait and see."

"My greatest failing: impatience." Martha attempts a small smile to alleviate her worries, at which point Kelman stops walking, staring down at her with an expression so tortured that her heart jumps in her breast.

"You have no failings, Martha. From the day I met you, I realized you were as close to perfection as can be imagined. And how unworthy I—"

"Unworthy?"

"Yes. That's the word I choose."

"Shouldn't I be the one to decide whether—"

"You know nothing about me! My history or—"

"What do I care for history when I have the real man in front of me? Someone who's kind and compassionate. Who can't abide injustice or cruelty, who's even now struggling to reunite a family—" The words vanish as Kelman takes Martha in his arms and kisses her. There's such ardor in their embrace that she almost forgets to breathe.

PERCY VANLENNEP

DESPITE THIS BOLD DISPLAY OF passion, despite the astonished passersby and carriage drivers and carters staring dumbfounded at a couple so absorbed with one another that they're impervious to being in a public arena, the afternoon continues. Kelman and Martha relinquish their embrace, their eyes now averted as confusion, embarrassment, and longing settle in their brains and on their shoulders. Then, in near silence, he returns her to her home. Martha accepts her place at his side but makes no comment on what transpired. Nor does he.

When at last she climbs the steps to her house and turns to wish him farewell, her speech and pose are as awkward as a shy child's. But so are Kelman's.

"Thomas . . ."

"Yes?"

"You'll call upon me later, will you not?"

"Yes."

"To . . . to let me know the results of your visit to Blockley?"

"Of course."

"And whether there's any hope of finding this awful Stokes?"

"I will."

"Well . . . I had better allow you to proceed. These are mighty tasks you have in store."

"I'll go, then." He doesn't move, however; neither does Martha lift her hand toward the door.

"Time is critical, as you suggested," she offers at length.

"It is." Following this terse opinion, Kelman seems to recollect himself. "Martha, I intended no disrespect to you when I . . . back in the street, when I—"

"You've always treated me with the utmost courtesy. What happened a few minutes past was no aberration. Besides, I . . . I also . . . It's not as though we haven't . . ."

"Yes."

He lingers; she lingers, both unable to give further voice to their emotions.

"I should make haste."

"Indeed. Yes. Yes, of course. Naturally you should. Dora must be found."

SO KELMAN CONTINUES ON HIS business, journeying again to the almshouse. During each encounter with those who either work or reside there, his manner is calm and his speech judicious, not because he deems that demeanor appropriate but because he can't risk showing his true feelings. He may be discussing Theodora Crowther and the unsolved city burglaries, or querying the men with whom Stokes was housed, but his mind pictures only Martha. Kissing Martha Beale in the middle of a busy thoroughfare for all the world to see. It is a proclamation.

MANY MILES FROM THE SCENES of Kelman's search, or Martha's afternoon of fevered contemplation; many miles from the hot and turbulent city, or the confining greenery of Blockley and the farmland that stretches along the Darby Road, a miraculous event occurs. Nicholas Howe enters the part of the forest where Percy lies wounded—and not only walks into an area of his property he's never before visited but pauses and listens until he becomes convinced that he can hear the faint sound of human speech among the dense and obscuring greenery.

"VanLennep!" he calls out. "VanLennep, are you nearby? I have news to impart. Difficult news, I'm afraid. A letter from one Thomas Kelman. It was sent down in a bundle of mail from Philadelphia several days ago, and I only just read it." He hesitates while his ears, so accustomed to the infinite variety of country noise—to the plaintive songs of crickets, the rustle of leaves no longer green and young, the migratory flights of grackles, or a changeable wind that heralds a shift of season—mark and identify everything.

"Percy! Are you here? If you are, be so good as to present yourself, or I'll move on. It's imperative I find you. Percy! Someone is close at hand. I feel it. If it's you, VanLennep, be done with your games. I must talk to you."

Howe stops speaking. The woods are thick, the buzzing of insects acute, and from high in the tree branches comes a raucous screech of bird life. At his feet, there's a sound of marsh water running; but added to this, like an echo, is a moan.

"VanLennep!" he shouts again. Then he plunges his farmer's boots into the brown and brackish liquid, trudging against a barely discernible current in hopes that he may find a stream and perhaps an open glade from which he can more readily view the terrain.

WHILE HOWE PURSUES HIS PHANTOM friend, Georgine Crowther sequesters herself in her boudoir, locking the door behind her with such a sense of purpose that it seems as if she has no intention of reentering the workaday world again. After taking these precautions, she sits at the chair beside her dressing table, where she lays out the mirror, buttonhook, and comb that belong to her daughter. With only fleeting attention does she notice how black and smeared with handling the silver has grown.

Instead, she gazes at the toilette articles, seeing not the engraved initial, not her daughter as a betrothed young lady, nor a mother's dreams of her only child's marriage day and how handsome the young couple will appear, or even visits to the newlyweds' home, or an infant for a doting grandmama to admire. No, what Georgine sees is the past.

Reflected in the tarnished metal is the round face of baby Dora, toothless and gummy one moment, then equipped with four front teeth that shine like seed pearls when the child beams. Oh, and little Theodora's hands! Pudgy, demanding, curious, grabbing at each and every object, heedless of danger—as are her wide and wondering eyes.

Georgine has no need of closing her own eyes in order to enter this land of memory and love, but she does . . . then wanders through all the seasons of growth and change as if a different room were assigned to each experience: Dora sitting on her mother's knee, patting her fists together in speechless glee as Georgine teaches her to count; Dora at three, lulled to near sleep while her mother reads a rhyming book; Dora sprawled on the winter hearth, building a magic castle from wooden blocks and chattering about the invented fairy princess who resides within its walls. Then there's Dora with ink-stained fingers, or with budding breasts, or begging for a "lady's" gown: a young woman now, pouting, winsome, and full of hope.

Georgine glides slowly through the remembered spaces, half smiling, half aching until her eyes open wide in revelation. In none of these visions does she see Harrison.

He doesn't bend dotingly above the infant's cradle; he doesn't hold the firm, fat baby fingers in his own; doesn't laugh at her childish tales or query her multiplication tables. In fact, he seems to have vanished. Georgine's mind's eye looks for him on the stair landing as she confers with the physician over a case of the croup; she peers into the parlor, where a ten-year-old Dora is practicing the piano, or where a seventeen-year-old Dora gathers with her friends.

But Harrison is gone.

What can this mean? the mother asks herself. *Isn't my husband devoted to our child? Surely he is, and has always been. Isn't that what our friends say? That Dora's the apple of her father's eye, while I'm demanding and stern? The parent who insists that her manners, like her handwriting, be letter perfect?*

Georgine frowns, pulling forward every reminiscence of her daughter's childhood and youth, but her husband remains an elusive figure: a shadow here and there, a disembodied voice full of bonhomie and easy gaiety. He's of no more substance than air.

The mother's dazed eyes grow wide. *He does love her; I know he does. And wants the best for her, too.* Then her mind burrows back to the confrontation with Percy VanLennep. *Harrison would never have thwarted the marriage; perhaps he was harsh that evening; perhaps I was overly stringent, as well, but he wants to see his daughter amicably wed. I'm sure he does. He must. No, no, he would never willingly do anything to mar Dora's joy. He would not. He would not.*

SO PASSES THE REMAINDER OF the twenty-first of September. Georgine rests in the seclusion of her rooms. An evening meal is proffered on a tray and returned uneaten. Her lady's maid prepares the bed for sleeping, but Georgine refuses to undress, or stir from her dressing-table chair, or even speak. So the maid withdraws, then crosses paths with Harrison, who has come to bid his wife good night.

No response is given to his gentle knocking at the door, and when he tries the latch, he finds that his wife has locked it. He studies his hand, resting uselessly on the cold metal, and all at once begins to weep. In the lighted corridor! Where any servant might pass by and notice this unseemly display! Harrison Crowther bends his big head and sobs.

THE RIFLE'S REPORT SHAKES MARTHA'S bed. She clutches the bed linens in fright, then immediately relaxes her grasp as she decides she must have been dreaming. Citizens don't shoot at one another on the city streets.

What folly is my sleeping brain creating? she thinks. *First a dying young woman, now a mortally wounded man.* Martha kicks the coverlet but can't dislodge the image: a virgin woods full of brambles and impenetrable scrub; a man lying bleeding within the concealing vegetation, and another fighting his way through a thicket as high as his shoulders. In the picture a flock of birds pulses through the sky, and the long yellow shadows of afternoon stretch from tree limb to tree limb. She can almost smell marsh waters, and the papery scent of leaves that have baked all day in the sun.

How foolish, she decides. *Why waste time inventing locales I've never visited, and men I've never met?* She climbs out of bed, but the dream follows, making her glance upward as though expecting to see a canopy of branches rather than one of lace. Then the analogy strikes her. Her brain has been so consumed with Thomas, she can't see the woods for the trees.

"Oh, honestly!" She shakes her head, releases an impatient breath, then marches across the room to yank aside the draperies. Real trees and real air must replace the illusory ones.

But there, she jerks backward in alarm. The beggar boy who watched her house two days prior is standing sentinel again. Although mostly concealed by the dark, his thin body looks as determined and menacing as it did before. As she glowers down, another figure approaches—a man who surprises the boy and causes him to spin around and forsake his watchman's stance.

A blow lands on the child's head. Illumined by the lamplight, the man's contorted face dodges close to the boy's as though cursing him.

That's who Thomas is searching for, Martha realizes. *It's the man we encountered listening to Amor Alsberg. It's Findal Stokes.*

She flies from her room in order to sound an alarm, but by the time a watchman can be summoned, Stokes is long gone.

TELL ME WE'LL SEE OUR DORA

THE MORNING OF SEPTEMBER TWENTY-SECOND dawns cooler than before. A mist that's not quite fog, not truly rain settles over the city, turning the paving stones a burnished black, the packed earth of the lesser streets a dense mud brown, while the sky clings to a leaden half hue that's more dusk than day.

Harrison Crowther steps into this cheerless world carrying the basket of linen he and his wife so assiduously prepared. His steps are brisk, echoing through the sparsely populated street, although the noise has an empty clatter as if his bones have been carved out with grief and fear. He trudges along, unseeing, intent on the successful outcome of his mission, and so doesn't notice that Luther Irwin has begun to trail after him. Or that Thomas Kelman, unbeknownst to either, is also keeping watch and pace.

When Dora's father reaches Dutch Kat's still-sleeping establishment, he places the basket upon the top step, then straightens and clasps his hands, although he makes no indication that he intends to depart. Instead, he stands as though in fervent prayer.

After several motionless minutes he sighs, bows his head in

acceptance, reaches down to touch the note atop the discarded clothing, and shambles reluctantly backward, sidling half sideways down the uneven road until he rounds the corner and begins retracing his homebound route with the same hopeless and echoing steps.

Luther Irwin is not as hesitant nor careworn as his employer. While Crowther concludes his seeming obeisance before disappearing from sight, the secret service agent fiddles impatiently within the shadow of a neighboring building, stamping back and forth, and growling and muttering to himself. His shoulders judder; his pugilist's chin jabs one way and then another; and his knees flex and extend, flex and extend.

Also hidden, Kelman studies Irwin, wishing he could clamp a restraining arm on the man or whisk him clear of the site. But he realizes the action would only call attention to them both and probably induce the kidnapper to keep a safe distance—if Irwin's continuous jouncing hasn't already achieved the same lamentable result.

Kelman is wrong to worry, however, for the moment Crowther is out of sight a figure darts from the rear alleyway entry to Dutch Kat's. It's a boy whom Kelman instantly recognizes as young Findal Stokes. He saunters toward the basket, all unconcern on the surface, all wily intent within. He licks his lips as though his mouth were parched while his remarkable ears twitch as if listening for a threatening noise. Findal's eyes leave the basket only long enough to glance about. He passes the front entry to the bawdy house, whistles as though trying to recall some forgotten air, then lunges backward, stuffing his fists within the folded layers of cloth.

Luther Irwin is on him in a moment, hauling the boy into the air, first by grabbing his thin jacket and then by wrapping his hammy hands around Findal's equally scrawny throat. "All right, my lad. That's it for you!"

Findal's response is to kick the secret service agent in an area where no gentleman wishes to be dealt a blow. The boy's aim is true; and Irwin crumples under the unexpected attack, releasing his prey with a curse and an exhalation of breath that's as loud as a butchered steer's. He sinks to his knees while Findal lights off down the street, running unfortunately toward the very place where Kelman stands hidden.

Before he's aware of it, the boy's flight is arrested by two long arms twisting his arms backward and pinning him in pain. "I didn't do nothing," he yelps. "I didn't take nothing. I just was passing, is all. There's no crime there."

It's all Kelman can do not to strike the child into silence, but as he considers that strategy, he wonders at his predilection for brutality. The boy is only a boy, after all. He's no match for a grown man. Not even Luther Irwin.

"Where's your father?"

"How should I know?" While Findal speaks, he struggles, but he can't break free of Kelman's grip.

"He sent you on this mission. If you don't reveal his whereabouts, I'll make certain you spend the rest of your worthless life locked up in the penitentiary."

"I can't produce what I don't have!"

"Your father's hiding place, Master Stokes! Unless you'd rather lead us to Miss Theodora Crowther yourself."

Findal tries to land a crippling kick to Kelman but fails in the attempt, which throws his slight frame off balance, allowing his captor to pick him up bodily, then throw him over one shoulder and march to South Street, where two members of the day watch await.

Still shrilly proclaiming his innocence, Findal is bound into custody while Kelman returns to find Luther Irwin again on his feet and a curious crowd gathering.

"Oh, you fool" is Kelman's only comment. At that moment, a shout goes up from the day watch as Findal makes his newest escape, and the morning's debacle is complete.

HARRISON CROWTHER RECEIVES THE NEWS of the calamity on Lombard Street in silence. Jumping up when Kelman is announced, he immediately sinks into a chair as he listens to the report; his seated wife retains an equally passive pose. Despair emanates from their two figures, but not disbelief, for that would permit a modicum of hope.

"Who's the boy?" is all Crowther asks when Kelman finishes his brief tale.

"A child out of Blockley, sir. Findal Stokes. I have reason to believe his father is the mastermind of this plot."

Crowther licks his lips in an unwitting replication of young Findal's anxious movement, but says nothing more. Nor does Georgine.

"I'll find him and his loathsome parent, sir. I assure you—"

"I did everything required of me, Kelman. I followed every instruction."

"You did, sir. I understand as much. But I fear Mr. Irwin was overzealous in stepping forward when he did—"

"From Blockley, you say?"

"Yes, sir. The son fled the institution. The father is also missing."

"I know the director there. I'll write to him at once. It would be appalling if the almshouse were harboring criminals."

"I discussed this matter with him yesterday, sir. Naturally, he and his staff are cooperating to the fullest extent."

Harrison Crowther sighs anew, then looks at his wife, but she's staring mutely into space. "Tell me we'll see our Dora soon."

"We'll catch these miscreants, sir. You can be sure of that. When we do, we'll have your daughter."

IT'S A BOY OF NO more than four who first notices the three fingers, so frail and white within the coal heap sloping down on either side of the alley near Erasmus Unger's shipyard that he imagines they were planted there—like sticks stuck in the mudflats at the river's edge.

He stares while his older sister, at a little distance, engages in a murmured conversation with a man the child doesn't know. The boy turns toward them, watching from the corner of his one good eye (the child's face is severely scarred from what appears to have been a burn), but he can't hear what the two are discussing.

Then the man vehemently shakes his head and strides away, and the sister turns and walks toward her waiting sibling.

"What were you two talking of?" the boy calls, and his mouth twists with the effort of speech. As he talks, his muscles work: the undamaged side displaying ordinary movement; the scalded half, a reddish mass of immobility.

"Nothing that has to do with you" is the bleak reply, and the boy, in order to cheer her, points to his discovery.

"See! A person's fingers! Like a magic sign, sticking up toward Heaven. Maybe that's a cure for me, like our mam sometimes said she was praying for—"

"Those aren't fingers. They're meat bones left in the coal cobbles by a rat. Come away now."

"But they are! Look—"

"Quiet, boy! We must move on. You don't want the day watch hauling us in for vagrancy, do you?" She begins to move off, but her brother grabs her thin cloak.

"Maybe it's a lady hiding there—"

"Stop this fanciful talk, at once."

"But we were looking for an omen. You said so yourself. A bit of magic to help us in our need. That's what you told me. And if the man you spoke with wasn't it—"

"Come along. I don't want to be standing here if there's river vermin about. You'd make a tasty morsel for them big things." By now the sister has wrenched out of her sibling's grip, but in doing so her eyes fall upon the pale fingers, and she starts backward with an oath. "What's that?"

"A lady, waving to us. Like our mam used to—"

"Enough, I tell you! This has naught to do with you or me. Them's chicken bones, most probably." Despite this statement, the girl advances upon the hillock of coal cobbles and commences scrabbling up its jagged sides.

"Ooof, what a stink. There's dead flesh buried here sure as sure. Long buried, too." She gasps as she nears the submerged hand, but before she can retreat, the crumbly carbon mound shifts, sending a roar down the alley as the lumps begin cascading downward, trapping the girl's feet and ankles while simultaneously unveiling the purple-white face and body of Dora Crowther.

YOU MUST BELIEVE ME

"WHAT WERE YOU DOING IN the alley?" Kelman demands, but the girl and her brother refuse to regard him, keeping their eyes pinned to the floorboards at their feet. In a neighboring room in the Moyamensing Prison, they can hear a man being interrogated. Despite the stout walls of the new county jail, the sounds of shouts and blows have reached their worried ears. Screams, too. Listening, the girl shivers on the wooden bench, and Kelman must repeat the question, raising his voice and speaking with such authority that the elder sibling jolts as if she's been struck.

"Talking to a gentleman. Just like I told your constable—"

"And his name?"

"I didn't ask."

"Stealing coal is more like it, sir," the constable tosses in. "Beggars like these." He's standing behind the pair's bench, and pacing back and forth as though they were livestock requiring constant prodding and poking. He has another odd manner, too, which the girl first noticed when he marshaled her and her little brother along Reed Street and up the prison's exterior steps toward the huge stone portal: He throws his wrists and hands backward as though tossing away bad fish. As the trio passed beneath a wall bedecked with such a fanciful display of battlements, turrets, and high and narrow windows that she considered it might be a painted stage design, she wondered at the man's peculiar habit and whether its cause was disgust or fear. Not that she said anything, for she was determined to remain as incommunicative as possible. Gabbing with the police was a guarantee of trouble.

"If I hadn't come running, sir, the entire populace of the dockyards would have swarmed in, pocketed the fuel, and probably trampled the corpse in their greed."

"We weren't stealing!" the boy's ruined face squeaks. "Sister was—" She lands him such a kick to his shin that the words vanish with a yowl of pain. "Tell no one our real names or what we were about in that place," she'd warned in a whisper the moment the watch appeared and cordoned off the fateful alley. "Let me speak, and you keep silent. If you don't, you'll have us both hanged for killing this poor lady."

"Your sister must be called by something else," Kelman observes. The voice is quieter now but no less commanding, although pity softens its edges as he speaks to this ugly child.

"Anne, sir," the girl lies. The sound is bright, defiant. "And this here's John."

The newly dubbed John frowns in his crooked manner. It pains Kelman to watch him. "Well, John, my lad. What were you doing amongst those coal cobbles?"

"Looking for magic" is the mumbled reply.

"And how can that be, I ask you, sir?" his sister interjects. "He can be quite daft at times."

"But you said—"

"Hush your tongue! You see how it is, sir. A poor mite such as him. We wasn't up to no harm. I told you that, as I told the constable before."

"John and Anne" is Kelman's sole reply. "You have no surnames?"

"None that I know of." She squeezes her brother's hand until he nods in agreement.

"And no parents?"

"Not at present, sir."

The reply obviously bothers the little boy, but his sister gives him a fierce look, then adds a definitive "None that we live with, sir."

Kelman studies her. "Your complexion is darker than most. Darker than your brother's—"

"It's on account of my falling into that mammoth coal heap, sir. My clothes is all bemired, too. John kept his distance. Despite his looks, he can use his noggin at times."

Kelman bends down to the child. "Do you know a boy by the name of Findal Stokes, lad?"

John shakes his head no.

"Or his father of the same name, perhaps? He gives work to small lads like you. And clever ones, too."

"You see, sister. I told you I was clever—"

But the girl's steely voice interrupts. "My brother works for nobody, sir. He's too little, isn't he? And oftentimes sickly, as well, on account of a misfortune that befell him when he was but a wee thing. I'd be a bad relative if I made him earn his own keep."

"So the body of the young woman who was discovered buried in the coal was a surprise to you?"

"An awful surprise, sir, as I said. More like a nightmare, really. Imagine, seeing a lady trapped in that unlikely spot."

Kelman's dark eyes stare, and this time the girl returns his gaze without flinching or dodging her glance toward the floor or the umbrous corners of the room. The noise in the adjoining chamber has ceased, and an eerie silence has replaced it. The thoroughfares of Reed and Passyunk streets with their carters, hawkers, and rag-and-bone men might as well not exist.

"Perhaps you don't appreciate the peril you're in. The young woman you discovered was abducted from her home by a man who runs a band of thieves. Small boys are his accomplices, and for all I know, girls your age, as well."

She bites back her tears. "We didn't do nothing, sir. You must believe us. We found that lady, is all—"

"I did, sister. Not you! I was the one who—"

"Hush, boy."

"But I did, and you didn't believe me when I told you about the—"

The girl sighs. It's clear that she would do more if there weren't two grim-faced gentlemen present. "All right, sir, I will explain why we were in that unfortunate alley. I needed money for our upkeep, and the docks are a good place for a lass like me to pick up a few coins. I'm sorry if I don't know this other gent you make mention of, and I don't like John to hear me telling you what I just did, for he's young and impressionable. But there's the truth of the matter."

"Oh!" her brother gulps, "but you said—"

"You see, sir? It were better he didn't know. But there you have it."

"And how old are you to be attempting that trade?"

"Old enough, sir" is the resolute answer. "Old enough."

Kelman's tight lips curl in distaste and defeat; then he looks over the girl's shoulder at the constable, who has now ceased his endless parade. "You and your brother certainly made enough noise on account of your discovery. You would have thought you'd witnessed the young lady's murder."

"It was the surprise, sir. The surprise, is all." As she speaks, she can't help but picture the scene again: the lady jouncing down the coal heap, her white skin swollen and gray, her fair hair full of noxious dust, and her eyes . . . Her eyes . . . As she remembers, *Anne's* eyelids jitter, and this small tic Kelman notices immediately.

"Do you know who murdered Miss Crowther?" he demands.

"No" is the adamant reply. Then she closes her lips and refuses to say any more.

Kelman signals to the constable. "Take them both away."

"The lad to be kept in custody, too, sir?"

Kelman nods. The gesture is curt but his expression pained. "Where else is he to go? We can't turn him out on the streets if we hold the girl for further questioning. Besides, I feel something crucial is missing in this tale—"

"It isn't, sir! It isn't," the girl protests, but Kelman overrides her.

"If the city has been turned upside down hunting for Miss Crowther, Constable, then how is it that two wandering children can happen upon her body—?"

"That's just how it was, sir. A bit of ill luck on our parts. If we hadn't ventured into that—"

"Magic!" John crows. "It were magic! Like the prayer Mam liked to—"

This outburst only earns him a cuffing from his sister. The blow is stronger than intended and sends him tumbling backward off the bench and into the wall, where his mouth opens in a wail of pain and protest.

"You're just like him, you are! Hitting me whenever you fancy—"

"Shut your lips—"

"I won't! I won't! I won't! Like him! Like him. Like him."

"Who's 'him,' lad? Stokes, is that who you mean?"

"Stop it, brother. Stop it now."

"Like him. Like him. Like him!" the boy continues to bellow, causing his sister to leap at him, grabbing his shoulders and commencing to shake him into silence. The constable's flaccid hands dart out to rescue the brother while Kelman just as quickly drags away his sibling.

By now she's also screaming, but her hands, instead of beating against Kelman or her brother or the constable, begin to strike her own body. "Don't keep us here, sir. Don't keep us shut up in this cruel place. I can take care of the lad. I can. Haven't I been doing it all these days? And don't send us to Blockley, neither. They'll separate us, and who knows what evil will befall us in that cruel place." Her sobs increase until they become a hiccoughing babble. "Queen of angels . . . Holy Mother . . . *Sancta Dei Genitrix*—"

"Take them away, Constable. And feed them something nutritious before you find a place for them to sleep."

"Not Blockley, sir! Don't send us there. Please, sir. Please."

Left alone, Kelman leans against a wall. Weariness weighs him down. Then he rises and slowly makes his way back into the noisome city.

"BUT IT'S THE TRUTH, I tell you," Percy pants between winces of pain while his friend dresses the wound with a poultice of slippery elm bark and pieces of charcoal crushed from the campfire that Percy had either fortuitously or foolishly allowed to burn out on its own. "A man shot me in the shoulder. I saw him take aim. I imagined it was another target he was hunting until I felt the . . ." Percy grimaces again, then grunts his supreme discomfort. "Must you inflict that awful thing upon me?"

"I must. Until I can get you home, and send for someone more experienced in medical practices than I."

"Will I die, Nicholas?"

Howe permits himself a wry smile. "Not from this, I don't imagine."

"But it's serious, isn't it? The hole, I mean?"

"Not as dire as it first appeared. Can you stand, Percy?"

"Oh, I don't believe so."

"I'm afraid you must if you want more professional treatment than a hastily constructed poultice." Howe grasps his friend around the chest and drags him to his knees.

"Oh, Nicholas, no! This is agony."

"You have no other choice. You must walk with me."

"Isn't there a cart you can send for?"

"We're not in the city, VanLennep, and can't avail ourselves of servants to dispatch hither and yon. I could leave you and make my way home and return with some means of carrying you, but that effort would take twice as long."

Percy stares at the grasses surrounding them and at the trees that seem to stretch out interminably: alder, scrub oak, birch, and pine as far as the eye can see. "I simply cannot—"

"You must." The asperity of this statement is softened only slightly by Howe's tone. "Now, stand up and let us go. If we retrace my route we have only a couple of hours before we reach the farm's outer pastureland."

While Percy struggles to put one foot in front of another, Howe keeps up a steady stream of conversation whose sole aim is to encourage his friend's forward motion. "It's not shameful to have accidentally injured yourself. You're inexperienced and—"

"But I didn't, Nicholas. A man—"

"Yes, I know. A mystery hunter. Or a would-be assassin, I should say." Howe's voice remains jovial, but Percy halts, drawing himself into as indignant a pose as he can.

"A man attempted to kill me. Why you find this a source for jesting is most peculiar."

"Well, I'm glad he did such a terrible job" is the rejoinder as Nicholas again half pushes, half pulls Percy along.

"You must believe me, Howe."

"I will."

"No. Now. You must believe me now."

"Oh, Lord, VanLennep, don't you city folk ever tire of existing in a state of heightened drama—?" The query is only partly formed when Howe interrupts his own words. "I forgot. The reason I came searching for you . . . A letter from an official named Thomas Kelman. Your fiancée has disappeared. Abducted from her home, it would seem."

"Dora—?" Percy gasps out. "Dora, what?"

"I apologize, VanLennep. I should have been gentler in breaking such disconcerting news. And she may have been found by now."

"But—?"

"Let us keep walking, Percy. I can tell you no more. Perhaps Kelman's letter will reveal information you can understand better than I."

"Oh, but Howe, I must go back there at once!"

"Back—?"

"To Philadelphia. If what this Kelman fellow writes is true and Dora's missing, then I mustn't tarry here. Don't you see—?"

"Percy. A moment ago, you felt unfit to travel to my farm. Surely you can't be suggesting sailing all the way to Philadelphia.

We shall write the gentleman and explain. And as I said, perhaps—"

"No! I must go. Today. At once. Or as soon as we can procure a boat—"

"You're in no shape for a ride on the river—"

"You'll come with me, won't you, Nicholas? Won't you?"

A MISUNDERSTANDING

As KELMAN DEPARTS THE YELLOW-GRAY temple to justice that's Moyamensing Prison he doesn't pause, as his two young prisoners did, to wonder at its massive columns and epic balustrades, or its central tower and flanking turrets, or even to question how a bellicose evocation of ancient warring Egypt and medieval Europe could have been built in a city whose foundation was the peaceable ideal of freedom of worship. Instead, he ignores the structure and its darker significance and sets his path toward the Crowthers' home in order to deliver the terrible news that the body of their beloved daughter has been recovered.

The intermittent rain that started the day has resumed, spitting at him in fits and starts while he plunges along, heedless of the drops beading up on his tall beaver hat or dripping from his black coat. At this hour of the afternoon and because of the stormy clouds swirling above, the commerce of the city has slowed and the streets have grown bare of peddlers and carts. Their absence lends the byways an uneasy quiescence, as though a savage beast were lurking close by and none but the foolish and unwary would dare venture abroad.

In fact, Kelman realizes, there is such a creature. Someone who would hide a body in a mountain of coal believing that the weight and pull of the substance combined with its desiccating properties would render the corpse unrecognizable—while that person would also make a handsome profit from the crime.

He clenches his teeth and strides northward, passing Ellsworth Street, League, Kimball, Carpenter, Christian—that name arrests him. *Do we learn nothing,* his thoughts demand, *we humans who claim to believe in the Divine? From one generation, one century to the next, do we merely slither about, snatching what we want, beating down those who stand in our way, hoarding, snarling, hating? Can we never look up into the heavens and cry: Forgive me! I have sinned and will sin no more. I've harmed my neighbor, my child, my spouse, and can no longer exist within the burden of my cruelty. I seek atonement. I repent. I, who have granted none in my life, beg for mercy.*

But there are no answers to be found to these queries, and so he moves on until he reaches the corner of Fitzwater and Sixth streets, where his footsteps again halt. This was the block where he spent the earliest days of his youth; it was on these pebblestones and cobbles that he learned to walk; it was these slanting windows he gazed up into, hoping to glimpse a happy face, a sense of love or welcome.

First the smells of long-gone cookery flood back: scraped bones or fish heads boiling in a pot, cabbage, turnips, black bread, and the stinging odor of lye that never fully masked the reek of human excrement. Then come the sounds: his father's petulant oaths, his mother's pleading tears. Finally, there's the watchful silence of "Young Tom" himself, gauging each moment, alert to every nuance of his parents' quixotic moods. Even when he could scarcely toddle around on his short legs, he knew to keep his back turned toward a wall, and his body out of reach whenever possible.

Kelman stands, lost in time. *Is it worse to be a bastard child like my father? Or to know both parents' histories, and recognize that all their faults and foibles are lodged within you?*

The buildings provide no answer, and the alley remains as mute and secretive as it once was. He dusts rainwater from his shoulders, pulls himself back to the present, and alters his plans. He must visit the Crowther household, it's true, but first he'll make a detour to the Beale brokerage concern and ask Martha to accompany him. The parents will have need of her soothing presence—as will he. Thinking of her, he smiles for the first time since they parted. The moment is like a ray of sun, wrapping him in light.

"A GENTLEMAN HAS CALLED TO see you, Miss Beale. I informed him that you were busy and asked him to wait in the receiving room downstairs."

The person making this announcement is one of her father's older clerks, a man for whom Martha has developed a special trust and empathy, but she knows full well that the present owner of the famed Beale brokerage and banking concern doesn't fly downstairs like a giddy girl. No, she must bide her time; extend gratitude (though not effusive) for the message; conclude what tasks lie before her; and then proceed (at a leisurely pace) to meet the caller. At least, that would have been Lemuel Beale's practice—but Martha isn't her father.

Surmising that the visitor is Thomas come to impart news about the Crowthers, she immediately rises from her desk, then hurries down the circular marble stair that leads to the establishment's ground floor. Each tap of her heel echoes upward as though she were dancing to a lively tune.

It's not Kelman who awaits her, however. Instead, she finds Nathan Weil, his hat resting on a nearby chair as if he were too busy to hand it to an under-clerk or servant. He steps forward as she approaches, and again she's struck by his dissimilarity to Thomas. It's the difference between midday and the long shadows of dusk.

"I hope you'll forgive my unexpected visit, Miss Beale," he says with the easy and intimate smile she remembers—and which causes her unexpected embarrassment.

"Of course. You're welcome to call at any time, Mr. Weil." Aware of her dearth of sophisticated banter, she makes an attempt at wit. "I hope you received my payment for the great debt I owed you."

"Indeed I did. And I thank you. Ice cream is a hideously expensive commodity, is it not? If we must borrow from near strangers in order to pay for it, then I wonder how Parkinson's Palace remains in existence."

"Perhaps that's because we're a city of strangers, and our interchanges in the gastronomic or financial marketplaces are our sole efforts at camaraderie."

Weil laughs. "Well said, Miss Beale, although I doubt those who frequent the bank of which my brother is chief director experience a bond of friendship and conviviality with those mortgaged to them."

Recalling the furious words of Findal Stokes senior, Martha considers questioning Weil about his brother's and his fellow directors' practices, but her visitor changes the subject before she can act on the impulse.

"I brought you a small token. A gift of gratitude for permitting me to rescue you and Mrs. Taitt." With that, he produces the same volume of Tennyson Martha read two nights past.

"How very kind, Mr. Weil, but I—"

"Don't admire Mr. Tennyson's works—"

"No . . . No, I do. Indeed, I do. But I already purchased the same collection. And noted your name as publisher."

Weil's reply is another congenial laugh. "You're thrifty, then, Miss Beale. An admirable quality and rare among the ladies of this city. Books are not bricks to be stacked into an immovable wall. Tell me, which of the poet's offerings do you most admire?"

Without thinking, she answers a rapid "*Dora*," then frowns. "No, that's not true. I found it terribly sad and, naturally, given the tragedy surrounding Theodora Crowther's disappearance—"

"Indeed, Tennyson's young heroine was cruelly and publicly spurned in love by her cousin William," he replies; then, beginning to quote from the poem, his voice takes on a more impassioned timbre.

> *"' . . . but the youth, because*
> *He had been always with her in the house,*
> *Thought not of Dora.'"*

When Martha makes no reply, Weil continues in the same serious vein. "I'm no callous 'William' to reject such a gentle, loving lady, Miss Beale, and I'm no 'William' with his 'harsh' and spiteful 'ways' who abandons home and future because he refuses the bride his father chooses for him. If I were to select a poem for your consideration it would be *The Miller's Daughter*, whose speaker is obviously besotted by emotion.

> *"'I loved the brimming wave that swam*
> *Thro' quiet meadows round the mill,*

The sleepy pool above the dam,
The pool beneath it never still—'"

Weil interrupts his own recitation. "Let me go further and state my case in the simplest and most direct of language. I'm asking if I might become a suitor to you, Miss Beale, and seek your hand in matrimony—"

She can only stare in astonishment, but he accepts the response with an indulgent smile. "Naturally, I would have sought the approval of your father before speaking so openly, but as you are now your own mistress, it is to you directly that I apply. I also recognize that I'm premature in my quest, as your year of mourning won't be fully realized until January—"

"Oh, but, sir, I have—" Martha begins, but Weil overrides her.

"I know what you're going to say, Miss Beale. That you and I have no true knowledge of each other. However, I hope and intend to rectify that situation. I'm not asking any consideration other than an equal standing among the numerous gentlemen who must be in the same position as I am, for I'm certain your suitors must be legion—"

"No, Mr. Weil, that's not what I intended to tell you. As for suitors, I have already—"

"Don't tell me you've pledged your heart to another, for I won't believe you, Miss Beale. If you were betrothed, the entire city would know of your choice, and I wouldn't be standing before you making a fool of myself. If you have other qualms, let me hear them. Perhaps you object because I'm of the Jewish faith, but I'll argue that William Penn created his colony on the precept of religious freedom and that marriage twixt Gentile and Jew isn't uncommon. Nor is it discouraged. Look at Mr. and Mrs. Isaac Levy, or Abraham Moss and his wife: both happy and devoted couples.

Like those fine gentlemen, I'm by no means poor, or without education or connections. If I seem hasty in my appeal, let me assure you that I'm determined rather than reckless. I'm not a person who allows indecision and diffidence to rule my life. Rather, I'm a man of conviction."

Finally, Weil draws breath and Martha has space to speak. "Mr. Weil, although I'm deeply gratified by your attention, you must understand that I—"

"'And I would be the necklace,'" he interrupts again, returning to *The Miller's Daughter*.

"'And all day long to fall and rise
Upon her balmy bosom,
With her laughter or her sighs;
And I would lie so light, so light,
I scarce should be unclasped at night.'

"Say yes to my petition, my dear Miss Beale, and make me a happy man."

It's at this juncture that Kelman prepares to rap upon the door, so he hears the request that concludes the stanza as well as the sultry vibrancy in the speaker's voice.

His hand drops to his side while he recalls every second of his previous encounter with Martha, how she felt in his arms, how her lips tasted, how her breath grazed his cheek, the promise in her eyes and the wonder of their public display. His fingers curl; he lifts his hand again, deciding he'll announce himself and question Nathan Weil's right to state his claim.

Instead, Kelman's former distress returns. Martha isn't meant for common folk like him. A father who was illegitimate, a mother who wouldn't have had even the basic skills to serve in a household like the Beales'—or the Taitts' or the Crowthers'.

What could he, Thomas, give to a woman as well-born as Martha?

His mouth tightens in a proud, defiant line. *This publisher with his poetry and facile speech will make a far more fitting husband,* he assures himself as he hears Martha respond in a tone so low and urgent that he can recognize the ardor of her appeal if not the words. *Haven't I already explained that I'm not good enough for her? Our embrace and the other private ones must be forgotten. For her benefit, as well as mine. That was my original intent, wasn't it? That she should marry among her own kind? Wasn't that what I desired for her all along? Safety, stability, an appropriate position amongst her peers. Isn't that what I choose for her now?*

Avoiding further opportunity to overhear Martha's continuing conversation, Kelman draws himself erect and leaves the building before he can be discovered lurking there. Then, alone, he makes his way to the Crowthers' home.

SECRET SINS

THE FUNERAL OF THEODORA CROWTHER draws so many mourners that the number of carriages and horses lining Pine and Third and Fourth streets nearly obstructs the entrances to St. Peter's churchyard. Men and women descend from their coaches only to enter a crush of bodies attempting to vacate the roads and sidewalks and pass inside the narrow gates. Horses neigh and whinny in protest at the jostling crowd; wheels turn backward and forward; and coachmen curse under their breath, extending whips and trying to extricate their vehicles from the throng without injuring the delicate paintwork on the carriage bodies or the animals themselves.

Inside the memorial garden's grounds, the amount of people moving toward the church proper is no less dense. In fact, it looks as though a large black tide had washed up from the Delaware. The ladies' gowns and mantillas flow like ebony-hued waves over the brick walkways; the customary funerary veils flutter around as if they were inky, seaborne clouds blown in to obscure whatever color the landscape might produce. The Ilsleys and Rittenhouses are among the somber, parading figures, as are the Shippens, the Cadwaladers and Levys, the Yarnalls, the Misses Etting, the Logans, Wolfes, Fischers, and Josephsons. Some knew Theodora Crowther personally; many did not and are attending the service for the parents' sake and because this tightly knit group of Philadelphia's elite considers itself a family.

Martha, who waits among the grave markers nearest the Pine Street gate, hears whispered conversation and *sotto voce* theories on all sides.

"It could have been our house the thieves entered . . . It could have been our child . . . The papers say the ring's mastermind has been residing at Blockley. Well, something must be done, if the institution is raising up criminals. Indeed, it should! And Crowther's daughter found in that deplorable condition! What kind of hellion would bury the girl's body in a mountain of coal cobbles and flee without a backward glance—"

Martha stops listening. Despite the balmy afternoon and the sticky weight of her dark clothes, she shivers, then watches the Taitts advance into the churchyard. As if Becky's connection to the murder were intentional rather than circumstantial, the crowd parts and the murmured tales chronicling Dora Crowther's slaying cease. Instead, eyebrows are raised and pointed glances exchanged.

"Miss Beale!" William Taitt exclaims in a baritone too loud and conspicuous for the occasion. "Terrible times. Terrible times. And to think the last time you and I met in this spot we had no notion of what evil lay before us. A genuine Pandora's box that storm opened in our town. Nothing's been right since then, you know." He nods as though agreeing with his own assessment while his eyes seek out nearby acquaintances. To some he touches his hat; to others he extends an abbreviated bow. The responses are polite but less than warm. Taitt is acknowledged but not his wife. No curtsy is dropped as she walks by; no lady's neck curves in recognition; no gentleman bows. "You'll sit with us, I hope, Miss Beale. I feel I owe you an apology. And to Mr. Kelman, too. Especially now that the thief's complicity in today's tragic gathering seems indisputable. My evaluation of his methods has been amended, I assure you."

Martha maintains her focus on Taitt's face, although she feels her eyes are betraying her discomfort. Thomas has neither called upon her nor written since Dora's body was uncovered. Although she recognizes how preoccupied with the Crowthers he must be, the neglect perplexes and pains her. "I'm glad to hear that Mr. Kelman's efforts have met with your approval" is all she says.

"You'll join us, won't you?" Becky asks; she fingers her reticule, and Martha notices it's the same one that was stolen.

Her friend's plea is genuine. It shows in Becky's face; it sounds in her voice; it stretches along her shoulders and in the forward bend of her encumbered body. Martha is torn as to what answer to give.

"I had intended to wait here until the last moment so the Crowthers would see me as soon as the funeral cortege arrives. I spent time with them following Dora's disappearance, and I believe my presence had a calming effect—"

"Oh, I don't believe Georgine is coming," Taitt interjects. "Harrison, naturally, but not the mother or aunt. It wouldn't be proper for them to attend. Weeping and so forth in public. That would never do. Unfortunately, the distaff side is prone to high emotion."

Martha doesn't challenge the pronouncement. Tradition is on Taitt's side; mothers and wives are all but ordered to forgo services for family members. Still, she reminds herself, it's the middle of the nineteenth century; the city is a cosmopolitan place, not a colonial-era backwater dwelling in the past.

"Besides, I don't think Harrison will recognize a soul he greets, Miss Beale. He'll be so surrounded by the priests and pall-bearers and the hired mutes decked out in their gowns and waving their official wands, and all the other attendant panoply—as well as the gawpers and gapers crowding around out there—I doubt a single face will seem familiar to him. You make certain to sign the church register. That's what I intend to do. Then the family will realize you were here. Names and numbers in attendance are all most people care about nowadays, don't you agree?" Having delivered this opinion, Taitt prepares to lead the two ladies inside. Martha makes no remonstrance, although she presses Becky's hand in covert recognition of their shared secret.

Then she glimpses Thomas, and a smile lights her eyes. "Mr. Kelman," she calls. "Here is Mr. Taitt, who has just been wishing you were at hand so he could render an apology."

The expression Kelman turns to Martha is so devoid of vitality that it makes her draw back in wonderment. "Mrs. Taitt," he says with a perfunctory nod. "Mr. Taitt, sir. Miss Beale. Good morning to you." He begins to turn away while a frown of uncertainty and dismay knifes across Martha's brow.

"It must have been a terrible burden for you to have found Miss Crowther as you did," she says, but the delivery is rote: a speech prepared by one semi-acquaintance for another.

"Police work isn't always a pleasant business. The results are rarely what one wishes" is the equally remote reply.

"But you've already discovered the criminal's identity, Kelman," Taitt tells him. "I'm certain you'll have equal success in tracking him to his lair. The name Findal Stokes cannot be a common one. And a reward, such as they're reporting Crowther has offered, will be an added incentive to those evildoers with whom he consorts."

"So the newspapers would have us believe, sir."

"You don't put the same faith in your own detective work, Mr. Kelman? Or is it the criminal element you mistrust?"

"If the man has escaped to another county or township, capturing him will be problematic. I need not explain how easily felons vanish into other areas. And if, as I begin to suspect, this Stokes boarded a ferry for New York, having left Miss Crowther's remains at Unger's dock, then I fear apprehending him may prove difficult. Our sister city is not always a natural ally." Throughout the exchange, Kelman's eyes neither seek out Martha's nor shy away; instead, they remain fixed on the air beside her bonnet. "I'm forgetting my manners, Miss Beale. I must congratulate you on your good news. Or convey my best wishes, as that is the more appropriate salutation."

"My good—?"

But Kelman slips away into the throng before Martha can finish her response. Then the organist commences playing, sending music spilling from the church's open windows and doors; and the crush of bodies moving toward the entrance propels the threesome along. "What good news is that?" Becky whispers.

"I don't know—" Martha begins as Taitt interrupts:

"Ladies, shall we? You'll have time for gossiping later." He hands his wife and Martha to a tall-hatted usher who conveys them to a box pew already so crowded with mourners that the seat cushions have vanished beneath the mounds of funerary fabrics.

"Perhaps we should sit in the gallery," Becky suggests as the pew door swings open.

Her husband glances up at the space, which was originally reserved for the parishioners' slaves and which remains a segregated area. "Surely you jest, wife."

"Why, no . . . There appears ample room—"

"This isn't a theater, Mrs. Taitt. One doesn't rove about in order to find a more commodious seat or a better view."

"I merely thought—"

"We'll sit here." With that utterance, Taitt almost pushes his wife and Martha up the half step leading into the pew while those inside hastily rearrange their voluminous skirts and their lengths of broadcloth coat to accommodate the addition. Martha can't see Kelman among the crowd, but her vision is hampered by so many veiled bonnets and headdresses that she realizes he could be several boxes away and she would be unaware of his proximity. Instead, she notes that the Rittenhouses are sitting with Erasmus Unger and a man who resembles an elder version of Nathan Weil, although the publisher seems to be missing from the scene.

Then the various pitches of the organ: the *viola da gamba,* the *cor de nuit, flauto amabile,* and *contra-oboe* surge through the sanctuary, and her search for Kelman ceases. The music builds and, peaking, shakes the very seats while everyone strains for a view of Dora's father. Speculation regarding the growing delay becomes stagy whispers; whispers turn into pointed queries; queries increase in tone and tempo until it seems that every group gathered in each individual pew is discussing the lateness of the hour. Then the heat, despite the open windows, seems to affect everyone at once. Jet-handled mourning fans are retrieved and begin darting back and forth, as shimmering against the drabber clothing as quicksilver. Still Harrison Crowther fails to arrive.

"Are none of them coming?" Becky turns her head to Martha as she speaks, but the wings of her bonnet, rather than muffling the sound of her question, amplify it.

"He may be too grief-stricken to attend," her husband responds with a fixed expression that serves as a warning for his wife to behave herself. "Who can blame him?"

"Who, indeed?" Other voices pick up the refrain. "And who could believe an act of such violence would befall a family like—?"

At that moment Crowther enters. Martha can't see him, but she's aware of a stir at the church's northwest entrance, and a shift of bodies straining for a glimpse of the unhappy parent. "Oh, the poor man!" she hears voices exclaim in unison as Dora's father walks toward his reserved seat. "And the wife under a physician's supervision lest she harm herself. What has our city come to?" The remainder of the comments are inaudible because by now all are noisily rising while the Order for the Burial of the Dead commences.

"'LORD, THOU HAST BEEN OUR refuge, from one generation to another.'" Martha recites from Psalm Ninety along with the others, although her mind lies a long way off. *What can Thomas have meant by my "good news"? And why his unhappy air? He can't have forgotten what occurred between us, or is he so overworked that—?* The musings are cut short by two simultaneous occurrences. One is the eighth line of the psalm: "Thou hast set our misdeeds before thee; and our secret sins in the light of thy countenance," which reverberates like a cannon blast through her brain.

The second is Percy VanLennep's arrival.

"YOU!" CROWTHER'S SHOUT SILENCES EVEN those in the farthest reaches of the sanctuary who haven't yet spotted Dora's betrothed. "How dare you enter this holy place!"

"Sir. My abject apologies. I didn't know . . . I was visiting my friend"—Martha can see Percy hobbling forward; he looks as drained of blood as Dora's father did when he first appeared—"Nicholas Howe, here, at his farm in the countryside—"

"I don't care how many friends you claim, sir, for you are none of mine."

"Please, Mr. Crowther. I didn't realize what had transpired. I was wounded, you see."

By now, all heads are swiveling back and forth, watching Percy's painful approach toward the man who would have been his father-in-law.

"Wounded! Well, my daughter is dead, sir! Dead and gone forever. And you not even bothering to show your shameful head."

"Mr. Crowther, sir, if I may speak—" Nicholas begins, but Dora's father cuts him short.

"No, you may not. And you're not welcome in this church, either." The tone has become so enraged, and Crowther's face such a purple mass of fury, that the priest attempts to interfere. He lays a consoling hand on Harrison's forearm. Rather than calming the distraught man, however, the gesture serves to catapult him into another violent emotion, and he raises his two thick hands to his face and begins to sob. The noise is as resonant as a howl.

RETURNED TO HER CHAMBERS, MARTHA stands drained; her mourning dress is half on, half off, her ringlets in disarray after the haphazard removal of her bonnet. Her maid pulls at one of her mistress's sleeves, then both, then slips the shirtwaist from Martha's sluggish form before beginning to tackle the many hooks that hold the upper skirt in place. She looks at Ella, who's sitting close by, idly swinging her legs back and forth while she watches the familiar routine.

Ella returns the maid's puzzled glance. "Don't be sad, Mother," she says.

Martha releases a breath that sounds more weary than sorrowful, although it's grief for the Crowthers that burdens her. "I won't."

"Didn't you tell me that good people turn into angels when they die?" Ella stops swinging her legs in order to pose this question.

"Did I?"

"Yes. Because of what Miss Pettiman said about the ghosts."

"Ah, yes . . ." The tone is devoid of emotion.

"Well, then, Theodora Crowther is an angel."

"Mmmm" is the still-distracted reply.

Ella looks at the maid, whose brow is now furrowed in concern.

"You know, Mother, when Mr. Kelman begins looking for my real family, I remembered something to help him."

The introduction of Thomas's name causes Martha's nearly naked shoulders to curve further downward and her corset stays to creak in their ivory satin pockets. "Did you?"

"Yes. It has to do with angels. And prayers, too, but not the kind you and Miss Pettiman teach me. I think my real mother must have recited it to my sister and baby brother and me."

"Ah . . ." Martha climbs out of her black skirts, staring at them as they billow downward, although what her mind's eye sees is not the cascading lengths of crepe nor the Turkey carpet nor the floorboards nor the cabriole legs of the chest-on-chest but the stunned faces at Dora's funeral as they reacted to her father's shriek of pain.

"'Queen of Angels. Queen of Peace. Pray for me.' That's what I remember."

"That's fine, Ella. That's fine." As Martha speaks, her thoughts are far from her ward; instead, she decides that tomorrow she must call upon Georgine. Tomorrow midmorning and no later. If the husband was capable of breaking down in public, then what must Dora's mother be experiencing in private?

"I'll write down what I recall, and you can send the message to Mr. Kelman."

"Yes, you do that." Martha looks at the child and forces a smile, although she hasn't heard a word the girl has spoken. "You do just that."

A QUESTION OF MOTIVE

KELMAN SITS IN HIS OFFICE. Shadows are advancing over the city, throwing a pall of flat gray over the lower elevations while leaving the higher storys bathed in a hopeful glow. Looking through the window, he notes the dichotomy, reflecting upon those who can afford to dwell in the sunny domains of light and air, and those who must live and work in the alleys where the gloom of dusk is a perpetual fact, and the atmosphere choking and rank. The thought is brief, however, and gone with the next tick of the clock standing on his sturdy mantelpiece. He has work to do and no time for introspection unless it pertains to Theodora Crowther's death—which is fortunate, although he doesn't yet appreciate how convenient this investigation is, allowing him to relegate Martha and Nathan Weil to the outermost reaches of his brain.

"Tell me again if you will, Mr. VanLennep, how this curious situation came to transpire. I refer to your departure from the city on the same day your betrothed vanished from her home. The timing is odd, to say the least."

"I've already detailed my sojourn and its rationale, sir," Percy declares, more emphatically than he should given the circumstances. "It was happenstance solely that brought me to my friend's farm. I could have visited any number of other acquaintances, and so remained cognizant of the awful events that transpired here at home. The estate maintains an almost eccentric seclusion from city life. Isn't that correct, Nicholas?"

Poor Nicholas nods. He would rather "happenstance" had not involved him in this wretched affair. As he gives his silent assent he also gazes out Kelman's window, although his eyes regard not the dimming cityscape but an imaginary view of cultivated fields and orchards, encroaching woods, and ancient buttonwood trees melding into the harmonious end of another peaceable day. "I shouldn't have let VanLennep wander off on his own," he offers in a faraway mumble.

"We'll discuss the wound your friend sustained in a moment, sir," Kelman tells him while his own eyes narrow as they contemplate Percy. "Callow" is the word that springs into his mind; but Percy is also handsome and debonair, and Kelman can well imagine a sheltered girl like Theodora swooning over such a compelling figure.

"Someone shot at me," Percy insists. "It may seem insignificant considering everything else that's transpired, but it's true."

"I have no cause to doubt you."

Percy frowns. He's not accustomed to this type of interrogation—or any interrogation except by a social peer. "You don't behave as though you believe me."

"Mr. VanLennep, a murder has occurred."

"I'm fully aware of that, sir. Miss Crowther was my fiancée, after all. As you can imagine, the shock is considerable. I left Nicholas's home believing her to be abducted—as your letter indicated, and which was horrible enough to consider—only to arrive in Philadelphia and find her dead. And gruesomely, too."

Kelman regards the young man, and two further descriptions enter his brain. One is *vain,* the other *cocksure.* Neither is a good attribute—especially in a husband.

"What can you tell me about a woman called Dutch Kat, the owner of a bawdy house on lower Lombard Street?"

Percy starts, then hurriedly settles himself, crossing one elegantly clad leg over another. "Is it my life you're investigating, sir?" he asks; the tone is more belligerent than is wise.

"Should I be?" is the calm reply.

"Establishments on lower Lombard are not for the discriminating gentleman," Percy states, intending to leave the discourse there, then purposely removes his focus from Kelman's face in order to reexamine the room. It's a shabby space; its furnishings battered rather than handsomely patinaed with age, its drab color scheme neglectful of the crimsons and greens that complete most gentlemen's appointments. Percy wonders at such an impecunious and unfashionable choice, and disdain shows in every muscle of his face.

"No, they're not, Mr. VanLennep. Which makes me inquire why you frequented one of them."

"Who is it that claims I do such an absurd thing?"

"The owner of the house herself."

Percy pauses, more than a little disconcerted. Here he is, newly returned to the city—and at the cost of considerable physical discomfort—only to be attacked by Harrison Crowther in the most public and inappropriate of gatherings, and now to come under scrutiny by the police. "You would take the word of a common slut, sir, rather than a gentleman?"

"I've known Kat a good many years, VanLennep; you, I've only just met."

Percy begins to bluster; his smooth and pinkish face grows pinker; his pale, soft curls almost quiver upon his head; but the more dire reaction is that his sudden choler increases the throb in his shoulder. "Ouch!" he yelps. "Owww . . . Nicholas, I fear I may have opened this damnable wound again."

Kelman remains unaffected by the young man's travail. "You didn't answer me, VanLennep."

"Nor do I intend to, sir. My private life is not under scrutiny here."

"There you're mistaken." Kelman regards Howe, whose glance sidles away again. In the confines of the two rooms that complete Kelman's private office, Nicholas Howe appears overly large, bumbling, and inept. It's hard to believe that two such different men could be friends. "I assume your former guest must have discussed some of his romantic escapades with you, Mr. Howe?"

Nicholas's oxen eyes grow heavier and more inward-looking while Percy sighs pointedly.

"Yes, I'm aware of the house to which you refer," he tries to sneer.

"Where you habitually request a blond companion."

"If I've frequented the place once or twice, I certainly cannot be expected to recall the encounters," drawls Percy. "The type of women found in such places isn't exactly impressive—"

"Where you habitually request a blond companion," Kelman repeats. "If your memory doesn't serve, the madam's does. She makes it her business to accommodate and anticipate her clients' wishes. A blonde—and especially one who appreciates your *prowess.*"

"Kat told you that?" Shock and dismay ping through Percy's

voice while Kelman sits back in his chair, watching the spectacle unfurl. Within his dove gray trousers, Dora Crowther's former fiancé's legs are jittering as though struck with Saint Vitus' dance; then the restlessness travels to his hands and finally to his face, which winces in rapid tics.

"My 'prowess'? She said that?"

"Among less delicate observations."

"But it's diabolical that she should be so free with her comments. Or that the girls should—"

"The women who work there are paid for that type of appraisal, VanLennep. It's what keeps customers like you returning."

Either the steeliness in Kelman's tone or Percy's own wilting pride calls a halt to the discussion. He sags while Kelman experiences an unwelcome sense of his own cruelty. VanLennep may be arrogant, but he's also foolish and too young for his years.

"I'm not the only blue blood who visits Dutch Kat's," Percy finally mumbles.

"So I was informed" is the thin reply. As Kelman speaks, he recalls precisely what Kat told him. *The cream of society,* she said, *and none of them enjoys being stirred up.* For a moment he wonders why she was so free with VanLennep's name and so secretive with others in her clientele. *Could it be that she was purposely exposing VanLennep? But what would be her rationale? Why risk losing a lucrative client?* Kelman thinks back, wondering why he didn't question her motives before, but the thought vanishes as Percy's querulous voice breaks the silence. With the sound, Kelman's mood of forbearance ebbs.

"Are you done with me, Kelman? For I've had a long and wearying day."

"As have the Crowthers."

Percy makes no response other than to drop his gaze to the

floor. "You think I didn't care for Dora, don't you?" he asks at length. "That I didn't really love her."

"It's not my business to judge private love affairs, sir."

"But that's exactly what you're doing. You're judging me right now and finding me inadequate, just as the parents did—and through no fault of my own. I loved their daughter. She was a sweet girl. Very pretty and lively when she wasn't under her mama and papa's stony surveillance. We would have been happy together, I believe. She worshipped the very ground I walked upon, and a man cannot ask for more than that in a spouse."

As Kelman listens, he can't help but compare these lackluster statements with his feelings for Martha. *Pretty and lively and sweet! Where's the man's devotion? Where's his ardor or his admiration for anything other than the most superficial qualities? If I were being interviewed, I would have no dearth of compliments: Martha's compassion, her honesty, her goodness of heart and spirit and mind, her loving soul, her wisdom, her beauty and intellect*— The list slams to a halt. *And come January, she will be officially betrothed to Nathan Weil.* The reminder thickens Kelman's voice. "What can you tell me about the connection between Kat's establishment and the ransom money?"

"Nothing" is the answer. "I wasn't here—as you're so quick to inform me."

"Precisely. You departed the city on the very day Miss Crowther was found missing. To some, that would seem highly suspicious. In fact, there was originally conjecture that she might have eloped with you—"

"Eloped! But I was forbidden to see Dora. That horrible father of hers drove me out of the house—"

"I urge you to be discreet, VanLennep. Mr. Crowther will make a substantial enemy."

"Don't I know that already? And wasn't Dora cowed by him, too? Didn't she jump every time her parents grumbled at her? And that daft old aunt always meddling and creeping about."

Kelman leans forward. Unlike the now defensive Percy, he has both feet planted squarely on the floor, and the set of his shoulders—indeed, his entire being—appears just as obdurate. "I advise you to take this matter more seriously, sir."

"I am. You just don't believe me—"

Kelman continues as if Percy hadn't spoken. "A lady you claim to have loved is dead—"

"It's no claim, sir. It's God's own truth. Else why would I have been engaged to be wed—?"

"And your connection to the bawdy house that served as a depository raises unfortunate questions. Do you understand my meaning?"

"I understand that I'm being wrongly suspected of an affiliation with a monstrous scheme! Dora was to become my wife. Why should I have wished her harm? Why aren't you offering me condolences rather than formulating ominous inquiries—?"

"If you seemed more stricken, perhaps I would—"

"Who are you to divine how I feel? If I'm a gentleman and choose not to wear my heart on my sleeve, that's my affair. Perhaps you should be concerned about who shot me in my friend's woods rather than how bereavement affects my—"

"I'm engaged in investigating a murder, VanLennep—"

"Well, I might easily have been a murder victim, too—"

"Go easy, VanLennep," Howe murmurs in his slow and unwilling tone. "You only sustained a shoulder wound—"

"And what would have become of me if you hadn't found me when you did, Nicholas—?"

"But I did, and so—"

"But you might not have, if that letter from this fellow hadn't inspired your search—"

"Gentlemen," Kelman interjects. He studies his reluctant visitors and is all at once aware that he'll learn no more of importance from either one, at least not on this particular evening. In differing ways and to differing degrees, both men are so utterly self-absorbed that they make poor witnesses and even more dubious defendants. "You're free to go," he announces, but then remains seated in an interrogatory pose, so neither Nicholas nor Percy stirs from his seat. "However, before you depart, I ask that you reflect again on Dutch Kat's. You needn't respond immediately, but I want you to consider your past patronage. Is there a girl employed in the house who might have participated in Miss Crowther's abduction? Do you recall anyone showing particular interest in your future marital situation, or expressing undue curiosity regarding Miss Theodora's habits—?"

"Those girls are too simple to—"

"Hear me out," Kelman growls. "The fancy house wasn't picked as a distribution site out of a hat. It may be you were an unwitting dupe who supplied a conniving woman—"

Percy bolts from his chair before Kelman has time to finish. "I'm not the only man who patronized the place. Go back to Kat and ask her the names of her other clients if you and she are such boon companions, for I won't be badgered in this fashion, nor made to feel like a pariah by Harrison Crowther, or a 'dupe' by you. I needn't remind you that I have important contacts in this city. The VanLennep name commands respect from our most notable citizens. Now, if you have no further inquiries, I'll bid you good day." Then, either sensing he's gone too far or compelled by an unexpected sensation of personal loss, he concludes with a pitiful "I loved Dora. I did. And I wish none of this awful tragedy had ever transpired. She and I would have been happy together. I would have made a good husband, no matter what you think."

THE LETTER BECKY GREY RECEIVES bears no signature, but the hand is both antiquated and florid, the kind of penmanship practiced by the lower type of public scribe:

> *Mistress Taitt,*
> *I am the person you encountered a fortnight past. I admit that I committed a small offense against you by removing from your illustrious self a private piece of property. Many's the moment I considered returning it, for I am by custom a righteous man.*

Becky frowns at the missive. Despite her safe home and the reassuring sound of servants passing to and fro across its polished floors, anxiety attacks her. She's fully aware that the man who sent this message is being hunted as a murderer and thief; and that she once touched his vile hands, accepted his handkerchief—and then concealed the ominous events of that day from her husband.

> *Circumstances have inveighed against me, however, madam, and I now find myself blamed for an act I did not commit. Nor never would have committed in this life. You will know to what I refer. The lesser accusations against my person may or may not be justified, but that singular deed is not of my doing. I may have sinned, but never, never that! Madam, you and I had conversation. I ask you as a good Christian lady who walks about in churchyards*

Becky stops reading; her fingers are slick and trembling as she tears the letter in half, and then in quarters. She hurries toward the bell pull to call the servant who delivered the missive and question him regarding the person who brought it, then stops halfway. She can't risk having William learn of this communication. *What would he say about me consorting with thieves and assassins? Or about the day I permitted this Stokes to rob me and then set his minions to work their crime in our home? What if William were to discover I lied? Not once, but twice—and had my purse jumbled up with a dead woman's stolen possessions, too?*

Becky rends the paper again. Her heart is beating very fast, and her breath is shallow and quick. *What can this Stokes want from me? Why did he write? Is he still in this city, and not fled from it as the newspapers report? Could it be he who carried this letter to my house? Can he be as brazen as that?*

Becky's feet tread in tight circles as she thinks. By now fear of Findal Stokes has begun to outweigh her concerns about her husband. *The man is a demon. He must be caught. But not with my aid. I've enough to fret over, and I'm soon to be a mother, after all.*

Then her nobler instincts again rise. *Stop this at once. You're a strong woman, not a mouse trapped in a corner. Consider the roles you played. Lady Macbeth wouldn't have whimpered like this. Lady Anne wouldn't have cringed before King Richard.* But the analysis fails, for neither of Shakespeare's two heroines was capable of saving herself.

"Oh, I wish I had Martha Beale's inheritance," Becky sputters, then resolves to visit her new friend. *Martha must take charge of the letter; she can take it to Thomas Kelman.*

And William need never know.

NIGHT

MARTHA REASSEMBLES BECKY'S LETTER, SLIDING the pieces together to form a whole: the curving tail of a *Y* to match its cup, the leg of a *T* to meet the crossbar. Nearby, the missive's recipient paces back and forth across her hostess's sitting room: chair back to chair back, table to chest-on-chest, window to curtained window, where her hands briefly flutter across the drapery fabric as though toying with a stage scrim while pondering the difficulties of performing an arduous scene.

> *... I now find myself blamed for an act I did not commit. Nor never would have committed in this life ... I may have sinned, but never, never that!*

Martha's frown deepens into a protective scowl; she continues reading in silence, then looks up to watch Becky's anxious procession. "I'm deeply disturbed that the man dared approach your house. His hirelings entered it before; they could again, and perhaps intent upon greater mischief."

"Oh, I don't believe so. Taitt has made the place secure as any fortress."

"And then, too, you walked here. Alone and in the dark, where anyone could have—"

"I was on our lighted city streets, Martha, and keeping fully cognizant of those around me. No sane person would have accosted me." Becky tosses off these words, but her restive pacing doesn't lessen.

Martha makes no answer for a moment; instead, she returns to the letter. Her gray eyes flash nearly as black as Thomas Kelman's. "And are you convinced this Stokes is *sane?* The garbled quotations from the Book of Isaiah with which he concludes his message seem like the ranting of a madman. Especially the list of physical afflictions perpetrated upon women. If those aren't threats, veiled or otherwise, I don't know what is."

"They're merely words."

"But hateful ones. 'Burning instead of beauty,' nakedness and desolation—"

"Sticks and stones," Becky interjects, but Martha interrupts her.

"Are you familiar with the preacher Amor Alsberg?"

"This has nothing to do with him or his lunatic devotees. There will always be those who condemn people other than themselves and find rationale by quoting the Bible—"

"Alsberg may be capable of exhorting his flock to genuine acts of violence, however. And this Stokes has listened to him. I know, because—"

"Yes. Yes, but so have a great many other impoverished people. Or not so impoverished. It's not Alsberg or his motives or methods I came to discuss, though." Becky stands still. "Oh, help me, Martha! I've begun a deceit and now am trapped in it."

"Not trapped, surely. And your deceit, as you call it, is mild when compared to—"

"I can't show this thing to my husband. That much is certain. Oh, why did this vile man write to me? What can he want—other than to rave about his supposed innocence regarding the Crowther death—?"

"And frighten you—"

"Well, he succeeded. Although perhaps not as he intended." Before Martha can reply, Becky's words rush forward again. "Take the letter to Thomas Kelman for me. Tell him all I've said, how I came by it—and impress upon him the need for discretion—"

"But Becky, wouldn't it be better to give the missive to your husband? If you conceal this—"

"I can't show it to William. I can't. I won't."

"What if Thomas wishes to question you or the servant who received it?"

"I don't see the purpose in that." Despite the stubbornness of her tone, Becky's pose remains irresolute as if she were pausing in flight. "Please, Martha, will you? Please. For me. Kelman should see this. You know he should. Despite Stokes's assertion to the contrary, the man must be captured and punished as the abhorrent criminal he is."

"And you have no notion why he approached you?"

"None! None!" Becky's hands flail at the air; her face is zigzagged with worry and self-rebuke. "Why did I hide the loss of that silly reticule? And my parasol, too. How foolish and stupid."

"Then put an end to your prevarications. Husband and wife should be honest in all they do and say. William will forgive this insignificant lapse in judgment, I'm certain. After all, a parasol and purse are of little consequence when compared to the greater human quandaries at issue here."

Becky's panicked state won't permit her to heed this reasonable counsel. "Now those small lies will give William cause to doubt everything else about me. Everything! My suitability as a wife, my fitness as the mother of his child—"

"You did what you did, Becky. You can't revise the past. As to your anxiety about being an inadequate wife and mother, it's wholly unfounded—"

"Oh, my dear, you're so naive." The words are like a moan.

Instead of taking the accusation amiss, Martha answers with calm and assurance. "I can't judge the strength of your marital bond. I can only state that you had an illustrious career, that you're a forceful personality, and that your husband must have wed you because of those excellent attributes. And I repeat my belief that man and wife should be candid with one another in all their transactions—"

"Taitt wooed me because I was a feather in his cap, pure and simple. What ardor he originally professed is gone."

Martha studies the bleak face confronting her and knows Becky believes every word she has uttered. "Perhaps your present condition has elicited sensations of delicacy and restraint in your husband; and therefore his behavior seems aloof or even chilly. After your baby is delivered, I'm sure you and he—"

"And if I'm found lacking then? You know as well as I do that Taitt could claim the child while banishing the mother. Especially if I give birth to a boy. Imagine how quickly the elite of Philadelphia will jump to his defense if he decides to divorce me. Then where will I be? Treading the boards again? Not in this city, that's certain. Not with scandal heaped upon my head."

"He wouldn't divorce you, Becky. He has no cause. Come, stop your fretting. As you just said, you have no idea why the reprehensible Stokes wrote to you. Surely your husband should take umbrage at the man's insolence rather than condemn you for an invented iniquity."

"Invented," Becky echoes, then lapses into silence while Martha again tries to reason with her.

"I've heard that pregnant women can experience confusion and even unhappiness at their altered state. In your case, having been so lauded for your grace and physical beauty . . ." The words trail away as Martha's brow creases with a newfound worry. "Taitt would not . . . He would never raise his hand to you? Despite your present feelings of unease, he's a fair man who behaves honorably, isn't he?"

But Becky's response is a repeated request that Stokes's letter be delivered to Thomas Kelman.

"Answer me, please. He would never strike you, would he?"

"Not yet, he hasn't" is the quiet reply.

"Oh, Becky!" It's now Martha's turn to pace the room. She sighs, and her whalebone corset stays creak out her distress. "But such an act is beyond contempt. Taitt is a cultivated gentleman, well educated and of good standing in our community. He's too urbane a person to—"

"To express anger or outrage?"

"Not in the horrid manner you suggest."

"Oh, Martha, no matter what you want to believe, husbands are masters in their households; and a wife is simply an adjunct to that property. Sometimes, I think he views me as being no different than the slaves he keeps at his estate in the Carolinas. I never saw such abject souls until I came to live in this country."

"You're not a slave. Nor any approximation of one—"

"What do you know of marriage, Martha Beale! You, who can choose to wed or not. Who can pick whatever spouse you desire—and rid yourself of him, too, I'll warrant." The angry speech is out before Becky has time to consider its effect. She flings herself down upon a divan. "I'm sorry. That was unkind. And to you, of all people. Please forgive me. I've never been able to bridle my tongue, and I seem to have grown even less circumspect recently."

"What you said is true nonetheless" is Martha's equitable answer, although her expression reflects her hurt. "My advice must sound antiquated and pedantic to a woman of your experience. A spinster dispensing words of wisdom on the vicissitudes of love."

"I didn't mean to wound you, Martha."

"I understand that."

"It seems I can do nothing right at the moment. Nothing at all. I lie when I could as easily tell the truth. I weep instead of showing courage. I snipe at my maid, and rail at my dressmaker when the fault is solely mine."

"You've become a master of pessimism and self-rebuke, at any rate," Martha tells her with a wry smile.

Becky's short laugh is bitter. "I'd rather impart optimism and joy—not cause pain to those around me. Especially to my friends."

"Then so you shall." That declaration delivered, Martha remains silent for a long moment. The clock upon the mantel ticks; the lamplight fizzles, ebbing and waning as the wicks burn, and stirring the familiar shadows of the room. Beyond the windows the sky is dark, lending the scene an even more sequestered air. "Your outburst is forgiven, Becky; and I want you to understand that you have a true friend in me. I will stand by you whenever—and however—you wish it."

Becky's features don't soften in relief, although her face gradually relaxes its preoccupied expression. "Thank you. I won't forget your kindness. Your many kindnesses." Then she also sighs, and a little of her former fortitude returns while Martha continues in a serious tone.

"But I also ask you to consider that your pregnancy may be

causing you to see hobgoblins where there are none. Think back to your first meetings with your husband, and what attracted you to him and him to you. I'm certain all will be well when you're safely delivered of this child. Better, indeed, than before because you'll be a family."

"Yes . . ."

"You can and *will* make it so. Don't forget who you are."

Becky sighs again, but the sound is more reassured. "That memory is always with me—for good or ill."

"For good, then. Make it for good."

"Yes."

"Promise me that. No more recriminations. Be the Becky Grey who was and you'll win over Philadelphia. I promise."

"Yes." She rises from her recumbent position. "Yes . . . Perhaps . . . But let us dispense with the vagaries of my brain and reattach this letter so you can give it to Kelman. Perhaps you could send a manservant to find him. I'll be gone before he arrives." She lifts a hand in protest to Martha's imagined retort. "Don't say anything more. I'll follow your advice and explain everything to William. I will. I guarantee I will. But let us address the issue with your Mr. Kelman first." So intent has Becky been on her own woes that Martha's dismay at the repeated mention of Thomas's name has gone unnoticed until now. "Oh, my dear! There's nothing amiss, is there?"

Martha's lips part to speak, but no sound comes. Her eyes rove from Becky's to the tattered letter, then to the table beneath it and finally to the carpet below that while her mind races through a variety of replies. There's glib untruth, delivered with a short and practiced laugh; there's coy secrecy, overt denial, or no answer at all. There's also honesty—which choice picks her before she's aware of having made a decision.

"Thomas and I have an understanding . . . At least, I believed we did—" Then the entire complex history comes rolling out, not the least of which is Weil's unexpected declaration.

When the narrative is finished, Becky knits her fingers together in concentrated thought. "What do you propose to do?"

"Well . . . Ella wants Thomas to help find her birth mother, and I—"

"No. You. What do you propose?"

"Send him a brief note, I suppose, and suggest he call upon us in order to speak with Ella. She recalled some words or prayers her mother recited. Then, perhaps, when he and I are discussing that situation I can ascertain—"

"Martha, for pity's sake! I came to you for help because you're strong and capable, and here you are blithering like a convent schoolgirl rather than following your own advice. Weren't you just cautioning honesty in all situations? Express your true feelings to Thomas. If there's been a misunderstanding, that's the only way you'll learn of it—"

"Perhaps, when he arrives to view Stokes's letter—"

"Oh, damn Stokes!" Becky throws herself back onto the divan, the movement so abrupt that several small pillows skitter to the floor.

"But he's the reason you came to see me."

"Very well. You need an excuse to visit Thomas in his private rooms. Let my letter be the reason—"

"Becky, no! Such a visit would be unseemly."

"Why? If your purpose is to help apprehend a murderer."

Martha stares back, wide-eyed at the suggestion. "People would talk. It's not fitting I be seen there. It would put us both in a terribly compromised position—"

"Would a man like Kelman care about such niceties, do you think?"

"Not for himself, certainly, but I'm sure he'd be concerned about my reputation."

"And what about you? Are you worried that the gossipmongers will tattle about your behavior?"

Martha thinks. "I was once. . ."

"But now you're questioning polite society's dominion over your life," Becky finishes the thought. "So I repeat my question: Why can't you call upon him, rather than he you? Because I fear this house and all its elegant possessions would dampen the ardor of all but the wealthiest of suitors."

"Oh, but—" Martha starts to protest, but Becky overrides the hesitant words.

"If you're in love with him and he with you, you must act upon it. I took my first lover when I was seventeen, and I assure you he was no elderly patron of the arts desirous of pretty speech and nothing more—"

"Oh!" is all Martha can utter.

"Is that too shocking to mention?"

"Perhaps not for others' ears, but I've never held this type of conversation—"

"Then it's time you do. I understand all too well the dictates of a modern and civilized community, and this Quakerish city in particular. However, if you study Shakespeare as much as I have, or Congreve or Sheridan, you realize that the world was an earthier place in our forebears' days. There's nothing wrong with passion; it's deceit and guile that are at fault. As you yourself have so ardently reminded me." Becky stands and marches to the table containing the shredded letter. "Let us paste this unpleasant thing together. You can carry it with you. But don't let it interfere with the real purpose of your visit. Another day of Stokes wandering free will hardly matter in the grander scheme of life."

Martha watches her friend. "I will agree to your plan if you also grant me a request—that you will allow me to have a footman escort you home, and that you explain the purpose of this visit to your husband. When Stokes is brought to justice, I believe, William Taitt will have cause to feel pride—rather than dismay—at his wife's involvement."

WITH THE LETTER IN HER purse and Becky returned home, Martha sets forth toward Kelman's lodgings. A sense of urgency impels her, but instead of hurrying along with her eyes pinned to the road and her shoe leather slip-slapping at the cobbles, she marches erect, studying the streetlamps, the fitfully lit brick facades of the neighboring houses, the windows behind which other householders are idling away the late evening hours by reading aloud to one another or playing musical instruments or listening to their children recite their bedtime prayers. For an infinitesimal moment, her eyes fill with panic, not because of her mission but because she may be proven wrong. Despite what occurred four days past, Thomas may reject her overture; he may think it coarse and unmannerly. Or he may become so engrossed in Findal Stokes that there will be no opportunity for personal discussion. But then she reminds herself that this is her only choice. The time for hesitation is over.

AS MARTHA WALKS, THE MAN whose message she bears continues to berate his son. For good measure, he also twists the younger Findal's left ear so hard the boy thinks the flesh will come away in his parent's hand.

"Owww," he mutters while tears of pain and fury course down his cheeks. "Leave off, will you? I told you everything I know."

"The little lad's crying, is he? Begging for mercy, eh? Beseeching his old da for forgiveness for his manifold wickednesses."

Findal yelps, but the cry, instead of eliciting aid from the passersby and residents of the unwholesome street called Blackberry Alley, garners minimal response. Steps are taken to avoid the two, or windows are shut, or slop buckets poured out in sour but silent protest. Despite the bucolic name, the small passageway is home to the city's most transient population. If any here have a memory of fragrant fields and sun-ripened fruit, they keep it secret, just as they keep their histories and their illicit dealings to themselves.

"You'll not get away so easy, I'm telling you, lad," Stokes continues as if no nearby person had made a stir. "I might have made a nice profit with those wares you so stupidly squandered."

"And been hanged as a—"

"Hold your tongue, boy! I'm smarter than that—"

"Smarter doesn't wind up in the poorhouse," the son spits back.

"Mind your manners!" Stokes thunders and reaches for Findal's other ear, but the child flinches away, dodging his head and gritting his teeth when his father gives the captive ear another ferocious wrench. "And haven't I done all right by you since then? Didn't I set up a nice little game, and earn us a pretty penny? And don't you accept a handsome share of the stash? Now, you tell me the truth about where you originally found those treasures, and why you deposited them outside a particular house without informing your father first. Because I don't believe one word of the feeble story you've been feeding me so far."

"It was to save you, Father—"

"Oh, aye. And next you'll be telling me the dead can speak—"

"They was on to us. That Kelman and the secret service agent—"

"And why do you think that unfortunate fact occurred? Could it be someone was careless in creeping close to that golden laundry basket—?"

"We shouldn't have done this thing, Father. Don't you know all the newspapers are calling you a—?"

"Don't tell me what we should or should not have done! I had the situation well in hand—"

"No, you didn't—"

"And now you've squandered our last chance. For who's to believe us if we've nothing tangible to prove we can finger the girl's killer. That portrait was only a start."

"But we have nothing more!"

"Thanks to you. Thanks to you!" Stokes eyes his son, but instead of dodging his glance away, Findal stares defiantly back. "You know something you're not revealing. I can tell by that shifty look upon your cunning face."

"I know nothing other than I've already told you, Father."

"Maybe you watched the lass getting murdered. Just as you watched that woman wading into the river."

"No, Father. I found only the—"

"Don't lie to me!" Stokes drags his son closer, twisting the imprisoned ear until the boy's agonized face is nearly parallel to the ground. "You saw who killed Crowther's daughter, is that it? And now you've got your own conniving scheme working, haven't you? You were creeping around that night, all by your lonesome the way you like to be. Then you happened upon the lass being hid in the coal cobbles, waited till the killer crept away, pounced, grabbed the goods, and maybe had a look beneath the dead lady's underdrawers before you came skulking home to your worried parent, pretending to have chanced upon newfound treasure."

"I spotted the parcel, Father. Just like I said. Only the package, not the lady. And nowhere near the docks."

Stokes is too caught up in his own theory to listen. "So you're working your own ploy, are you? And cutting your fond parent out of the profit. Sending a private message to that pinch-hearted banker."

"No, Father. It's as I said—"

"Ten thousand dollars, boy, you cost us. Do you know what that could buy? The whole world, is what."

"I told you, Father; that were a mistake. How was I to know the damned secret service agent was lurking there?" Then Findal ceases pleading and adds a challenging "If I hadn't been there, you would have been nabbed instead of me. And you wouldn't have been able to scarper like I did."

"I do believe I'm squeezing the wrong appendage," the father sneers. "Maybe twisting something else will aid your memory."

Instinctively, Findal crouches and his hands rush to cover his private parts. His father breaks into a croaking laugh.

"That's right. Cover up the silly thing before I have my way with it. You don't mind pulling at it yourself, do you? As I have no doubt you and that filthy band at Blockley were doing while you watched that woman giving birth—"

"We weren't! We only happened upon her when she waded into the river—"

"Oh, aye. Certainly you did. And you tried calling her back—"

"We did!"

"Don't you lie to me!" Stokes rages again. "I know what you were up to. And it wasn't perdition for her sin-filled soul you were fretting over . . . Now, tell me what you know about Crowther's daughter and the loot."

"Leave off, Father. We've earned enough from—"

"You simpleton!" Stokes finally releases his son's ear, but instead of letting the boy go, the father lands a blow to the side of his son's head, sending Findal reeling sideways and banging hard into a clapboard wall that then resounds with the attack, which earns the pair a number of hisses of impatience and a few hoarse shouts of "Take it elsewhere." Those dwelling in Blackberry Alley may be secretive, but like their more elegant neighbors' their patience finally reaches a limit.

"I'll take it where I wish and when I wish!" Stokes bawls back. "This here is my boy, my own flesh and blood, and I'll discipline him as I see fit when he misbehaves." Then he mashes his face so close to Findal's that the son's view consists only of one red-streaked eye and a nose that looks like a strawberry left in a monger's basket until the fruit has turned pulpy and purple.

"Whoever killed that girl is driving us out of business. If you don't comprehend that, you're an idiot as sure as you were born—"

"Forget this, Father. There'll be other opportunities. Better ones."

"That's right, my lad. But not for you and me together. I'm acting on my own now. So let this be a warning. You're no son to me, nor never will be any longer. I don't want you trailing after me, complaining you're hungry or cold or ill shod; and I also hereby order you to keep away from a certain rich lady's house, for those kids of hers is mine. You may have found that pretty girl, but I claim her for myself. The lofty shall be repaid, boy. Remember that. Evilly repaid."

By now, through either preoccupation with this ardent speech or fatigue from holding his son captive, the elder Stokes's grasp has loosened, and Findal leaps away, shouting abuse at his parent. He overestimates his agility, though, and the father makes one flying lunge toward his child that brings them both down upon the cobbles, young Findal's head clattering like a plate breaking on a stone.

AS FINDAL FALLS, MARTHA RISES, passing with confident steps up to the third floor of a building on Spruce Street, where she raps upon Kelman's door. The answer from within is gruff, as he's in the midst of pondering the more elusive aspects of the Crowther case: the involvement of Dutch Kat being a sizable conundrum.

Martha takes no notice of the tone. "It is I, Martha," she calls back. "May I come in?" It doesn't occur to her that her presence at this unorthodox hour and in this inappropriate place might take him by surprise, so she's perplexed by the flurry of movement within: the sound of chairs being pushed along the floor and of plates and other serving pieces being hurriedly cleared away.

Then the door is flung open.

"Martha. Is something wrong?"

She stands in the entry, seeing him as she did the first time: the thin, expressive scar, the eyes that either reveal more than they should or hide too much, a reservoir of feeling that only the thinnest layer of flesh prevents from overflowing. "No. Nothing. I . . . I brought a letter Becky Grey received." Despite her bravado, Martha's efforts begin to falter. "From Stokes."

Instead of a reply, Kelman holds the door wider, gesturing her inside as if part of him had been waiting for this moment all along. "I see." The tone is polite and cool, but his expression is the opposite; every emotion flies across his face.

"Becky tore it in pieces, but she and I glued it together again." Martha produces an envelope. "You may peruse it now—or later." She holds the paper, neither relinquishing nor retracting it while her body and brain steel themselves to her task. "In truth, Thomas, although this missive has obvious bearing on your work, my bringing it to you is a ruse—"

"A ruse?"

"Yes. Or, rather, not entirely." Again Martha hesitates, and again urges herself forward. "The fact is that I've come to ask if a misunderstanding has arisen between us. I believed we shared a strong feeling for one another, but now—"

He removes the envelope from her grasp and places it on a table at the center of the small room, although his eyes remain fixed upon her face. "You've promised yourself to another. No good will come of this."

"No. I haven't" is all she can utter, but he doesn't heed the protest.

"You've promised yourself to Nathan Weil. As is appropriate, given your rank and station. I won't claim that your choice makes me happy, because that would be disingenuous, but I believe he will be a fitting husband for you, which I could never be; and I wish you—and him—abiding joy—"

"I'm pledged to no one," Martha interjects with more force. She gazes at him, then away, her glance taking in the Spartan space: the single deal table, the two ladder-back chairs arranged on either side, the window bereft of either wood shutters or drapery as if creature comforts were of no importance. "I'm pledged to no one," she eventually repeats. Kelman's response is a nearly whispered:

"This is wrong, Martha. We shouldn't be alone in my lodgings. Let me examine the missive and then escort you home." He crosses the floor to the far side of the table, opens the letter, and pulls the paraffin light closer while she shakes her head in disagreement.

"No one, Thomas. I repeat that fact. If you learned of such a rumor, it was unfounded and untrue."

"How did Mrs. Taitt come to possess this?" is the sole reply to this declaration.

Martha explains, although her thoughts are equally distracted.

"Another scribe," he murmurs. "Another hand entirely. What can this mean? How many people are involved in this crime? And why did Stokes approach William Taitt's wife?"

"Thomas, tell me why you believe I'm betrothed."

Kelman's frown deepens. He runs his fingers across the letter's rumpled surface. "I heard the declaration myself," he says, although his perplexed stare never leaves the words scrawled upon the page.

"And didn't query me directly?"

"There was no need. Weil spoke and—"

"And you overheard without—?"

"I called at your offices in order to request your aid in breaking the news of Dora's death to her parents." Then he adds a muttered "Crowther was sent two messages concerning Dora . . . then a contradictory and poorly written note arrived with her effects . . ."

The incipient smile that had entered Martha's eyes vanishes, and her backbone grows stiffer. "You listened to my private conversation but didn't make your presence known?"

At last Kelman looks up, and Martha reiterates her question.

"Weil was quoting poetry and whatnot. It was an intimate moment, and I assumed—"

"You assumed." Martha's expression hardens; her tone has turned edgier.

"Yes. Yes, I made an assumption." By now Kelman's voice is also rising in frustration. "If a gentleman recites love poems about necklaces and bosoms to a lady, what else can be the reason—other than a display of mutual affection?"

"Oh, Thomas!" is the swift retort. "Nathan Weil is the publisher of the book he quoted; I met him only recently, the day you found me at Parkinson's Palace. He brought me a gift of Tennyson's latest works, which volume I already owned. It wasn't my wish that he visited, nor did I ask him to declaim any verses—about necklaces or anything else. You're too conscientious a person to act in this high-handed manner—"

"And how would you have wished me to behave when I stood in the anteroom, Martha? Should I have interrupted your *tête-à-tête*—?"

"Yes! If you cared for me and believed I returned your affection; by all means, you should have protested."

Kelman makes no answer, and Martha also remains silent while the house stirs around them: a fellow resident's clattering footfall on the lower stairs, the opening and closing of a door, a conversation that carries sound but no audible meaning. It's as if even the air is waiting for these two to break their proud silence.

"If you truly cared for me, you would have," she repeats in the same resolute fashion, but the words have scarcely left her mouth when Kelman is at her side, his lips covering hers and his arms clasping her close, holding her so firmly that she couldn't move away even if she wanted. His hands move to her shoulders, to her neck, to the bodice of her gown while Martha gives in to his embrace, reaching out her own hands to caress his shoulders and head.

Her movements are tentative at first but soon grow bolder; her fingers twine through his long hair, trace his cheekbones and the scar that seems to hold the secrets of his heart. "Oh," she breathes while the scent of him swells around her: hot skin, hot wool, and something pungent and musky like a forest floor in April or farm fields newly tilled.

"My dearest," he murmurs as his fingertips brush the curled plait at her neck. "How could you doubt I loved you?"

Martha doesn't answer the question. Speech pales when compared to what her body and soul are experiencing. Instead, she whispers his name, then succumbs to the wondrous pleasure of being enfolded in a man's strong arms.

Somewhere a clock chimes; somewhere the watch cries out the hour; somewhere a wagon's iron-bound wheels echo across the cobbles. She hears the sounds although her sensory perceptions are concentrated on the feel of her skin against his, the heat that becomes one heat, their flesh melding into a single unit.

THE BANGING ON THE DOOR jolts them apart, as the sound of Kelman's sergeant issues from the hallway. "Sir. My apologies, sir, for rousing you so late. But I must speak with you at once."

Kelman calls out a response; he leaves Martha's side and hurries toward the entry, business-like and efficient in a moment, then gazes back, obviously worried about having her presence discovered. She returns his glance with a shy shake of her shoulders.

"Has public scrutiny discovered us so soon?"

Hearing this female sound although unable to identify the speaker, the sergeant on the stair landing grows more abashed. "I didn't realize you were entertaining, sir."

Kelman walks to the portal while Martha steps into shadow in order to conceal her identity. For a sickening moment, she imagines that the sergeant has come to summon her because of a problem at home, but then realizes such a thing could never be. No one but Thomas knows where she is. And Becky Grey.

"I'll come with you," she hears Kelman tell the man. "Wait for me downstairs." Then the flame of the sergeant's lamp flickers out while the exterior door shuts against him; and Martha quits her hiding place.

"Bad news, Thomas?"

The expression he turns to her is so bruised that Martha's chest constricts in fear. His answer is equally somber. "There has been a suicide attempt at the Crowthers'."

As he speaks, he holds up his overcoat and hat as if he's forgotten what the things were for. "I'm afraid I must go there at once. I had intended to escort you home, but with my man waiting downstairs—"

"I require no escort. I found my way here, after all. And don't worry, I'll wait until I can steal away in secret." She tries for a light and competent tone, but the effort rings false; instead, the monstrous word "suicide" opens a chasm between them, and Martha wonders whether it could have been mere minutes ago that their arms were intertwined and their minds focused wholly on each other. "I've been so fearful for poor Georgine," she adds in a subdued voice. "I imagine her mother's heart is broken. But to try to take her own life . . ."

Kelman regards her across the spare furnishings of his rooms. "It's not the wife, my dear one. It's the husband. It's Harrison who swallowed poison. Apparently, the surgeon in attendance isn't certain he'll survive."

NOT IF I CAN HELP IT

"OIL OF VITRIOL," THE SURGEON repeats as if Kelman hadn't heard him the first or even the second time. "Why would anyone choose such an excruciatingly painful substance? There are far easier means of seeking death. If Crowther does survive, which is uncertain, it will take time to repair the extreme damage the caustic liquid did to his mouth and stomach, although I doubt he'll experience anything approximating complete recovery even then." The surgeon pauses to shake his head and release an unhappy sigh. He's an august person, silver-bearded and reluctant to show emotion, so this overt display of his feelings takes Kelman by surprise.

He doesn't interrupt, however, but permits the surgeon to gather his thoughts. Around them in the hall outside Harrison Crowther's rooms a muffled flow of servants hurries back and forth, eyes averted and scared, footsteps hardly seeming to touch the floor. All appear exhausted, for it is now approaching two in the morning.

"I've dosed him with magnesia in milk-and-water and applied

leeches to the exterior of his throat in order to ease his breathing, but it's still dangerously labored. It's a wonder the man didn't suffocate owing to the swelling that undiluted oil of vitriol can induce upon the tongue, larynx, and epiglottis. Of course, he has expectorated flesh as well as blood, which has further damaged the trachea. I've also applied leeches to his abdomen—"

"You're positive the acid could not have been administered accidentally?" Kelman finally interrupts.

"Accidentally?" the surgeon repeats. "Perhaps. But not *swallowed* erroneously, for the merest sip would warn a reasonable man that he was imbibing something poisonous. Then, too, we must consider the missive Mrs. Crowther recovered at her husband's side. Despair at losing his daughter and only child is the recurring theme—"

"Or intentionally poisoned by someone else's hand?" Kelman persists. Although he's only given the letter a brief perusal, there's something in the present circumstances that troubles him, and it's not the overt message of a father's overweening grief.

"Murder's not my province, I'm relieved to say, Mr. Kelman. Besides, who would commit such a repulsive deed? Not Mrs. Crowther, surely, or the elderly and diminutive Miss Lydia? And how would you imagine anyone—man or woman—forcing Crowther to drink a concoction so foul?"

Kelman's initial response to the queries is silence. "I take it Mrs. Crowther identified the handwriting as her husband's?" he asks at length.

"It didn't occur to me to ask. Before your arrival, it was all I could do to persuade her not to throw the missive into the fire Poor lady. What a sight to behold. Her spouse in what she assumed were his death throes—" The surgeon's words cease as he sighs anew, his white-gray hair and beard standing out in contrast to the dusky walls. Dawn is a long way off, and until it comes, the house will remain in fitful chiaroscuro with puddles of bright lamplight pushing against the enveloping shadow. "I've left instructions as to how to remove the leeches when they begin to fall off," he states, returning to the cool comfort of scientific fact, "and how to apply a poultice of warm poppy fomentations in their stead."

"And Mrs. Crowther and Miss Lydia? I assume the servants are aware of special medical needs their mistresses may have?"

"Miss Lydia has a strong will for self-preservation. Quite a remarkable determination, in fact. I offered her a sleeping draught, but she refused it, saying she would profit from using her waking hours in prayer. Mrs. Crowther I dosed with laudanum, as her behavior seemed as potentially self-destructive as her husband's. I doubt she'll awaken till midday. I suggest you question her in the gentlest fashion when you begin your inquiry, Kelman, for her psyche, understandably, is in a perilous condition. Indeed, it may be impossible for her to endure should Crowther perish. To have this loss added to the first . . ." He leaves the thought unfinished, then adds an unexpectedly hesitant:

"However, during the course of your investigation, if you do determine that this *is* a case of attempted or actual murder, I must repeat that the means are barbaric, because the agony Crowther suffered and is continuing to suffer is almost unbearable. It would take a callous soul to inflict such anguish. Now, if you'll excuse me, I feel I've done all I can at present. You, too, I would imagine. I'll call again at breakfast time."

"Yes, of course. Good night, sir."

"Or good morning, as the case may be. You should get some

rest, too, Kelman, for the hours and days ahead may bring worse news rather than better."

AS KELMAN CONCLUDES THIS CONVERSATION, the younger Findal Stokes opens his eyes and finds himself staring at the few and distant stars that gleam down upon Blackberry Alley. For a moment he can't remember how he came to be lying here on his back in what he assumes is the middle of the night. Then the throbbing of his head recalls the argument with his father and the blow that sent him crashing into the street.

He pulls himself into a sitting position so his hands can prod his skull. They come away sticky with blood when he finds the tender place. "What a fine parent I have," he mutters, then all at once retches with pain, spewing out only bile because there's nothing in his belly. Unwelcome tears streak his clammy cheeks as he heaves again, then groans again while his eyes flicker shut against the ache in his skull. "What an honest, upstanding gent!"

But these caustic words, and the tight-lipped bravado with which they're delivered, can't match the misery etched on the boy's face. Not that anyone is there to read the expression, for the alley is long abed and only the scuttling creatures of darkness are present: a long, hairless tail slithering along a gutter, a snarl from a tomcat protecting its turf, the grunt of a thin and feral pig. Listening, Findal bows his head and presses it against his knees, letting the shameful tears well up and fall where they may.

"Oh, what a prince you are, Da. What a living, breathing saint." Then he swipes at his nose and eyes with an angry hand, and stifles another groan when his heaving chest and swelling eyes cause his head to shoot with renewed pain. *Well, I won't let you harm that girl Ella. Or the little mulatto, neither. You won't be "abducting" them or holding them "hostage" or whatever blasted thing you're scheming. Not if I can help it.*

Findal stands, shaky and nauseous still, but also filled with a ferocious energy. *And who will you call an idiot then?* his thoughts demand. *For that Mr. Kelman was on me like glue back at Kat's place. And he'll stick to you, too. Just like the stink of curing leather when you worked an honest trade. I may be smaller than you, but I'm smarter. I'm far, far smarter.*

For good measure, the boy wipes his eyes again, noting how curious it is that his sore head should cause such a ceaseless and silly flood of tears.

DESPITE HER PROMISE TO JOURNEY home immediately, Martha remains rooted in place long after Kelman and his sergeant are gone. If she's aware of the singularity of her circumstances, of her shoes resting on sloping and unfamiliar pine floorboards, of the whitewashed ceiling beams and the uneven plaster of the walls—or the fact that she is in Thomas's chambers—she doesn't reveal it. The paraffin lamp he left lighted shines upward into eyes that are staring not outward but inward. *Harrison Crowther,* she repeats in silence, *not Georgine. The father tried to take his own life, rather than the mother.* The flatness of Martha's expression divulges nothing further than these simple pronouncements; what other opinions her brain is examining are as yet too unformulated to disclose.

Then, as if an external force is impelling her into action, she relinquishes her statue-like pose, finds her mantle, sets her bonnet upon her head, and retrieves her gloves. *The father,* she reiterates, *not the mother. The father, who was instructed to deliver his daughter's ransom monies to a brothel—and who insisted Thomas keep his distance.*

By the time she hurries up the steps to Dutch Kat's house, Kelman is concluding his conversation with the surgeon.

"AND WHAT IS IT YOU wish to inquire of me, Miss Beale?" While the madam poses the question, she closes the door to her "private parlor," a small and claustrophobic space whose entry is on the landing between the first and second floors. Martha suspects the room was once reserved for the storage of household linens and the housemaid's carpet brooms and brushes, as it barely fits a desk with its account books and a narrow upholstered chair squeezed in beside it.

Kat gestures Martha to the chair while she seats herself upon a three-legged stool that was hidden beneath the desk. "It's an unusual hour for a grand lady such as yourself to be abroad—if my timepiece is correct."

Martha can feel the madam's suspicious eyes appraising her. *I must appear precisely what I am,* she decides, *a woman who has just left a gentleman's lodgings.* The notion produces a sense of rebelliousness rather than guilt, so she smiles instead of bowing her head in humiliation.

"I have no doubt your timepiece is correct," she states, then continues with a lie so seamless it might as well be the genuine reason for her visit. "In truth, I chose the hour because I thought it might be less taxing for your establishment and therefore a better hour to pose a number of questions I need answered. I have every intention of paying you for your assistance. Let me be forthright, madam. I hope to ascertain some history of a girl from the streets I took into my home. She's now eleven. Or so I believe—"

"Not born into this house, I trust?" Kat interrupts. Martha can see both avarice and alarm splotching true pink on the rouged and powdered cheeks and knows the ruse is working.

"Alas, I'm afraid I can't answer that," Martha says in a voice that sounds remarkably free of subterfuge. Her newfound proficiency at deception makes her want to laugh aloud; instead, her expression remains composed and serious. "With you to help me, madam, perhaps we can discover the truth together."

Kat thinks. Martha intuits that the fancy house's owner is considering demanding her payment in advance but also questioning the wisdom of the action. It wouldn't do to aggravate someone with the name of Beale. Especially a lady so obviously on a mission of charity. "I do my best watching over the girls who earn their livelihood while in my keeping," she grumbles in her most wheedling tone, "but you can't spend every waking moment guarding their activities. Some of them are sly, you see. They sneak off, saying they're going to visit a relative they've never spoken of before. The next thing you know they pop back again, thin and exhausted and unwilling to work. So I suppose your ward could be one of those unwanted babes. Eleven years of age, you say?"

"Yes." Martha pauses again, considering what her next maneuver will be. She touches her reticule as if the activity were merely reflexive, but the gesture isn't lost on Kat, who now begins to regain a little of her composure.

"I don't like inferring that a lady like yourself might be wrong about a subject, Miss Beale, but misunderstandings do occur," says Kat. "If the child weren't of this house, then there's no need for us to be yammering away in the dead of night, is there?"

"You're right, of course." Martha opens her purse, retrieving notes and two gold coins. "My apologies. In my haste to accomplish my task, I came out without additional funds. Perhaps you'll accept this as an initial offering? In case my Ella was clandestinely born to one of your ladies."

Kat's meaty hand covers the stash almost before Martha has finished speaking. "I'm glad to help in any fashion I can, Miss Beale. In fact, it does my heart proud to think that a child who might have been born to a lowly lass in my employ could rise in the world."

"Your thoughtfulness will be amply repaid," Martha tells her with a feigned and courteous smile.

"Let it be the child you reward, Miss Beale. That's all I ask." Kat sighs as though her deepest wish in the world has been granted.

"And the lady who may have also aided her parent."

"If it pleases you, Miss Beale, who am I to argue with generosity of spirit? Ella is the girl, you said?"

"She escaped from another fancy house in the vicinity because she believed a customer intended to harm her."

"Not last winter, was it?" Kat's eyes widen until they're no longer greedy slits sunk into her ample flesh but owlish orbs of fear. "When that lunatic was strangling the youngest girls and slicing out their tongues?"

"Yes." Martha leans forward in her chair while Kat simultaneously slumps back.

"He was here," she mutters at length. "Killed one of my most promising young pieces. It got the other girls in such a state: an investigation with a sergeant and that zealot Thomas Kelman who works for the mayor. You wouldn't know the man, I imagine, but he appears when a crime is *of consequence,* as they say in the penny press. We were scared for our lives after that night. Thought the monster might return because he'd found such easy pickings here. So your ward had traffic with that devil? And survived to tell the tale? A charmed life, she must lead."

"Yes, she was very fortunate." Martha explains no more, neither her own part in the rescue nor the murderer's identity.

"You never know, do you, Miss Beale, who's going to walk through your door?" Kat states, still preoccupied with her anxious musings. "Gentlemen can be odd creatures and have peculiar tastes. You wouldn't be familiar with such things, but it's true."

Martha makes no answer while the madam begins to compose herself, fluttering a hand through her ringlets as if dispensing with the past were as easy as brushing off dirt. Something in her demeanor has changed, however. In place of servility, there's resolution and vigor. Martha remembers everything Thomas has told her about the madam's associations with the city's crimes but can't comprehend this altered behavior. "The name Ella is an unpromising start to this search, I'm sorry to tell you, Miss Beale. Those who work for me choose saucier sobriquets. Clients like a bit of spice when they're paying for female companionship. Especially our more refined gentlemen. We've had Gabriellas and Josephines and the like. So no, I can't imagine one of my girls dubbing her infant Ella. It would be too bland and ordinary, you see. In my experience my employees, like the gents they service, admire a modicum of illusion. Once they've established a taste for it, that is."

"Ah . . ." Martha realizes she's underestimated her adversary. Kat is going to prove difficult to entrap. Even if Martha knew the correct questions, the madam probably would be adept at deflecting them. "So nothing as plain as Dora, either?"

"Gracious me, no, Miss Beale! Theodora, perhaps. Although I doubt it will become popular anytime soon, don't you? What with that young person of quality being murdered. May God rest her tortured soul."

Martha nods as if only considering the likelihood of Theodora becoming a fashionable name. "Your house was connected to that tragedy, was it not?"

"By happenstance solely, I'm relieved to say. The gazettes and journals invented a number of melodramatic tales—how the criminal band chose the spot, how a beggar lad served as an accomplice, even how I conspired to obstruct justice. Well, that's a reporter's business, isn't it? To make mountains out of ant heaps. I'm glad to tell you that nothing came from the palaver. My customers don't appreciate the constabulary's presence, so it's fortunate my house never came under scrutiny from the authorities."

Oh! Martha thinks, *the first falsehoods I've uncovered,* but the discovery is followed by the recognition that she doesn't know what course to follow next. *How does Thomas manage this?* she wonders. *All I've managed to learn is that Kat is lying about his investigation. But wouldn't that be her normal behavior? To pretend her house was as free from taint as possible?* "It's fortuitous your business wasn't adversely affected. I imagine having the day watch in sight while you're open for commerce might be detrimental."

Kat regards her. Martha can feel the scrutiny, the shrewd eyes probing hers, the brain gauging her dress, the time, the amount of money exchanged. The woman almost seems to sniff as though she were an animal scenting prey she couldn't quite identify.

"On the contrary, Miss Beale, some folks like a whiff of danger. I daresay, now that the situation is past, I may see a rise in trade. Especially among those who look the most staid and humdrum, or the better class of customer who fancies dipping into treacherous terrain." With that, Kat lurches forward, leaning hard upon her desk. "Why are you here? If hunting a vanished mother is what you're about, I'm sure you could find professionals to help you. Secret service gentlemen and such."

Martha considers her response. The madam may have been fooled by flattery and monetary gifts for a while, but she's too clever for the trick to last. "You're correct. A secret service agency would better serve my purposes than this random inquiry. In fact . . ." Martha also bends over the desk, lowering her voice as if to share a private confidence. "I believe you may have guessed my motive. I'd hoped to discuss some of these 'staid' gentlemen to whom you refer. And their desire to 'dip into treacherous terrain.'" Martha's ears burn as she speaks, but she keeps her speech level and prays her cheeks haven't colored in mortification. "Some wellborn ladies keep lovers, as I'm sure you know. And it . . . it behooves us to be as pleasing as we can . . . and . . . to anticipate particular desires."

Kat barks out a laugh, then sits up straighter, smoothing her flounced and beribboned gown into a tighter line as if she's contemplating a business acquisition. She's now very much the mistress of her terrain. "So, you didn't come a-hunting this Ella child's mother? Or is your ward an invention, too?"

"The girl is genuine, but I'm not looking for her natural parents at this moment."

Kat considers this answer. A grin stretches across her pudgy cheeks. "And did she or did she not escape the murderous fiend of which I just made mention?"

"She did."

"Ahhh . . . Now I begin to understand. You should have been plain with me earlier, Miss Beale, and not squandered these late minutes in idle discourse. You want to learn the gory details, is that it?" Kat's left eye winks with a sinister leer. "How I found our lass with her severed tongue lying on a pillow and all the blood soaking into the bed linens. Is that the sort of dark tale you're after, mistress? Some folks crave those ugly facts, I know."

Martha stifles a gasp while forcing a conspiratorial smile. "No. Not those particular details . . . other unusual and disturbing fancies your clients might have. As I mentioned, I have a personal need to know more."

"So, you've got yourself one of the rough ones, do you?" Kat laughs again, the sound bursting out to fill the tiny room. "I guess the fanciest of ladies like yourself are no different from them we dub 'fancy' ladies." She snickers broadly again, tossing her yellowish curls and wriggling smugly on her seat. "Beats you, does he, your fine fellow? Or makes you crawl about naked and wet? Or swallow all sorts of putrid things you'd rather not? Well, I'd show him the door, if I was you, my dear. They can be dangerous, that type; unless you've got neighbors, which you would in a house like this, bad things can result. Though look what happened here despite the others."

Martha nods. The need to uncover the truth vies with a physical distaste so potent she can feel it on her tongue. "I just want to hear the stories," she murmurs, her voice so low and slow each syllable stands on its own.

The statement draws an even louder guffaw from Kat. "Don't that top everything! So all you're after is lurid talk. Well, my dear Miss Beale, you should have informed me from the start; there was no cause for the pretense of bastard children and murderous clients. I'm a business woman, I am. And if my conversation doesn't suit, I've got plenty of other females to keep you company: old, young, large, small. You have only to look them over and take your pick. But I must insist on additional funds. Pungent tales don't come cheap to someone with your fine name—if you understand my meaning."

"I'll supply them" is Martha's steady response, but Kat shakes her head in disagreement.

"I'll take that brooch off you in the meantime, if you don't mind. Lest you forget my humble manse."

Martha removes the piece of jewelry and hands it to the madam, who weighs it in her palm. "For safekeeping," she says and stuffs it inside her bodice. "Now, oddities . . . Let me see if these appeal. We have a couple of educated young fellows who like their girls unwashed. Claim they admire the *aroma* of the piss pot—and require them in pairs, too: two for two, although sometimes they forget the girls and find more pleasure in each other. Then there's a gent who demands female companions whose hindquarters are as slim as a boy's, and he's no more than a lad himself. Most particular he is, and he refuses any with decent bosoms on them. And, of course, the customers who insist upon the young ones, which can be a trying enterprise. What with the need for new product all the time. Although sometimes the girls can be clever and feign virginity—until they begin to bud, of course."

Bile rises in Martha's throat. It's all she can do not to clamp her hand over her mouth. *This is the trade Ella was sold into,* she thinks. *What parent would knowingly perpetrate such an evil? What kind of woman would encourage it?* Martha's face stiffens in outrage, but she continues the charade, although her tone when she speaks again is husky and rough with effort. "You mentioned gentlemen of breeding, I believe—"

"Young Mr. VanLennep, is that who you wish to discuss? You do like your stories mixed with a bit of gore. Though I regret to say his tastes may disappoint—"

"No," Martha interrupts. What compels her to ask the next question is unclear to her, but the words emerge as if she'd been considering them all along. "I mean older, fatherly types—?"

"Ah, so there's where your inclinations lie," Kat crows. "Indeed

I do! There's Mr. Harrison Crowther and the girl he—" Too late, her fingers fly to her lips.

"The girl he what?" Martha demands, but Kat makes no reply other than to glower at her visitor. Then her hand returns to the desktop as if all she'd done was dab a bit of moisture from her face.

"I'm afraid I must ask you to leave now, Miss Beale. The hour's grown too late for reasonable conversation, and I'm likely to utter any silly thing that pops into my head. I'm sure you'll forgive my rudeness." With that the madam pushes back from the desk and stands. Although she's a good head and shoulders shorter than Martha, her weight and heft make her look as forbidding as a bear.

"What about Crowther's girl?" Martha insists as she also rises.

"His poor daughter, do you mean, Miss Beale?" is the cool reply. "Let us ask God to bless the dear child's soul."

"And the father's, too," Martha spits back. "Because he's lying at death's door even now. And your Mr. Thomas Kelman is with him."

JOURNEYING HOME, MARTHA'S FEET ALMOST fly across the paving. *Thomas and I must query the madam together*, she decides as she leaves somnambulant Lombard Street, then hurries north toward Delancey and Cypress and finally Chestnut Street. *If he interrogates her alone, she'll evade the truth, claim she's never met Dora's father, and has no woman in her employ who is his favorite—*

Here her thoughts slam to a stop as she realizes that they'll need to act quickly lest Kat sequester the girl or attempt some other lie. For a moment, the resolute march also halts while Martha considers returning to Thomas's apartments to await his reappearance. Then the imagined idleness of such a mission sets her on course again.

No, I cannot spend my time pacing the floor and anticipating Thomas climbing the stairs. It could be hours before he finishes his official conversations and interrogations. And then, he may waste time chiding me for visiting the madam. I'll send a footman to find him—either at the Crowthers' or his own chambers. When we speak again, it will be under my own roof, and it will be as equals. After that we can address Dutch Kat.

The decision made, Martha proceeds. So intent is she on her deliberations that she fails to notice the sights around her or recognize the smallest sound. If she were being pursued by footpads, they'd have an easy night of it. For despite what she considers her haphazard appearance, her garb is clearly fashioned of the finest materials, and her posture and bearing are those of a lady of wealth and prominence.

In fact, Findal sees her and recognizes her as Ella's benefactress. He frowns in consternation. *The lady should be home protecting those two children in her keeping,* he argues as he creeps forward in Martha's preoccupied shadow. *What's she doing out here, and who's guarding her home while she gads the night away? What if my father has sneaked into the house? What if he's already working this new plot of his?*

IF IT OFFEND THEE

Findal is correct, because his father did decide his designs on the Beale children called for a bolder approach. When the boy so rudely challenged him, he made a rapid alteration to his plans. He knew he had no time to spare lest his son regain his senses and attempt to thwart him again.

Approaching the house, though, Stokes finds it isn't the sleepy place he expected given the advanced hour and the otherwise slumbering city. Too many interior lamps are glowing; too many exterior ones, as well. He surmises that the mistress isn't home, but her absence at an hour that's neither night nor morning strikes him as unusual. Where could she be, and why? And who waits up for her? For Stokes guesses that a mansion this rich and filled with servants wouldn't settle into dreamland unless all was in accord. Whoever anticipates the mistress's return will be extra vigilant to the noise of a window sash sliding open or a stranger's footfall creeping up the stairs.

Protected by the night's black shadows, Stokes regards the place and thinks. *Damn that son of mine,* his brain fumes. *How did*

I beget an ungrateful whelp like him? Who's he to grow a conscience now? Who's he to lecture me on good and ill—or have the right to suggest I'm lacking in intelligence and cunning? Then, perhaps more significant: *And who will help me slither into that citadel of a home with young Findal missing from the scene? Damn the boy! Damn his eyes. He'll never be a child of mine again. I'll find another boy I can trust. A better lad. And he can be my rightful heir. My chosen one.*

Nursing his many wrongs and his equally numerous lost opportunities, and recalling Amor Alsberg's righteous words of prophecy and doom, Stokes spots a female figure hurrying toward the house, then rapidly entering. He can see a groggy footman standing at attention within the foyer before the front door is shut with an echoing clang. Stokes waits, but the first-floor lamps remain lit, and soon the door flies open again, and the same servant rushes off down the street. Not a quarter of an hour passes before the hireling returns, only to be dispatched a second time. "What the devil is this?" Findal's father curses under his breath. "Don't these people believe in godly rest at the close of the day? Aren't they Christian folk?"

Now he can spot the woman, whom he assumes is Martha Beale, walking through a large room fronting the street. Despite the layers of drapery, he marks the abruptness and determination in the way she paces, which makes it clear to him that she has no intention of quitting her post. She strides to a window, thrusts aside the overdraperies as well as the sheerer undercurtains, and stares at the road, then retreats back into the room only to repeat the activity a moment later. "Damn her," Stokes seethes. "What's she doing? Not waiting up in childbirth, that's certain."

As he hesitates, undecided whether to give up his scheme for the night or wait for the contrary Martha to finally retire to bed, the footman returns. With him is a man Stokes recognizes only too well. *So, the fine Miss Beale has called in Mr. Thomas Kelman, has she?* he thinks. *Why would she do that, unless my worthless son exposed my intentions? But how could he have played such a spiteful trick on me already? Didn't I leave him as limp as the dead?* As Stokes rails against his ingrate of a child, Martha and Kelman quit the home, hurrying away down Chestnut Street; and the footman, clearly on his mistress's instructions, begins dousing the lamps.

At last, Stokes watches the lights blinking off one by one until nearly all the building lies in stupefied darkness. An exhausted household is an easy one to enter, as he knows. There's no need for lithe boys or chimney hooks when the servants are too tired to hear anything but their own snores.

TO SAY THAT DUTCH KAT is pleased to see Martha and Kelman standing on her doorstep would be as gross an overstatement as suggesting a caged sparrow enjoys watching a feline approach its small prison. Fear springs into the madam's eyes, followed by hopelessness, which is finally replaced by obstinacy and belligerence.

"More tricks of the trade for you, Mistress Beale?" she demands as her face works itself into a sneer that's both genuine and uncertain. "Isn't it time you were abed? For this household certainly is."

"Watch your speech when you address a lady" is Kelman's taut reply. He doesn't raise his voice, but a threat is evident, and not only in his tone.

"You been bought and paid for, too, *Mr.* Kelman?" Kat snaps back. "Just like our other city officials? Well, I wouldn't set too much store by what this *lady* of yours says on any subject, if I was you—"

"That's enough."

Kat is far from finished. "What difference does it make if Harrison Crowther was a customer of mine? This house had nothing to do with his daughter's death—nor her abduction, neither. If you think Dutch Kat's at fault, then I'll argue your companion here fed you misinformation. And she's not such a lady, neither. She was a-whoring earlier tonight. Or didn't you stop to question what she's doing up and abroad in the wee hours of the morning when even the fancy houses are calling it a day?"

In response, Kelman pushes his way into the now quiescent house, driving Kat out of his path by dint of his determination, although it's obvious to both women that his hands itch to shake the madam's insolent shoulders. "Bring me the woman Harrison Crowther kept on your premises," he thunders.

"Kept, is it?" Kat snaps while she squares herself against the intrusion. "There's a lovely word! Do you think I run a house of assignation where gentlemen ensconce their pretty bedmates so as to be exclusively at their beck and call? The 'girl,' as you call her, is a top earner hereabouts. Old Crowther isn't the only one—"

"Bring her to me, or I'll close down your establishment."

"On what charge, Mr. Kelman? Or can't a law-abiding citizen ask?"

"On aiding and abetting a kidnapping and murder."

"I've done no such thing!" Despite this avowal, a trace of fear has crept into Kat's voice. "Or didn't you hear me the first time—?"

"Then how do you explain your doorstep being chosen for the delivery of the ransom money?" is the measured reply. "Or the fact that both Theodora Crowther's father and fiancé were known customers? From my perspective, it looks as though a nefarious plot had been hatched within these walls."

Kat starts to interrupt, but Kelman raises a hand in order to request silence. The gesture lingers, full of fury. "You may bluster all you wish, but I'm assuming that either you or someone in your employ arranged to abduct Miss Crowther from her home. Otherwise, why did you hide the fact that her father was also a client when you were so willing to expose her betrothed?"

Kat glares at Kelman. Her lips work; she seems about to speak and raises her chin in a show of defiance, then suddenly tosses her head, turning toward the door leading to the front staircase and the remainder of the house. "I'll fetch the young lady in question," she states in a tone as contentious as before. "She's asleep, so it may be a moment or two until she makes an appearance."

"Send a servant for her instead," Kelman says. "I'd rather you and she have no conversation prior to my interrogation of her."

"Do you see a servant anywhere, *Mr.* Kelman? The house is abed—"

"Yet you answered the door" is the calm reply.

"I'm the owner, sir. I work longer hours than those in my employ. And this fine lady here kept me up."

By way of answer Kelman inclines his head, although his black eyes never leave the madam's face. "Miss Beale will accompany you. Lest you become tempted to hold a private discourse you shouldn't. You don't mind, do you, Martha?"

Martha nods her assent but makes no further response. Kat's nostrils pinch at the familiarity, then flare as if several mysteries had been resolved. She seems on the verge of making a lewd remark but thinks better of it, although a sense of superiority remains in her tight spine and upthrust bosom. "This way, miss," she says. "Mind where you step. Some of our ladies are careless when doffing their garments, or too much in haste to be particular. You may not be accustomed to such behavior, but I am."

If Martha wonders how a woman raised in her circumstances could find herself following the madam of a bawdy house in the middle of the night, she's unaware of posing that question. Instead, she walks in Kat's wake with footsteps that are as certain as if the situation and path were familiar. The only thing that seems unusual is the smell; in the confined space of the stairway, in the narrow upper halls, there's such a collision of stale perfumes and dirty hair and female sweat as well as a residual acrid maleness that the air feels almost too thick to breathe.

"Cat got your tongue, Miss Beale?" the madam cackles.

"No more than yours" is the composed reply, then Martha says no more.

"YOU MEAN HE MAY NOT be able to speak again?" is the girl's first question after Kelman has described the purpose of the visit.

"If he lives—which is uncertain."

The answer generates another little yelp and a fresh spate of tears. The girl looks toward the door through which Kat was banished, then sniffles in a petulant manner that Martha finds both conniving and disagreeable. Every instinct of empathy she first felt has vanished.

As if she understands Martha's feelings, the girl ignores her, fidgeting in a dressing gown that is too sheer and too loosely clasped to serve any purpose other than be intentionally revealing. "Well, I certainly didn't do anything to make him despondent, if that's what you're thinking. A nice old gent like that—why would I want to hurt him? And he doing nothing to harm me. Not like some of them others who say all they want is a bit of chitter-chatter and maybe a little tickle, and then end up hitting you when you do as you're told. He was generous, too, the old gent, though Kat keeps most of our stash." The girl shifts on her bare feet, wiggling her toes while she twirls the sash of her garment around her hand, then unwraps it again before gazing up at Kelman in a sham of wide-eyed innocence. "You're not suspecting I had anything to do with the other Dora, are you?"

"The 'other Dora'?" Kelman stands straighter, his head nearly touching the beams of the low-ceilinged room.

"The one who died, I mean. The one whose body was found in a coal heap. Kat said the constabulary thought this house was involved with the deal on account of the boy who served us sometimes. Findal, his name was. But you'd know that, I expect, because—"

"What do you mean, the 'other'?" Kelman interjects.

"Well, that's what the old gent called me, isn't it?"

"You're Dora, too?" Incredulity floods Kelman's face.

"No, of course not. Who'd want a commonplace name like that? Even if it were, I would have changed it as soon as I arrived here. What I meant was that's what the old dear called me—"

It's Martha who interrupts. "Harrison Crowther called you by his daughter's name. When he—?" Revulsion stops the query in her mouth.

"Well, he wasn't doing anything except blithering about this and that, now, was he, miss? At least, not always. So where's the harm if he liked me to call him Papa or wear a blond wig—?"

"Blond, too?" Martha exclaims as her glance flies to Kelman before returning to the ill-clad girl before her.

"Blond- or auburn-tressed, what's the difference? You must be unfamiliar with men's wants and desires, miss, to carry on so. The old fellow was nice, even when he asked for more than a polite little parley with 'Papa'—"

Martha draws in a sharp breath, causing the girl to round on her. The peevishness in her face is gone, replaced by damaged pride that mottles her cheeks a raw red and white.

"It's not the first time a gent said I reminded him of his precious little girl," she insists. "And why not? I'm a petite and tidy bundle, not like some of the other drabs who labor here. Why shouldn't I be as pretty as one of those toff's darling kiddies? Though I'd be living a hell of a lot better if I were. Just like you, miss, with your fancy dress and your horrified *oohs* and *aahs* about how we working girls earn our keep. It's my poor luck that he's gone and poisoned himself. But I guess it's like the Good Book says about cutting off your hand if it's doing evil deeds. The old gent must have a powerfully bad secret."

Martha looks at the girl, who continues to talk on and on to Kelman. The passage from the Gospel of St. Matthew to which she refers is familiar, and Martha recites it in silence. . . . *Whosoever looketh on a woman to lust after her hath committed adultery with her already in his heart./And if thy right eye offend thee, pluck it out, and cast it from thee . . . And if thy right hand offend thee, cut it off.* When she repeats the final sentence aloud, the girl stares at her with something akin to admiration, then immediately returns her focus to Kelman.

"Is that all the questions you have for me? Because I'm dead on my feet, and business hours will be here sooner than I'd like."

KELMAN WALKS MARTHA HOME. DAWN is only an hour away, and the city will soon be stirring, but for now it remains quiet as if all breath had left it. This same enervated mood has settled over the two who slowly traverse the dusky streets.

"Could he have killed his own daughter?" Martha murmurs after several moments of silence. This is the third time she's uttered the same words, and left them hanging in a similar and doleful fashion.

"I see no motive, Martha. A whore he liked to call Dora and whatever other vile secrets he may have had don't provide an incentive for murder. Let us also remember that Crowther hired Luther Irwin and was anxious and willing to obey the felon's instructions."

"Yes" is the ambivalent answer. "Although, couldn't such actions have encouraged everyone to believe that the crime was the work of another person? Stokes, as you have suspected, or—?"

"What manner of man would invent and then execute such a scheme? Are you suggesting that Crowther concealed his own child in a heap of coal? And then wrote letters to himself demanding ransom for a person already dead?"

Martha shakes her head. She's removed her bonnet, and her hair, its plaits and waves too long unrepaired, falls into her eyes. "You're correct. My hypothesis seems preposterous. No parent could carry out such a cold-blooded plan. Unless—"

"Unless?"

"I don't know." She brushes the locks away with a careworn hand. "What if Dora's death were some sort of ghastly accident? Suppose her father went to her room that night, argued with her over something, and raised his hand in frustration. Yes, I know, a distasteful situation. But parents do beat their children . . . Perhaps he did hit her and she fell. If he then panicked when she didn't revive—? No, you're correct, Thomas; I can't conceive of such callousness. The man was obviously devoted to his daughter." Martha stares into the dull gray air, then looks at Kelman. "You don't intend to tell Georgine what we learned tonight, do you?"

"No. And I think we can rest assured that the information won't leave Dutch Kat's house. As far as I'm concerned, she and Crowther's bawd remain under suspicion for their role in this affair. I don't yet know to what extent they're involved, but I will when I discover who orchestrated the scheme. The fact that the father and fiancé frequented the same establishment seems more than coincidental. Who knows what information was coaxed out of those two during—?" Kelman's words die in his throat. "I apologize. That was indelicate talk. Sometimes I forget you're not a male colleague in whom I'm confiding."

A small smile shoots across her face. "I would rather you view me as something more than a *colleague*."

He stops walking and gazes into her eyes. "Martha, my dear one, my dearest—"

She puts her fingers to his lips, her smile grown brighter and steadier. "Say no more. Let us savor those moments we recently enjoyed. We'll have ample time to discuss the future. What transpired in your rooms tonight is enough for now."

"I—"

"No, Thomas. No protests. No speech. Let us revel in emotion only."

So they continue on their way until they come to within a block of her house. By now the sky is transmuting itself into the silver-rose of an imminent sunrise while the sound of anxious voices breaks the stillness. It's Kelman who first notices the noise. "What's that? Not muleteers engaged in an early-morning wrangle, surely? They have no business in this section of the city."

The clamor grows, building into what must be a heated argument, and Kelman and Martha increase their pace until they spot a throng of people gathered near her home. A fire gang is in their midst, the horses pawing and snorting and attempting to rear in their traces while the habitual oaths of their drivers are flung far and wide. At this disreputable hour, the men who compete with each other to subdue the city's blazes are often drunk, although the same can be said of them midday, too. Something in the middle of the roadway has attracted everyone's attention, but neither Martha nor Kelman can yet detect what it is. Then she notices her majordomo standing on the front steps and hastens toward him.

"I shouted out when I heard the man," he states, obviously distraught. "With you gone, Miss Beale, and the night so peculiar and me awake on account of worrying over your absence—" The words tumble out without a pause for breath. "Of course I heard him. Why wouldn't I with the house so still? I knew it was a burglary attempt and that someone must have been remiss with the window latches. I didn't spot the fellow, though. Not inside, that is. But I did see a figure darting away on the house's east side. A boy was hurrying after him; I did notice that much. Then the fellow hauled off and landed a blow across the lad's face—"

"Where are the two now?" Martha asks.

"That's him, the man. He's lying in the street. The fire gang was rounding the corner when he jumped into their path. Oh, Miss Beale, my pursuit must have killed him, I think."

Martha leaves the safety of her steps, pushing her way into the jittery throng. Kelman is there already, bending over the figure in the road. "He's dead" is all he says, then adds a toneless: "It's Stokes."

"Stokes! The murderer?" someone shouts, and this news races through the group.

"The same."

The crowd draws back in alarm as if the dead man could rise up and slay everyone there, and Martha is caught up in their horror and fear.

"You mean he was in the city all along, hiding amongst us while we were unawares. That's a crime for you. Leaving honest citizens unprotected." An anonymous voice screams out this assessment while one of the members of a fire gang disentangles himself from the crowd in order to step forward and address Kelman.

"A boy chased him down. I saw the fight, even though my mates and I were still far off. My eyes are accustomed to the dark—"

"Accustomed to the inside of a rum barrel is more like it," one of his mates scoffs before also approaching Kelman and commencing a similar account. "I took the pair to be father and son, but then the boy threw a stone or brick, so I doubt they could have been blood-related—"

"And who else would have greater cause for villainous thoughts than kin and kith?" another fireman interjects. "Especially the offspring of criminals. Live by the sword. Die by the sword. Isn't that what the Good Book tells us?" The man plays to his audience with these comments, which draw nervous guffaws but don't deter the previous speaker.

"The lad struck this Stokes fellow in the back, which made him spin around. If I'd been closer, I would have heard the blow; it was that hard. Then the fire wagon came roaring along and the boy rushed at the man and pushed him into its path. At least, that's how it looked to me—"

"Where's the lad now?" Kelman interrupts. The question seems to take the group by surprise.

"We was so worried about the wounded man. If we'd known it were Stokes, though . . . I wouldn't want to say I'd rescued a demon like him—"

"And the horses, too. We was worried over them," someone else adds. "They're trained not to trample folk underfoot and they get edgy and nervous when something like this occurs—"

The most voluble witness hasn't finished. "It were no accident, sir. That lad knew what he were doing. He killed that fiend

Stokes, sure as sure. He should get a reward for what he did. Indeed, he should."

Kelman says nothing. If Stokes is guilty in the slaying of Theodora Crowther, he's gone to his Maker with his secret intact.

"Saved the city from a hanging, sir. That he did. And the quicker wicked folk like this demon here are dispatched, the better for us all." A flurry of hearty agreement greets these observations; then all begin to discuss the case, and opinions, either informed or not, circle among the spectators.

Kelman stands. The undertaker's cart will be arriving shortly, but for the moment the road is empty except for the group encircling Stokes's corpse. Or so it appears. Instead, young Findal hides nearby, watching and weeping in the shadows.

KEEPING WATCH

MARTHA PICKS UP THE LETTER, puts it down, taps her fingers upon its soft surface, turns away—indeed, takes an entire step backward—only to return and take the paper in hand again.

My dear Miss Beale,
Now that this cruel mystery has been resolved, and the man reputed to have slain my dearest child has received retribution, I wonder if you might consider calling upon me. Your aid in our times of distress was a blessing, and although Mr. Crowther can no longer verbally express his thanks, I wish to extend gratitude on behalf of both my husband and me . . .

Martha rubs the page between her fingers, replaces it on the desk, and gazes toward the windows. Of course, she must pay a call upon Georgine. Today. This afternoon, certainly. No. Now. She must visit the bereaved lady now. This very morning. Why else would she have written if she didn't desire a comforting presence, someone she believes was a friend to her daughter?

For a moment, Martha considers sending a message to Thomas and requesting that he join her in this mission, but then tells herself it's the coward's path. Georgine needs a woman to lend sympathy, not the man who failed to save her only child.

Martha releases a pensive breath, walks to a window, and looks into the street. It's been two weeks since Findal Stokes senior met his death on this same spot. Two weeks since she and Thomas interviewed Dutch Kat, two weeks since she climbed the stairs to his lodgings. For a flickering moment, she allows herself to remember that visit. She can recall every sensation induced by Thomas's caress, and how hot and strong his shoulders felt within her fingers' grasp. Then the present situation commands her attention and her expression is transformed: Her eyes grow darker and sadder; her mouth sags into a discouraged line. The day is dank and misty, the temperature not the chill of late autumn nor the warmth of Indian summer. It's weather for an uncertain time.

She leaves the window, drawing a stern and steadying breath as she walks to the bell pull and rings for her maid. When her mantilla and bonnet are brought, she settles her shoulders for the task ahead and leaves her house. There's not the slightest hint of joy in her figure or on her face.

"ARE YOU ACQUAINTED WITH MR. HOWE, Miss Beale?" are the first words Miss Lydia says when Martha is shown into the Crowthers' withdrawing room. The tragedy surrounding the old lady seems to have left her unaffected, for she smiles complaisantly, holding her ear trumpet in anticipation of a lengthy conversation. Georgine isn't yet present, so the aunt commandeers the guest as her own. She pats the seat beside her as Martha approaches. "Not as handsome a specimen as his forebear Lord Howe, nor as urbane, but we live in a modern world where courtliness counts for little."

"I was unaware Mr. VanLennep's friend was descended from the British general" is Martha's preoccupied reply. Thinking she hears Georgine's footsteps in the foyer, she turns away and walks to the door but finds she's mistaken.

"When Lord Howe's army occupied Philadelphia, he held a great celebration. The Meschianza, it was called. All the Tory ladies attended, dressing *à la Turque* in turbans and exotic apparel. I'm happy to say none in our family were among those invited, as it was a terrible scandal. Some of the scarlet creatures later lost their tresses because of their attachments with the enemy soldiery. I'm glad young Percy has such an illustrious companion, however. I told Harrison he was very wrong about the boy. Not that I expected a reply. That poison my nephew swallowed may not have killed him, but his life is hardly worth living any longer, is it? Forced to keep to his rooms and reduced to no more than dumb show. I wouldn't wish to continue under those circumstances, would you?"

Before Martha can think of a reply to this callous assessment, Georgine enters. Dressed in mourning black, her face drawn, her eyes ringed with smudgy shadows, she carries herself with a careful air, as if a nearly superhuman effort at self-control were lurking beneath the crinolines, the chemisette, and the stays.

"Miss Beale." Rather than walk forward to greet her guest, she waits, so Martha must come to her. When she takes Georgine's hands, their needy grip is undeniable.

"Mrs. Crowther, I'm so terribly sorry for all you've suffered. For all you're continuing to suffer."

Dora's mother accepts the declaration with a grave nod. "I tell myself over and over that God doesn't visit us with sorrow unless He provides the means for us to bear it, and that I should give eternal thanks that at least my husband survived the calamity he inflicted upon himself . . . and that . . . and that our Dora has gone to a better place . . . but still—"

Grief threatens to overwhelm her. Georgine draws a shaky breath, gazing around the room as if seeking solace from the many memories stored within it, or even from the inanimate objects that fill each corner and that have made up the whole of her married life. Her eyes rest on a settee, a table, a vase, a mirror shrouded in the black silk of death, and finally the somber walls themselves. The draperies are pulled shut to indicate the family's bereavement, and so the hour could be late or early, night or time for midday dinner. "But still, I'd like to have my Theodora at my side. And Percy, too, and . . . and babies . . . Dora was . . ." Whatever the mother intended to say, her words fade into a whisper.

Martha's eyes fill. "You've endured a terrible misfortune," she finally responds.

Georgine regards Martha. Misery flows from her as though it were a physical commodity like heat or cold. "Women's hearts must steel themselves to pain, Miss Beale. If we've been blessed with children, we soon come to recognize how fragile their little lives are, and that we parents, try as we might, are often not strong enough or clever enough to protect them. Consider Harrison and his efforts when Dora vanished. Wasn't he the picture of a doting father, tireless, relentless in his insistence that there would be a happy outcome to the tragedy? Do you remember his determination, and how patient he was with my frailty? Do you remember the enormity of his compassion? I think back and am shamed by my weakness. And I, who always appeared a pillar of strength. I failed my dearest daughter, Miss Beale. I did."

"Oh, no, Mrs. Crowther, you did not. There was nothing you could do." What Martha doesn't add, but what both she and Georgine now understand, is that Dora's body had been buried within the coal cobbles soon after vanishing from her home. "You mustn't blame yourself—"

"Oh, blame!" is the bitter retort. "You know nothing of the guilt I feel at permitting this catastrophe to occur. Not even guilt! I am condemned."

Martha squeezes Georgine's fingers but makes no reply while her mind's eye plays an unkind trick, conjuring up the girl at Dutch Kat's, the "other Dora." *Did I pay the trollop enough?* Martha frets. *Will she quit the city as I insisted? Or might she and Kat begin to suspect my motives in demanding their silence—?*

The questions are interrupted as Georgine draws her guest closer. "Miss Beale, you've been a genuine friend to our family. No mere words can express my appreciation of your solicitude. Come, let me show you Dora's chambers. They've become my favorite spot in the house because they still retain her loving spirit. I don't believe you've ever seen them."

"No" is all Martha can manage before Georgine pulls her from the room, then almost marches her toward the front staircase.

"Georgine! Wait!" she hears, but her hostess answers with a peremptory:

"No, aunt. You must remain below." As if the order were too harsh, Georgine adds a softer "Dora's rooms were in the back, you know. On the third floor. It's a difficult climb for my husband's elderly relative."

She says no more but leads the way up the main staircase and into the second-floor corridor, passing numerous shut doors until they reach a smaller rear flight of steps. The pair proceeds in silence: the sounds of skirts swishing over carpets and bare wood and the creaking of risers the only noise. Although that noise seems loud in the mournful space.

Georgine almost seems not to breathe. Martha knows her own breaths are shallow and apprehensive. She wishes she could be gone and dispense with this grim parade; instead, she moves stoically along in her hostess's wake. *Think of the mother, not the father,* she tells herself over and over. *She's the one who requires solace now. Whatever Crowther did outside his home must remain a secret. It has no bearing here.*

When they reach the landing outside Dora's chambers, Georgine stops. "This is where my daughter died," she says. "Right there. Inside."

"Oh, I don't believe so, Mrs. Crowther. Surely the abductor—" Martha's protest is cut short as Georgine spins her large body around until she backs her visitor into a corner. Her face is so contorted that it looks as though the flesh were ripping from the bones.

"There was no 'abductor,' Miss Beale. No Stokes and his felonious gang. No mystery men holding my child hostage. There was only Harrison."

Martha's lips open in objection, but Georgine's ferocious glare obliterates her effort at speech.

"Only Harrison. My husband. Harrison. He killed my daughter. Killed her with his own hands—"

"Oh, Mrs.—"

Martha might as well not have spoken, for Georgine continues, her mouth like a gash, her eyes wild. "Oh, yes. Oh, yes . . . I realize it must have been some type of hideous accident. I believe that. I do. I do. Don't I understand each and every one of his deficiencies? A choleric man like Harrison, given to fits of rage whenever his wishes weren't realized. Ask his aunt if you doubt me. Ask her about her dear nephew's ill-tempered ways. But however my darling child's death occurred, what I can tell you is that every act he committed after that . . . every act he—" The speech halts. Georgine's head sags, her wrath now supplanted by a sense of such hideous loss that the emotion seems unendurable. Taking Martha's arm, she drags her through the door. "Let me read to you from the letter he wrote before swallowing that damnable poison. I keep it here in Dora's apartment. I keep it because I . . . because . . ." The words clatter out like stones. "Why did this happen, Miss Beale? Why? Weren't we good enough? Devout enough? Kind enough? Is this God's punishment?"

Martha makes no reply. What can she say in the face of this extraordinary confession? That Georgine is mistaken? That Stokes—or some as yet undiscovered person—was to blame?

"Harrison closed the missive by quoting from the Revelation of Saint John. However, he made two telling alterations to the text." She picks up the letter. Martha notices how creased and rumpled the paper is, and how roughly the lady handles it. "In times past, we were schooled by memorizing long passages from the Bible. You may not have been raised in such a fashion, but I was; and aged as I am, I still remember my lessons, so I can tell you what words my husband excised." Holding the page to her eyes, Georgine's fingers almost rend it in half.

"'*It is done!*' he writes. '*He that overcometh shall inherit all things. But the fearful shall have their part in the lake which burneth with fire and brimstone.*' The words my husband eliminated after 'fearful' include 'murderers' and 'whoremongers.'"

She throws the letter on her daughter's bed. "I see how those words affect you, Miss Beale. Perhaps you know more about this than I realized, and are also aware of a certain fancy house my husband frequented—and young Percy's connection to the same establishment? Or the hunting accident that wasn't as arbitrary as it seemed? Don't speak. Your expression has answered for you. As mine must have also when I discovered Harrison's involvement in that hateful matter." Georgine's chest heaves; her cheeks redden, then turn icy white. Her mouth opens and closes, opens and closes; and Martha steps toward her, fearing the lady will faint.

"Dora's betrothed dead in the woods," she cries out. "Wouldn't the incident have assured his guilt? Or if not assured, then made him forever suspect, gossiped over, his complicity never proved nor disproved." She crumples her husband's missive; then, heedless of her actions, begins tearing it in pieces. "My citified spouse tramping the forest while my girl's poor body rotted in a filthy heap of coal. What fiend would undertake such an act, do you think? Burying his child in coal cobbles!"

Martha doesn't answer; instead, she watches Georgine's hands as they shred the words her husband has penned.

"If I'd examined those two ransom letters with greater care, Miss Beale . . . if I'd questioned Harrison concerning where the monies were to be left, or why his reaction to the return of my little girl's daguerreotype was so uncharacteristic and full of dread, perhaps I would have detected the lie sooner. But what good would that have done? My darling was dead by then! My daughter, my dearest, dearest daughter was already—"

The mother begins to weep, her tears as noisy and copious as a child's. Martha makes not a sound. It seems to her that there's enough pain in these two small chambers to fill the entire house several times over. Enough to cast a long, dark shadow over the entire street also. She looks across the room, imagining Dora alive, sitting at her *escritoire,* writing in her journal, gazing out a sunny, spring-filled window, happy, fun-loving, considerate of her parents' wishes, then tumbling headlong into youthful love.

In her mind's eye, Martha sees the girl pacing back and forth in front of her window, waiting for a glimpse of Percy, her slender frame nearly shivering in anticipation. She laughs aloud, catches sight of her pretty face in the looking glass, and beams at her own reflection.

Then without warning the lighthearted vision turns sinister, and Martha witnesses an uncompromising father and increasingly obstinate daughter. Their bodies are illumined only by a single candle resting on Dora's bed table, although the girl herself is fully dressed and seated near the now night-filled windowpanes. Martha hears voices begin to rise in querulous argument; there are remonstrances and pleas; there are parental commands and haughty contradictions; there's ill-considered opposition and petulant tears, then a strangled oath, a shout, a startled yelp, while a blow seems to descend upon Martha's body as if it had been aimed at her and not at Theodora. As Martha reacts to this illusory attack, there is also the echo of a scream.

"How could he have committed the crime he did, Miss Beale? How could he have harmed his own child? And then hidden—?"

"Mrs. Crowther, don't torture yourself thus—"

"Torture! You don't know what the word means. My daughter gone. My husband destroyed in mind and body. No, don't talk to me of torment, because I can see my child dying as though I were witnessing the scene. I see it over and over and over again. Here. Right here. And Harrison, too. He lives with the memory every waking and sleeping moment. When he told me—" All at once, she lunges toward her husband's torn letter, swoops up the pieces, and deposits them in Martha's hand. "Take these to your Mr. Kelman. Let him solve the conundrum of who first discovered Harrison's crime. For some devil did—and intended to profit from that knowledge."

Georgine's hands cup Martha's; her grip tightens until Martha feels her fingers nearly imprisoned in the larger woman's. The grasp grows more rigid; Martha's own flesh begins to tingle. "But I have a request to make first."

Martha's heart sinks as she looks into Dora's mother's eyes, for she intuits the petition will not be an easy one to honor. "A request?"

"Yes. That he and you tell no one of this matter."

"Oh, Mrs. Crowther—"

"I see you wish to pull away. You desire honesty. You want and respect truth. But the man who was reported to have stolen my child from her home has perished. His reputation was sullied already; let him remain guilty in the public arena. Let it be as everyone believes. That Stokes murdered my Theodora, and that the hand of God has dispatched him . . . Whoever attempted to blackmail us by returning Dora's portrait and the possessions taken from this room, I'll deal with myself after—"

"Oh, Mrs. Crowther, what you're asking—"

"Is against your scruples, is that it, Miss Beale?" The words fly out, knifing through the air. "Or your fine Mr. Kelman's?"

"No, madam" is the austere reply. "What I was going to say is that it's against the law."

"Oh, the law! The grand and illustrious decrees of this commonwealth. Did those verdicts protect my child? Did they?" Georgine's voice has risen again; her fingers have become like vises. "Did they, Miss Beale? Did they save my little girl? Or Harrison?" Then she abruptly opens her locked hands and flings Martha's from them.

"Grant me what I ask. My husband may be guilty of the worst sin a father can commit. He may be a coward. He is a coward. I know he is. What he did was terrible; and then to compound the one mistake with so many craven and heartless acts . . . But haven't we been instructed to follow Christ's example? Haven't we been taught that no one is perfect except our Father that is in Heaven? That we must love our enemies, and bless those that curse us? That we must forgive and forgive, and that even our anger is wickedness?" By now Georgine's voice is so close to a howl, and her focus so inward turned, that she seems unaware of another person beside her. "Oh, God, help me to show mercy. Help me to walk in thy path, and feel thy presence sustaining me. Fill me with love, instead of hate. And for what I did to my husband . . ." The words disappear in a moan.

Martha's lips part to speak, but no sound comes; the two rooms at the top of the house also remain hushed as if interpreting those final words. Then a curious noise begins to shiver through the walls; it's like a breeze gusting through the chimney, although the damper is shut and the day relatively windless. The sound grows and swells until it half moans, half sings within the flue, and a spurt of air bursts out upon the floor.

"That's my Dora," the mother murmurs at length in a sluggish tone. "She comes home like this. To watch over her parents. Wretched sinners that we are."

HOW MARTHA DEPARTS THE HOUSE and finds herself again on the street she isn't certain. She recalls a footman opening the door, another footman delivering her cloak, someone bowing, asking if she wishes to be escorted home—and her murmured refusal. Then the door shuts behind her, and she's aware of praying that she'll never have to enter the house again.

Walking away, her feet wander. She's mindful of nothing except one shoe stepping in front of the other. So lost is she to outward sensation that she doesn't notice how threatening the sky has grown or how her fellow travelers are beginning to hasten for cover.

Crowther attempted to kill Percy . . . her thoughts echo. *How did Georgine discover that fact if not from her husband? And how did she learn about Dutch Kat's? And when? Or the ransom letters . . . What did Georgine mean? That Harrison created them? Or that it was an act of blackmail?* The questions roil through Martha's brain, repeating themselves but providing no solutions; instead, they spin into further dilemmas. *I can't ask Thomas to lie. I can't suggest he leave the blame on Stokes. No matter how reprehensible the man may have been, he can't be falsely accused.*

Then those quandaries are superseded by a memory that bursts into her consciousness. *And for what I did to my husband . . .* Martha's body jerks to a halt as she recognizes the import of those words. Georgine poisoned Harrison.

Before this new revelation can unfold, the storm hits; water descends slantwise upon the roadway as though being poured from a giant and bottomless bucket. Martha looks up in bewilderment. She has no idea how she came to be in the section of the city bordering the Delaware River docks. In a second, she's soaked through: her fine bonnet limp and soggy, her mantilla clinging to her gown, her gown and petticoats wrapping themselves around her legs. She makes no attempt to escape the deluge but continues to stand in the middle of the street, gazing incomprehensibly into the angry sky.

"Watch out, miss!" a boy's voice calls, but Martha doesn't hear.

"Miss! Watch out. That horse is—"

The warning finally penetrates her brain. *Horse?* she thinks while simultaneously remembering the careering fire wagon that ran down Findal Stokes. No sooner has this picture surfaced in her mind than a boy barrels into her, knocking her out of the road and onto the opposite walkway while a runaway dray horse, still dragging a heavy cart behind it, gallops across the cobbles she occupied not a second before. Then the animal's traces tear loose; the cart crashes onto its side, and the increasingly frenzied and frightened beast plunges on amid shouts and oaths.

"Miss? Are you hurt?" Martha hears as witnesses press round her. Hands reach down; faces peer; someone picks up and returns her now trampled mantilla. "If it hadn't been for that lad over yonder pushing you out of harm's way . . . You've got yourself a guardian angel there, miss—"

She looks in the direction indicated but can only see a figure disappearing into the crowd.

SO THIS IS HOW THE day ends: Martha is returned to her house, bruised and sore and shaken but otherwise undamaged. With the aid of her lady's maid, she's ensconced on the chaise in her private parlor, where she reclines surrounded by all the comforts of her home, a silk-covered quilt across her legs, a down pillow at her head, another under her feet. Thomas arrives, taking charge as he paces the room, ordering a concoction of brandy and water for the patient, and an emulsion of extract of lead to treat the swelling and lacerations on her face. If he's oblivious to his uncharacteristic domesticity, Martha is not. She watches his movements with eyes full of private delight.

"You must take greater care, my dearest heart," he repeats. "Indeed, from all reports you were fortunate to escape with your life."

She accepts the admonishment (his several admonishments) with a small nod but has no opportunity to defend herself, because Kelman is far from finished. "And venturing into that area of town, as well. What were you thinking?"

"Of Dora . . . and Percy. And Crowther—"

"But not about your well-being if you took yourself down to the docks. It's a blessing you weren't robbed."

Martha ignores his badgering. "Oh, Thomas, it was such an insignificant accident when compared to all else that has occurred."

"It's not insignificant to me. You could have been killed." With that, he finally ceases his restless steps and draws a chair close to Martha's divan.

"But I wasn't." She tries to smile. Even her face feels pained and achy.

"What will happen to Crowther now? And Georgine?"

Kelman doesn't answer for a moment. "I don't know. He's very ill."

"And when he dies?"

"I don't know, Martha. If the wife is willing to publicly attest to what she told you in confidence . . ." The words trail away.

"Could you . . . could you delay your investigation—?"

"Until he succumbs to his supposedly self-inflicted dose of oil of vitriol?"

She nods again, although that small activity hurts more than it should.

Kelman releases a troubled breath. "That's a treacherous path to embark upon, my dearest."

"Yes. I know. And there's your reputation and position to consider."

"Hang my reputation." Despite this outburst, Kelman says no more on the subject, instead reverting to grim self-assessment. "Why didn't I recognize that the first ransom letter was Crowther's creation? That no professional thief would have delivered it, as there was no method for payment. Or the peculiar manner in which he dealt with the second request? The return of Dora's portrait, too. The wife was correct. Despite all symptoms of a man overcome by grief, there was something more: a state of panic and inflexibility. I couldn't reconcile it with the situation, but I overlooked its significance . . . And his motive in hiring a man like Luther Irwin—why didn't I query that decision more effectively? Crowther was trying to thwart the investigation from the beginning—while attempting both to buy off the person he believed had uncovered his crime and to cast suspicion on young VanLennep. The daguerreotype must have seemed proof positive to Crowther that he'd been caught. And when Percy reappeared—"

"Oh, Thomas. How premeditated and brutal that seems."

"It does. It was. But, as his wife indicated, he'd begun a deception he was incapable of ending."

Neither speaks for a moment while their thoughts scrutinize every facet of the case. "Poor Georgine," Martha finally says. "And Dora . . ."

"Yes." Then Kelman's logical brain returns to the unanswered question. "Who could have discovered the ruse, I wonder?"

Martha looks at him. It requires a moment for her mind to adjust. "Could further examination of the second letter reveal—?" she offers, and Kelman interjects an energetic:

"Perhaps. Perhaps. I can order every hired scribe in the city questioned, and their statements may yield—" Then he interrupts himself with an impatient sigh. "But the enterprise comes too late. Learning the identity of the person or persons who knew that Crowther killed his daughter is immaterial now. The damage can't be remedied." He leans back in his chair, his face dark with regret.

"Thomas, my dear, you mustn't castigate yourself. Even if you'd had all the information at your disposal originally, you still couldn't have saved Dora."

"No . . ." is the eventual reply.

"Nor the parents," she murmurs.

"No."

Ella explodes through the door at that moment. She's just returned from school and has been regaled with the tale of her adoptive mother's accident by Miss Pettiman, who's had no qualms about explaining the gravity of the situation. "You might have been killed, Mother! A runaway horse just like the one that trampled the man to death outside our house." So intent is Ella on the drama of the moment that she doesn't notice Kelman's presence until she's halfway across the room.

"Oh, Mr. Kelman! I didn't realize . . . Miss Pettiman didn't say that Mother was entertaining. Only that she was very badly injured—"

"Which you see isn't the case," Martha tells her. With effort, she pulls herself more erect and thus farther from Kelman. Ella frowns. The truth confronting her isn't the truth she's conjured up. Except for a bandage on her adoptive mother's face, she looks no different than she normally does.

"I'm only bruised, and a little scratched. Nothing worse. I think you sustained greater injuries when you fell out of the apple tree last spring and got such a large bump on your head."

"But Miss Pettiman said—"

"She was probably trying to impress upon you the need for caution when you cross the street, don't you think?"

Ella's frown grows. She senses that Martha's smooth speech is concealing something, but what that secret is she doesn't know.

"Miss Pettiman says you're often rash in your behavior, Mother. And that's why troubles like this one occur."

"Does she?"

"Yes. And that you don't always consider where your actions will lead, either."

"She said all that, did she?"

Ella hasn't recognized the chilliness that has crept into Martha's voice, but Kelman has. He smiles as he regards the woman lying on the chaise. "Miss Pettiman is quite right, Ella. Your parent can be reckless at times."

"Oh, Thomas! How can you?"

Kelman's smile grows. "But that trait isn't necessarily bad, Ella. In fact, it can be a very good one to have. People who are brave are often considered reckless, because courage takes many forms. Doing what you believe in your heart to be right—even if you're criticized—takes bravery. Do you understand?"

Ella nods as Martha's expression softens. She looks at Thomas; he returns her gaze.

"Shall I tell you what I remember about my real mother now, Mr. Kelman?" the child asks. "And a sister and little brother I had, too. He was badly hurt when he was a baby and had a disfigurement—"

"I want to hear everything you have to say, but not at this moment. Let us allow your adoptive mother some quiet. When she's better, you can explain what you recall." He rises and takes the girl's hand.

"You needn't go," Martha tells them.

"I'll return in a few minutes. First, I'd like to see that Ella has what she needs after her busy day of schoolwork. And that Miss Pettiman understands how potent opinions can be, especially when delivered to children."

Left alone, Martha feels her thoughts drifting. Beyond the closed door, the household hums with its commonplace chores. There are soft footfalls, muffled words, the quiet swish of an upstairs maid's long apron, the plink of a cornice brush hitting the edge of a ceiling. She listens, cataloguing each sound until reverie and memory become dream-like states. There is Ella—and Cai—and Thomas and this chamber and the street below, from which reflects upward the spinning light cast by a polished carriage wheel, or a flight of birds flinging shadows across the walls. She grows drowsy and her eyelids flicker closed while her mind carries her back to the Crowther house, jumbling together each hour she spent there until a pattern gradually emerges and she begins to see the situation with Kelman's clinical eye.

The missteps along the way become increasingly apparent: the father's terror and anguish; the mother's incipient passivity and her final revelation. Percy makes an appearance, then fades from sight; Miss Lydia whispers; Dutch Kat beckons; the separate messages delivered to the household flutter forward—then unexpectedly creep away into Becky Grey's possession.

Finally, Martha recalls Georgine's prayer, but no sooner have those tormented words been uttered than Martha's disembodied self is propelled outside toward the docks along the Delaware, where she's again sent sprawling across the rain-washed roadway as the boy who saved her vanishes from sight.

It was young Stokes, she tells herself. *The boy who called out to me. Young Findal Stokes. I'm certain it was he.*